P9-CNE-980

WITHDRAWN

No longer the property of the
Boston Public Library.
Sale of this material benefits the Library

FOREVER
IS THE WORST
LONG TIME

OTHER TITLES BY CAMILLE PAGÁN

The Art of Forgetting

Life and Other Near-Death Experiences

FOREVER
IS THE WORST
LONG TIME

CAMILLE PAGÁN

LAKE UNION
PUBLISHING

This is a work of fiction. Names, characters, organizations, places, events, and incidents are either products of the author's imagination or are used fictitiously.

Text copyright © 2017 Camille Pagán
All rights reserved.

No part of this book may be reproduced, or stored in a retrieval system, or transmitted in any form or by any means, electronic, mechanical, photocopying, recording, or otherwise, without express written permission of the publisher.

Published by Lake Union Publishing, Seattle

www.apub.com

Amazon, the Amazon logo, and Lake Union Publishing are trademarks of Amazon.com, Inc., or its affiliates.

ISBN-13 (paperback): 9781503941618
ISBN-10 (paperback): 1503941612

ISBN-13 (hardcover): 9781477818381
ISBN-10 (hardcover): 1477818383

Cover design by David Drummond

Printed in the United States of America

First edition

For Xavi, who wishes this book were about dragons

ONE

"This story ends with loss," said your mother. "I'm only on the first chapter, but I can tell."

It was the spring of 1998, and I had just let myself into Rob's apartment. Your mother was sprawled out on the sofa with her nose in a novel; a messy knot of golden-brown hair peeked out from above the edge of the pages. The late-afternoon sun cast fractured light over her body, and she looked celestial—sort of like a miniature angel, I remember thinking. Of course, I didn't know she was your mother then. It was the first time I had ever laid eyes on her.

"Don't they all?" I quipped, trying to act as though I weren't unnerved. Rob had told me she would be there, but I was expecting someone generically pretty, dimly bright, and socially adept enough to sit up and greet a stranger when he walked into the room. That is, someone more like the type of women Rob had always dated.

She set the book on her stomach. Her eyes were suddenly focused on me, but she didn't seem to be taking my measure. Instead, she was looking at me like—well, like she already knew me. "They do," she said, still lying there. "They really do."

"Then why bother?" I asked, pointing to her paperback, which was Wallace Stegner's *Crossing to Safety*. (Read it sometime.) I was getting my master's degree in creative writing and was in the habit of asking rhetorical questions, particularly about books.

"Because there's no such thing as life without heartbreak," she said, swinging her legs around so she was right side up. The novel fell neatly into her lap. "And just as well. Otherwise none of it would matter."

I stared at her, slack-jawed, trying to come up with a semi-intelligent thing to say in response. It was a relief when Rob strode into the living room.

"I see you've met Louisa," he said, smiling broadly. "James, Lou. Lou, James." He walked to the sofa and slung Lou over his shoulder. "Big news, my friend," he said to me, Lou's feet still in the air. "I'm literally holding the future Mrs. Logan. We got engaged two days ago."

Lou squealed, and he gently put her back on the ground.

"*You're* getting married? No way!" I said, my voice cracking. I've never been a particularly cool cat, and this was no exception. Meeting your mother was not unlike having my home hit by a meteorite. The odds of it happening were impossibly slim, and yet there it was: this incredible incident that had just left a hole in the middle of everything.

"Way," he said.

Rob being as lumbering as he is, and Lou being a pocket-size person, he had to bend down to kiss her. As their lips met, I bristled, as though I were witnessing a crime against nature rather than two twentysomethings in love.

"Um," I said, glancing around, wishing for another person to commiserate with, someone who would shrug and say, "Insane, right?"

Instead, I caught Lou's eye. And what did she do but shrug and give me a look that said, "Insane, right?"

I thought I might die.

Instead, I took a deep breath—*James, man, act like someone with a fully functional frontal lobe*—and forced my mouth into a smile. "When did this happen?"

What I meant was, how was I just hearing about it? Rob had been my best friend since the fourth grade. If I knew anything about him, it was that while he wanted a wife, some kids, and the whole white-picket-fence package, he didn't want any of that until he had banked several million and was on the losing side of forty.

When he called the month before to tell me he was dating someone seriously, and that I should fly my miserable ass (sorry to be profane, but that *is* what he said, and by the time you read this you'll know it and dozens of other expletives I've never even heard of) to New York to meet her, I understood that he was in love.

His invitation was a welcome opportunity to temporarily abandon all the writing I wasn't actually doing, as well as the thirty-two undergraduate creative-writing papers I was supposed to be grading (no fewer than five of which would be at least partially plagiarized). But I was anticipating a meet-and-greet nestled in a relaxing weekend. Not a wedding announcement.

Rob put his arm around Lou's narrow shoulders, and she beamed up at him. "It's sudden, to be sure," he said to me. "But when you know, you just know. You know?"

"Absolutely," I said.

But as Lou turned from Rob to me, I knew something that was at distinct odds with what he was describing. And that was that Lou was wrong—completely wrong—for my oldest friend.

"And now I've finally brought my two favorite people in the world together," he said. "Let's go somewhere nice to celebrate and charge it to the company."

Rob had attended the University of Virginia on a full ride, graduated in three years, and gone directly to Columbia Business School.

Afterward, he had landed a plum position at a large international bank that is no longer in existence. At the time, even he suspected the company was perhaps a skosh evil, but none of us yet knew that he was working for an institution whose financial solvency revolved around destroying people's dreams.

Lou pulled Rob closer. "No, no, let's do something fun and easy," she said. "Fun and easy, right, Jim? Do you like Italian?"

I liked Italian well enough, but I was stuck on the Jim part of her sentence. No one called me Jim; that had never been my name. And yet now it was, at least to Lou.

"Sure, I'm flexible," I said, and by this I meant, *You may refer to me as Larry or Pookums if you're so inclined, and I'll eagerly answer.* Something in me was unfurling fast, and it was wonderful or terrible, depending on how you looked at it. Maybe both. I had no business being envious of Rob, or paying any heed to the feral attraction I was feeling for his fiancée, even if I thought it was strange that he *had* a fiancée. I was his best friend, and it was my job to act as such—toward both of them.

After I stashed my suitcase in the corner of the living room and ran to the bathroom to make sure I didn't smell like an airport urinal, we grabbed our jackets and headed out.

Rob and I had to work hard to keep up with Lou, who walked awfully fast for someone with such short legs. We stopped at a liquor store—back then, there weren't so many wine shops everywhere, even in New York—and bought an unchilled bottle of champagne and a bottle of red wine. Then we wandered over to a restaurant on Avenue A at Eleventh Street. It was the kind of place that looked like it was one health inspection away from being shuttered, but Lou said the pasta was handmade and we would absolutely love it.

"So where did you two meet?" I asked after we had been seated at a four-top in the corner.

"It's kind of a funny story," Rob said, turning to Lou.

She laughed—a deep, throaty laugh, not at all the jingle I was expecting based on her squeal when Rob was holding her upside down—and began. "I was at Starbucks at Astor Place." (Yes, we had Starbucks back in the Dinosaur Days, though perhaps it, too, will be extinct by the time you read this.)

"And I bumped into her—" said Rob.

"More like spotted me from across the café and made a beeline for me—"

"All right, I saw her sitting at the bar and made a beeline for her."

"Ah, the meet-cute," I said.

"No, no," said Lou lightly. "It was more romantic than that. Almost serendipitous, really."

I flushed; I wasn't trying to make it sound unromantic, per se, even if a small part of me wasn't particularly enthused by their tale. "Okay, no meet-cute. Meet-serendipitous. Carry on."

She was instantly appeased. "As it happened, I was reading Neruda," she said. (*The love poet. Of course you were,* I thought.) "And Rob looked at me and said, 'Before I loved you, love, nothing was my own.' So I let him buy me a second cup of coffee."

I resisted the urge to snort at Rob, who was looking quite pleased with himself. "Neruda, huh? I thought you were more a case-study kind of guy."

"I'm an educated man," he protested.

"Yes, Mr. MBA, I am aware. I'm just saying—"

"That I don't know poetry?"

"That at most, you might have memorized a line or two to facilitate your pursuit of women."

Rob put his hand on Lou's shoulder. "I won't argue with that. But as far as I'm concerned, there are no *women.* There's only Lou."

"We went on a date the next day," said Lou.

"And by the following week, she had moved in with me," said Rob, not bothering to hide how proud he was of his evolved status as half of a cohabiting couple.

With her legs twisted like a pretzel beneath her and her head held high, there was a fierce elegance to Lou that I couldn't recall ever noticing in another woman; and if I had, I certainly hadn't stopped to admire it. Unfortunately, I couldn't take my eyes off of her. Which meant I had to continue to make conversation or risk coming off as her fiancé's weird staring friend who had to be tolerated, if only for a weekend. "Are you a dancer?" I asked lamely.

She smiled. "I wish! Dance is an expensive hobby, Jim. My mom didn't have money for that sort of thing."

I let my gaze drop to her caramel-colored sweater. It was pilling in some places, and worn thin in others. She had managed to make it look stylish, but upon closer inspection, it probably wasn't the kind of garment she would choose were a newer item of clothing available. "Sorry," I said.

"Don't be. I'm flattered that you'd think that of me. But no. I'm a poet."

Be still, my beating heart! She announced it like she was the queen of England. As mentioned, I was in a writing program at the time and so every other woman I knew was a writer, with a good percentage of them dedicating themselves to the craft of poetry. But not a single one of them ever said it like *that*.

"Do you have your MFA?" I asked.

She laughed lightly. "Oh, Jim. No, no, no. I work in the mail room at a literary agency and spend seven hours a day sorting other people's ambitions."

"And the eighth?" I prompted. To be honest, I wanted to know how she occupied all twenty-four hours, but it seemed ill-advised to ask just then.

She gave me a wry smile. "I spend it crying in the bathroom."

The proud poet, crying in the bathroom. What a flurry of contradictions she was; what a whirl of emotions was washing over me. I tried to imagine something unpleasant—say, an anesthesia-free root canal—but as I turned my thoughts inward, Lou was still right there in the center of my mind.

"Not for long," said Rob, and for a moment I almost thought he was telling me that I would only feel the way I was feeling for a short while longer, which probably would have been the best-case scenario. As he continued, however, I realized he was talking about Lou's agency job. "Soon she'll be able to stay home and write all day and do whatever she pleases."

The waiter had uncorked and poured our red wine, and I took a long drink from my glass, then another, and a third for good measure. "You're twenty-five?" I asked Lou. Rob and I were twenty-five, and I guess I expected she would be our age.

"No, twenty-two," she said, reaching for her wine as well. She looked at me over the edge of the glass as she took a sip. "I graduated last spring."

Twenty-two seemed awfully young to be a full-time writer, but at that point in life, I had very particular ideas about how writing was to be done.

"So you'll write poems part of the day and spend the rest of it baking, Sylvia Plath–style?" I said.

Lou and I chuckled, but Rob frowned. "Uh, didn't she commit suicide?" he said gruffly.

Lou put her hand on his arm. "A little writerly humor, sweetheart."

"Did you forget about my raging case of foot-in-mouth-itis?" I asked Rob.

"You think you're bad?" said Lou. "Two weeks ago, my supervisor's boss called down to the mail room, and I accidentally said, 'Love you!' before hanging up the phone."

"That's a good one. But have you ever been the jerk who told a blind man to watch his step as he walked into the street, as I did last week?" I asked.

Rob, who had finally started to laugh, added, "Worse, I was walking down Sixth Avenue the other day and saw my friends Jess and Aidan walking toward me. So I yelled, 'What's up, assholes?!' It wasn't until I saw the looks on their faces that I realized they were total strangers!"

"You didn't—did you?" cried Lou.

"I did!" he said, and the three of us looked at each other and laughed even harder, until our laughter became howls and tears leaked from the corners of our eyes. It was one of those moments when you feel unbelievably lucky to have been placed on the planet at the same time as the people in your life. As I wiped my eyes and looked across the table at Lou, I silently thanked her for so swiftly smoothing over the situation.

"What about you, Jim?" asked Lou later that evening. We had moved on to a tiny bar that played old jazz and were standing around waiting for Rob to fetch us drinks (his treat; he always tried to buy the first round). "Rob says you're a writer, too."

"I am," I said, sounding far less resolute than she had.

"Fiction, right?" she said.

I nodded. "I'd like to write novels. I'm hoping to land a teaching job to support myself."

She was staring at me so intently that I thought maybe I had pesto stuck between my bicuspids. "Rob says you're crazy smart, but sounds like you're practical, too. I like that."

I shrugged, simultaneously embarrassed and flattered. "You want to pass that on to my father? He's holding out hope that I'll become a mechanical engineer."

She laughed and accepted a glass brimming with red wine from Rob, who had just returned. "Being something for someone else is a perfectly good waste of a life, isn't it? At any rate, I get the impression you're great just the way you are, Jim."

Don't swoon, don't smile, don't think about kissing her, I told myself, sticking my nose into the wineglass Rob had just handed me.

Unaware of my angst, Lou picked my brain about books for a while, then quizzed Rob and me about our childhoods and how we had become friends. (In brief: He walloped me on the playground one afternoon during elementary school, and though I may or may not have cried instead of fighting back, we were both given detention. A few evenings of mopping the school floors together—yes, in our day child labor was not just permitted, but actually encouraged—and we realized we could both quote ninety-seven percent of *Star Wars Episodes IV* and *V* and lived seven blocks away from each other. The rest, as they say, is history.)

The bar had been a good choice. Whereas some people get rowdy while drinking, I suffer from an alcohol-induced narcolepsy of sorts, and when we returned to the apartment I instantly passed out on the sofa without having to think about Rob and Lou retreating to the bedroom they shared.

The next morning, I awoke to the sound of Rob tinkering in the kitchen; Lou was nowhere to be seen.

"She gets up early on the weekends and goes out to write," said Rob, answering the question I had not asked as he walked into the living room. He was clutching a cup of coffee for dear life, and his eyes were as bleary as I'm sure my own looked. But at once he perked up. "Well?" he asked, sitting on the end of the sofa. "What do you think?"

What I thought was that there was a perfectly lovely woman I had been seeing back in Ann Arbor—Kathryn Pierce, her name was—and I would have to go home and end things with her. And that was because I had just discovered that there was a void in me, and "perfectly lovely" was never going to fill it.

"She seems great, Rob," I said.

He ran his hand through his hair. "Isn't she? She's had such a rough life, and yet she's so unjaded. And God, is she gorgeous or what?"

I recalled Lou's almond-shaped eyes, which were a greenish hazel in some light, and brown in others. I thought of her golden mane of hair, her impossibly small wrists, her rose of a mouth. "Yeah," I said.

"I feel like I just won the lottery."

"You did. You really did."

"You'll be my best man, right?"

The wedding. Of course, there was going to be a wedding. I squinted at him. "When is it?"

He frowned. "Does it matter?"

My conscience kicked in, thank God, and I was able to string together the phrases that I should have immediately blurted out. "Of course not! Stupid question. Get married on New Year's Eve—or my birthday, for that matter. I'll be there with bells on, and would be honored to be your best man."

"That's great, James." Rob took a sip of coffee, then looked at me. "You're like a brother to me, but better. No one knows me like you do, and if you're there, it means I'm making the right decision."

"Right." I nodded, wishing that the sofa contained a portal that would suck me in and transport me back in time, or forward, or to any point at which I was not bending beneath the horrible weight of the lie I was about to utter, and all the lies that would inevitably follow. "I'm already looking forward to it."

~

The internet was a fairly new thing in those days, and I didn't have a personal computer, let alone a cell phone, on which to conduct impulsive searches for useless trivia. And so, on Sunday night as my plane lifted over LaGuardia, I scoured the cobwebbed corners of my mind for a few lines I had read years earlier as an undergraduate.

The plane was touching down at Detroit Metro when they finally came to me. They were Neruda, too, but from a very different poem.

I could not recall the exact phrasing, but it was along the lines of, dark things must be loved secretly, in the space between the soul and the shadows.

Oh come on, you ridiculous sap, I chided myself as Lou's sparkling face surfaced in my mind yet again. It was true that I knew—just as sure as you know you're alive when you begin to rouse in the morning—that she would be an important part of my life, and not only because she was going to be Rob's wife.

But was it really love? Or had I simply placed Lou on a pedestal and given myself permission to idealize her, all things right and rational be damned—and this decision set love in motion?

I still wonder about that. If I had made different choices then, such as telling Rob what I really thought about his impending nuptials, he would have married Lou all the same. Then I would have estranged myself from him—from both of them—and everything else that came next would have been different. And that, I will admit, is a version of history I can't bear to imagine, as fraught as the following years may have been.

But as you know, that's not where this story ends.

TWO

November 1998

"So, douche nozzle, are you *sure* you're ready?" I shouted at Rob, who was standing next to me at the crowded dive bar where we had gathered for his bachelor party. "*Really* ready?"

It was the week before Thanksgiving, and Rob and Lou had recently arrived in Michigan for their wedding. Lou's family was scattered across the country, and your grandmother—a troubled woman, though I'm still sorry you never had the chance to meet her—claimed she no longer believed in the institution of marriage and refused to attend the wedding. Because of this, the ceremony and reception were to take place in Rob's and my hometown and would be primarily paid for by Rob, who was already making three times as much as his father.

Being Rob's best man, I was expected to plan a raucous night out for him and the rest of his groomsmen. This group included a bunch of his friends from business school, his cousin Justin, and our other closest friend from childhood, Jason, whom everyone called by his last name, Wisnewski.

We had just arrived at our third stop of the evening, and I was doing what many a best man before me had done: making sure the groom was actually prepared to yoke himself to his beloved for the rest of forever.

Plenty of people get married in their twenties and do just fine, but somehow Lou's twenty-three and Rob's twenty-six felt tragically young. It was not just that my opinion was muddied by misguided longing. It was that Lou seemed more like Rob's quarter-life crisis than a true match for the rest of his adult existence. As long as I had known him, he had favored tall, glossy girls who played tennis and lacrosse and spent their summers somewhere other than their primary residences. Their enormous white teeth lined up just so, and they were in possession of or in the process of accruing multiple degrees they intended to use only until they began producing flocks of perfect offspring. Lou was petite, unmoneyed, and—well, nothing like those other women. How could Rob be so certain that she was more than just a phase?

"Never been so ready for anything in my life, dick widget," slurred Rob, who had already been much fêted by the beefy wunderkinds who had flown in from Manhattan and Boston for the celebration.

"That's great," I said. I was on the verge of being stone-cold sober myself and waved in the direction of the bartender, who glanced my way and took the order of the woman standing behind me. As I turned my attention back to Rob, I realized his eyes were wet. At that point I had never seen him cry. I wasn't sure how to react, so I just stood there nodding like an idiot.

"I only hope to God you find someone who makes you feel like Lou makes me feel," he added, and took a swig from his pint.

As much as I was tempted to make a snide remark, I understood that this was his soon-to-be wife we were talking about and that I was to endure his sappy inanity and at no point mention that my dinner was resurfacing in my throat. (Funny, isn't it, how we can't stand the behavior of other people in love yet turn around and act the same way when we're smitten?) Anyway, I was used to it. Every call from Rob included a fresh anecdote about how curious and bright Lou was, each email a laundry list of their most recent adventures.

"To love," I said to Rob, raising my empty glass.

"To love!" hollered Wisnewski.

Rob smiled drunkenly in Wisnewski's direction. I was relieved to see that his eyes, while still moist, were no longer threatening to drip sentimentality into his beer. "And to think you guys knew me when. To love," he said, though it came out as *tuh luff*. He turned back to me. "How's Karen?"

"You mean Kathryn?"

"Right!" barked Rob.

I had attempted to break it off with Kathryn Pierce, but she had not taken it well. And by not well, I mean she simply had not taken it: "I don't believe you, James," she said, arms crossed over her chest. "We spend hours together without getting bored. We like the same movies and restaurants. We even have similar taste in books." (This last part wasn't actually true. She was wild about the Williams—Shakespeare and Faulkner—neither of whom I could muster much enthusiasm for.) She was an English professor and a well-reviewed novelist; I was her student when we began dating, though I'm a little ashamed to admit this to you. She had high cheekbones and perfect prose, and when she continued to show up at my door, I invited her in because I didn't understand how hurtful it could be to say yes just because you weren't sure how to say no.

I laughed. "She's fine—but you're not. We need to get you home soon."

"Nah," said Aidan, another one of Rob's groomsmen. "It's bad luck if he doesn't puke."

I eyed Aidan's left hand. His ring finger was bare. "You ever been married?"

"Nah," he said again. "Not for me. But I've been to a lot of bachelor parties."

"'Not for me'—I said that once," said Rob, wobbling a bit. "But look at me now."

I *was* looking at him, and beneath the fluorescent bar lighting, it appeared he would soon be lucky all over himself. "How about some food?" I asked. "A burger, maybe? Some fries?"

"Fries sound like just the thing." He threw his arm around my neck. "You're a good friend, James. The best, even. *Way* better than a brother."

"Thanks, man. You, too." It was true, even if it was a shame that it took alcohol to get us to confess such things.

Eating gave Rob a second wind, which led to more celebrating, and we didn't make it back to his parents' house for two more hours. The back door was open, just as it always was. I managed to get Rob down the stairs into the basement, where I deposited him on the worn leather couch where he had slept more often than his own bed during high school. He passed out as soon as his head hit the cushion. I left his shoes on and located a bucket in the laundry room, which I placed on the ground beside the sofa.

I tiptoed back up the stairs, hoping that I had not woken up Rob's parents—or Lou, who I assumed was asleep in the guest bedroom. I had just reached for the doorknob when I heard someone say, "Hey, Jim."

"Christ on a cracker!" I yelled, jumping straight up like a spooked cat. As I looked over the kitchen island, Lou came into focus.

"It's Cheesus to you," she deadpanned from the recliner in the corner of the living room.

I laughed, even though I was cringing inside. Against my better judgment, I had been looking forward to seeing her. Yet I was bone tired and presumably splattered with Rob's vomit (even after the fries—or maybe because of them—he had bent over and spewed on the sidewalk next to me on the way home). My looking forward involved more alert, sanitary conditions.

In the nine months since I had seen Lou and Rob in New York, I had completed my master's program and had been hired as an adjunct writing instructor at the university I had attended. The position didn't pay much, but it kept me mentally and logistically occupied, which in turn kept me from spending too much time ruing Rob's poetic waxings about Lou. In the evenings, I had started writing a dystopian novel that I hoped would put me on the literary map—or at the very least, land me an agent and a minor sale to a major publisher.

My thoughts of Lou swung from frequent to sporadic. But every time I was doing better, Rob would call to tell me about some clever thing she had done; or I'd see some knockoff version of her walking around campus; or I would read a poem and find myself wondering what Lou was reading, and whether her own work was any good—and I would resume acting like a man who has been lobotomized.

During these periods, I had to shove so many questions and conflicting thoughts onto the cluttered shelves of my conscience. How could I occupy dozens of hours thinking about someone with whom I had actually only spent two days, total—and in the company of her fiancé, who happened to be my closest friend?

And now there she was, wearing an oversize t-shirt and a pair of footless tights, exhausted and weary and every bit as beautiful as I had remembered her. As I met her gaze, still neither of us smiling, my mind flooded with nonsense. What did she look like sleeping? Were her eyelids light lavender or the palest seashell pink? Did she leave her hair in a pile on top of her head while she slept, or did it float around her like seaweed in a shallow pond?

"Sorry," I said sheepishly. "Hi. Were you there the whole time?"

She rose from the recliner and walked over to the kitchen island. "Hi yourself. I just came downstairs. How bad is he?"

"Fine," I said, walking into the kitchen. "Well, not really, but fortunately the wedding isn't tomorrow."

She rested her elbows on the counter and cracked a smile. "There's that, at least."

I shifted from one foot to the other. "How are *you*, Lou?"

"Great," she said, but her eyes flashed with something—doubt? Uncertainty?

I glanced around. There was the floral wallpaper, bleeding from the kitchen into the dining room. The hunter-green sofa and matching recliner. The framed photos of Rob at various stages of his early life, scattered on shelves and nailed to the walls. These domestic trappings were more familiar to me than those of the apartment I had lived in for the past three years. But they were new to Lou.

"Is it weird being here?" I asked, though I already knew it was; maybe asking was my way of telling her it was okay.

"No." She sighed. "Yeah, a little. It's . . . I grew up, um. Kind of not like this. You know? And the Logans, they're just—"

Like the newbie professor that I was, I pressed for detail without letting her work it out for herself. "How has that been? Have Bobby and Nancy been nice to you?" Bobby was much like my own father: quiet but prone to flashes of anger directed at the state of the modern world. Nancy was friendly in that distant Midwestern way, though once you got to know her, it was impossible to overlook her frenetic anxiety. I leaned in toward Lou conspiratorially. "Has Rob's mom been picking up your glasses and washing them before you've had a second sip of your drink?"

I expected another smile—a small laugh, maybe—but she bit her bottom lip and looked toward the stairs, like she thought Rob's parents might be listening in. "They're really lovely."

I was no longer tired. "Remind me, where did you grow up?"

Lou unbent her torso and rested one foot on the inside of the opposite knee, flamingo-style. "Here and there. Mostly Virginia. And Pennsylvania, a bit, and Ohio for a while."

"You've lived everywhere."

"If you consider interchangeable coal-country towns *everywhere*."

I chuckled. "I guess I don't."

"Nor should you." She yawned, her nose scrunching up as her mouth opened. Then, God help me, she rubbed her eyes with both hands, looking so sleepily adorable that I wanted to scoop her up into my arms.

Instead, I balled my hands into fists, forcing myself to concentrate on the sensation of my fingers pressing into my palms. "Well," I said in what I hoped was a neutral tone, "we should probably go to bed."

Lou arched one eyebrow, and all of the blood in my body made a beeline for my face. "I didn't mean it like—"

She held my gaze for several electric, terrifying seconds. Then she laughed. "Of course you didn't."

"It's my foot-in-mouth-itis," I said limply.

"Oh, I remember. Sorry to see that you remain afflicted." She smiled. "I suppose I should go check on Rob and head upstairs. Need to get my beauty rest for the wedding, or so they say. I'll see you tomorrow at the rehearsal, if not sooner, yes?"

"Yes. Looking forward," I said as she made her way around the kitchen island.

She was at the top of the stairs when she turned and glanced at me over her shoulder. "Me, too, Jim."

∽

It was nothing. Whatever I had sensed while Lou was looking at me was the result of my being a writer—a person who, for all intents and purposes, lived in his own head and was prone to fantastical thinking. Even if I *hadn't* imagined it, it didn't matter. Rob and Lou were about to publicly proclaim their intent to spend the rest of their lives together. The rest of their lives!

As for me, I was a grown man with free will. I could, and would, rein in my thoughts.

These were the things I told myself that night as I walked back to my father's house, where I was staying for the weekend. I reminded myself of them yet again as I dressed for the rehearsal the following evening, and as I drove to the church, walked into the nave, and watched an ecstatic Lou and Rob practice their vows.

See? I thought as I pretended to hand Rob a ring, which he pretended to put on Lou's finger. Forever was forever. By the end of the rehearsal and dinner afterward, I had almost convinced myself my fabricated convictions were true. After all, Lou had been beaming at Rob all through the preparatory ceremony. And Rob: I had never seen him so happy. This was how it was going to be, and it was time for me to adjust accordingly.

~

The actual ceremony was lovely, as these things usually are. With Lou's father out of the picture, Rob walked her down the aisle himself. Prayers were said, poems were read, teary vows were exchanged. There was a passionate, lingering kiss, then applause. Rob and Lou strolled back down the aisle as husband and wife, to much cheering. With their bright eyes, flushed cheeks, and shared air of exuberance, I was able to forget my tangled feelings and wish them a beautiful forever.

The reception was more of the same. Silverware clanking. Champagne glasses filled, raised, and drained, again and again. Then it was time for my speech. I had labored over it for days, trying to find the perfect balance between generic and honest. Truth be told, I didn't know all that much about what made a marriage happy—or how Rob and Lou were together. They seemed happy enough, though most couples do at first. Were they? Their day-to-day life remained a mystery to me. Their shared dreams were equally elusive. How many children did they want? Were they planning on a big house in the country or a jet-setting life with apartments in various cosmopolitan destinations?

Having been together less than a full year, perhaps they hadn't figured out these things yet. The most I had gotten out of Rob was that he would do everything in his power to give Lou the life she deserved. The particulars of this deserved life remained undefined.

So I centered my speech on Rob. "When Rob asked me to be his best man, of course I said yes. But as so many of us here can attest, *he's* the best man here. He's always the smartest guy in the room, but never acts like he knows it. He's bighearted, and—" I glanced at him and chuckled. "Well, he's just big, period, and I'm not just talking about the fact that he's six four. Everything he does is larger than life. When he told me about Lou, I assumed she was going to be like the hundreds of other women he dated." (For this, I received requisite laughter, and a few hoots from his business school buddies.) "But of course, if she *had* been, Rob wouldn't have told me about her." (More laughter.) "And then I met Lou and—" I was standing at one end of the long table where the wedding party was seated. Over bouquets of pale purple flowers, Lou's eyes bore into my own, questioning: *What will you say?*

Breathe, I told myself. *Swallow. Speak.*

"This lucky bastard found a woman who, while a heck of a lot smaller than he is, is also larger than life, and just as amazing. Lou, I've never seen Rob happier." Raised glasses, murmurs of approval. I shifted my attention back to Rob. "May the two of you find meaning and much joy in your life together."

Glass clinked against glass. Rob nodded at me, his eyes wet; I had made him cry a second time. This was not nothing. I myself wasn't fond of crying, which seemed to conjure up funerals and the worst parts of childhood. And yet I remember the rare feeling of triumph I experienced when one of the short stories I workshopped during my graduate program—a fictionalized piece about my mother's death—had half my cohort in tears. It is not easy to make people feel something beyond the state to which they are predisposed at any given moment, and here I had managed it with a few words about Rob and Lou and love. (In retrospect, it occurs to me that this had as much to do with the two of them as it did with my speech.) I raised my glass to Rob and nodded back, satisfied that I had gotten it right.

As soon as the other speeches were given and the band started back up, I escaped to the restroom, desperate for even a moment to myself. I sat in a stall for a while, listening to my pulse in my ears and waiting for my heart, which was still racing, to resume a normal beat. After a few minutes, I reluctantly left the bathroom and headed down the hall toward the ballroom.

As I turned the corner, I nearly ran into Lou, who had just stepped out of the women's restroom. Her gown was a simple silk sheath. It suited her. She was smiling, but like Rob, tears were swimming along the rims of her eyes.

"You okay?" I asked.

"That was beautiful, Jim. Thank you. It's just all so wonderful that it's a little overwhelming." She gestured toward the ballroom. "Come dance with me?"

There was no amount of alcohol or encouragement that could make me attempt to move my body to a rhythm in front of other people. "Okay," I said.

"You look nice," I said as we made our way to the dance floor. She put her arm on mine, and we began to sway. "Is that strange to say?"

"It's my wedding day. If I don't look nice, then there's no hope for me."

"Your wedding day," I repeated. Yes, I understood she had just gotten married. But up until that point, I had mostly questioned Rob's motivation rather than consider why a woman like Lou would wed at twenty-three. Love is the obvious answer, but I knew at least a hand-ful of people around our age who loved each other deeply and had no immediate plans for matrimony. My parents had married in their early twenties, but the result of this was that they spent the next three decades acting like they regretted it; my mother had barely mustered a

21

smile at their twenty-fifth wedding anniversary party. When she died of a massive heart attack a year later, I half assumed it was a broken heart that had really killed her. "What's next for you and Rob?" I asked Lou.

She held up her left hand, which sported an engagement ring with a diamond nearly as wide as her finger. Beneath that was a thin white-gold band, which would be the only ring I would see her wear after that day. "Well, I left the literary agency last week. So I'm going to write more. And there's talk of Rob going to Hong Kong, so of course I would go with him."

I spun her around, trying not to step on the edge of her dress. "Really?" This was the first I was hearing of their plans. "What will you do there? Won't you be lonely?"

"You know what Chekhov said, right?"

"Ca-caw, ca-caw?" I said, doing my best seagull impression.

She grinned. "No, you lunatic. What he said about *marriage*."

"I'm less familiar with Chekhov's thoughts on human coupling."

"Prepare to be enlightened. He said, 'If you are afraid of loneliness, don't marry.'"

"I'll be sure to use that one on my future wife."

"Where's the woman you're dating?"

"Pardon?" I said, losing my footing for a split second.

"You know," said Lou, guiding me back into step. "Rob said you were dating Kathryn Pierce. I loved her last book. Why didn't you bring her?"

"I thought it would be rotten to bring her if she had to sit alone during the ceremony and most of the dinner."

"You're not in love, then."

"Not so sure."

"Rob desperately wants you to be as happy as he is, you know."

"What about you? Are you happy?"

"Of course. I love Rob, and he's so good to me. He—"

Lou was interrupted by one of her bridesmaids, who was suddenly standing next to us with an expectant expression across her face. "Lou*isa*!" she cried out. "When are you going to let me have a dance with this cutie?"

Lou turned to her friend. "Jennifer, love, would you mind giving us one more minute? I promise I'll hand Jim over to you as soon as we're done."

"You'd better! There's a line of men waiting to dance with you! And you!" Jennifer said. "Come find me and we'll boogie!"

"She might be good for *you*," Lou said.

I watched Jennifer clodhop across the dance floor. "Think I'll have to pass."

"Does that mean you're going to try to make it work with Kathryn?"

"Something like that."

"You know, the two of you could come stay with us for a week. We'd have a blast."

"That does sound fun," I said. As I looked at the couples twirling across the dance floor to a song I hadn't heard since high school, I was hit with a pang of homesickness—not for my actual home, but for Kathryn. The creamy pillow of her stomach; the way she ran her fingers through my hair while I read beside her on the sofa. If her familiarity was a trap, then her desire was the bait that lured me. Because what I was really longing for at that moment was for someone to long for me. As much of myself as I gave, Kathryn wanted more, and that in and of itself was addictive. (Not that this was fair in any way; I know that. But we so rarely hear the truth because it is unfair, and even so ugly that we can barely admit it to ourselves, let alone another person.) Maybe that spark of longing, I thought, could kindle a fire.

"Come *on*!" It was Jennifer again. She pointed at me, made a lassoing motion, and pretended to pull me toward her with an invisible rope.

"Yee-haw," I said, letting Lou go. "Guess that's my cue."

Her eyes were sparkling as she laughed. "I'm so glad you're Rob's best friend, Jim. You wouldn't believe just how highly he speaks of you."

I just barely managed not to wince. "Feeling's mutual," I mumbled.

Jennifer seized me around the neck and began wiggling her hips in what appeared to be a drunken samba. I sighed and made a halfhearted attempt to match her moves. Over Jennifer's shoulder, I saw that Rob and Lou had begun to dance. As I watched the two of them glide across the dance floor, her head resting on his chest, I was surprised to realize that of the many things I was feeling, envy wasn't one of them. My oldest friend had made his vows before God and man, and now he and Lou were embarking on a life together. And of course, I wanted them to be happy.

I wanted to be happy, too, so I made a vow of my own. I would forget about Lou and throw myself wholeheartedly into my relationship with Kathryn, toward whom I was feeling more and more warmly as the night wore on. And if for some reason committing to Kathryn proved to be impossible, I decided, I could, and would, make a concerted effort to find a partner who made the rest of the world disappear when she was near.

THREE

Spring 1999

"Joan Didion said it's harder to see the ends of things than the beginnings," I said, regarding the two dozen undergraduates who were in various stages of slouch around the table.

It was my last class of the semester, and what a relief to have made it through. My father liked to say that if something was worth doing, it was worth doing well, and I spent hours preparing for any given lesson. Maybe, just maybe, it had begun to pay off. While I had not quite figured out what worked, I had begun to establish certain patterns. I had started to determine what *didn't* work.

"Who's Joan Didion?" called a male student from the back of the classroom.

I glared at him. "She's the writer whose essay was part of your last assignment." (Okay, so I had more determining to do.) I paused, then addressed the rest of the group in a more neutral tone. "Do you think that's true when it comes to writing? Do you begin your story with the end in mind?"

"It's impossible not to, right?" said one student, flicking her glossy hair over her shoulder. Sorority girl, East Coast accent, dressed in head-to-toe black. The car she drove around campus probably cost twice as much as mine.

"No, writing should be an adventure," said another student. He was beige—skin, hair, opinions. He would go far in life.

"You're both correct, at least when it comes to your own work," I said. "There's no one right way to approach a story." I tapped the stack of papers on the table in front of me. "Before I return your finals, let's talk about process. Did you begin with the end in mind?"

After what I hoped was a decent discussion, I passed their assignments back. I had graded kindly, maybe too much so—rookie mistake, owing to my nervousness about how they would fill out my teaching evaluation. After all, I had not yet been officially hired for the following year, and I needed the work.

At least most of the class would be happy about their marks. But my heart was pounding as I reached the last student, whose paper I had deliberately placed at the bottom of the pile. Nora Roderick. She had deep copper skin and short hair and favored oversize cashmere sweaters and tall leather boots.

"Can you please see me after class, Nora?" I said, raising my eyebrows in what I hoped was a semiauthoritative yet nonthreatening way.

She cocked her head and looked at me. Her voice was low and relaxed as she responded. "Sorry. I have another class to be at."

"All right." *Amateur,* I chided myself. *Grow a pair.* "Then come see me during office hours. Three to four today."

She looked down at her paper, which lacked the red scribbled grade I'd given the other students. I saw it click for her: she had been caught. "Okay," she said. "I'll see you then."

A few hours later, she knocked on the door of the small office I shared with another adjunct instructor.

"Come in," I said, gesturing to the cheap bucket chair in front of me. I was jittery. As mentioned, I was no stranger to plagiarism. But usually it was blatant—some glittering piece of writing that could not possibly have been written by an undergraduate who slept through most classes. Nora, on the other hand, had stolen a story, only to go through the trouble of rewriting almost every line. And why? She had written a few pieces before, and they had been fine. Good, even.

"So?" she said.

"Well. Nora. Here's the thing."

"What's your deal, Professor Hernandez?"

I sat up straighter. "*My* deal?"

"Yeah," she said. "You're acting like you drank a pot of coffee for lunch."

"Don't change the subject," I said sternly. *Spit it out already, Professor Hernandez.* "When I said steal, I didn't mean it literally. Remember my caveat? Steal if you must, but make sure you make it your own?"

In fact, I had stolen this bit of wisdom from Pascal, my onetime instructor turned mentor and friend. "Since there is nothing new under the sun, steal everything!" he declared in his melodic French Guinea accent. "*Every single thing you love!* Then make it your own!" (No doubt, Pascal did not have my best friend's wife in mind when he dispensed this advice.)

"I know the better part of your story came from the *Kenyon Review*," I told her. "So I ask, why?"

Nora crossed one long leg over the other and leaned back. "Are you going flunk me?"

I stared at her, then felt self-conscious about doing so and glanced away. "Should I?"

"No."

"And why's that?"

She eyed me warily. "If this is the part where I'm supposed to give you a sob story, you've got the wrong woman. I grew up in an enormous house in Bloomfield Hills and attended one of the best prep schools in the country."

I frowned; this conversation was not going the way I had planned. "It has nothing to do with where you grew up, Nora, or where you went to school. It has to do with you cheating. I know you can write. So why didn't you?"

For a moment it seemed she was going to protest, but she just shook her head. "I don't know. I started something that seemed good, and—I just couldn't finish it."

This I understood; I had not written a single paragraph in my dystopian novel in more than two months. Try as I might, I couldn't seem to figure out who the hero was, and while this doesn't have to be a plot problem, it was for my book. "That happens. But why not ask for an extension?"

"Because I assumed you'd say no."

"You know what they say about assuming, right?"

"That it leads to a clichéd saying about asses?"

"Nora."

As she tried to repress a smile, I sighed. "It's fine. And yes, I might have told you no. But wouldn't you rather miss one assignment than risk flunking a class or being placed on academic probation?"

"I guess. How'd you figure it out, anyway? I chose an obscure story on purpose."

"Fate, maybe, or bad luck on your part." I shrugged. "I read that piece as a graduate student. Didn't really like it, and what you don't like often stays with you even more than what you enjoy. Anyway, if you're going to rewrite, you might want to choose a piece that sounds more like your own voice."

She smoothed the front of her skirt. "Sorry. It was really lame of me to do that. May I have another chance?"

I stood, indicating we were nearly done. "You already know the answer's yes, though your final grade will have to take a hit. Have a new paper to me in forty-eight hours. I don't care how long it is, just make it your own."

"I will. Thank you."

"Don't thank me just yet. Do the work, then we'll talk."

Nora stood and extended a slender hand to me. Her handshake was firm. "I'll have a new story in your box right away. Oh, and Professor Hernandez?"

"Yes?"

She released my hand and grimaced as she glanced at my pants. "Your fly's down. Might want to deal with that before you leave your office."

I blushed and turned toward the wall to yank my zipper up. "Um. Yes, it is. Thanks," I said.

When I turned back, she was gone.

~

Two days later, I was en route to California with Nora's new story tucked in my carry-on and Kathryn beside me.

"You're going to adore Napa," she said, squeezing my arm.

Through the dome window of the airplane, San Francisco began to come into focus. "I bet I will. Our first vacation."

"May it be our first of many." She rested her head on my shoulder. "It'll be good for us."

We were on our way to meet Rob and Lou, with whom we'd had dinner in Ann Arbor a few months earlier. Lou and Kathryn were similar in many ways, but since Kathryn was nearly a decade older than Lou, I hadn't anticipated that they would become fast friends. Of course, they'd taken to each other immediately, and by the end of our meal they had planned an entire vacation for the four of us.

Hong Kong was out, as Rob had deferred his transfer a year. Instead, Kathryn and Lou proposed California's wine country. Given my anemic adjunct salary, I would have preferred something less expensive—say, a nice trip to a bedbug-free motel on the Jersey Shore, or even a stay at Lou and Rob's place in New York. But Kathryn was from the Bay Area and knew all the best places to see, and Rob and Lou had always wanted to visit. Napa it was.

We rented a car, and Kathryn drove—no map needed, she cheerfully informed the man who assisted us. I hunkered down in my seat and watched brightly colored buildings give way to brown earth, then the green canopied spread of grapevines. We pulled off the highway and onto a dirt road, where the inn we were staying at was located. It was a rambling Victorian nestled between vineyards, with steep hills visible in the distance.

Our room was cozy, if a bit fussy for my taste. The bed whined loudly as Kathryn and I sat on its edge, and we looked at each other and laughed.

"Should we go find them?" I asked.

"No, let the newlyweds spend some time alone. Why don't we explore a bit?" said Kathryn. She was wearing a loose blue dress, and her lips were stained a raspberry color. She was beautiful, and I said so. We had been together about a year and a half at that point, and though I still did not think I was in love with her, I had grown to love her, which was a confusing state—sometimes I thought they might be the same thing.

"You think?"

"Should I say it again?" I teased.

"Yes," she said, dead serious. "You don't compliment me all that often, and it makes me wonder sometimes."

"You're beautiful, and I'm sorry. I'll do better," I told her, making the same promise to myself.

We wandered around the inn, which was charming in a musty sort of way, then took a stroll down a dirt path between two vineyards.

Though Kathryn attempted to explain the difference between grape varietals to me, I quickly decided that if you had seen one trellised grapevine, you had seen them all.

When we returned to the inn, the sound of familiar laughter rang out from the lobby. We found Rob and Lou nestled together on one of the upholstered sofas.

"You two!" said Lou, jumping up to hug us.

She squeezed me so hard my stomach hurt, then pummeled Kathryn. The two of them immediately jumped into the gratuitous ritual of burgeoning female friendship.

"Look at you," Kathryn said, holding Lou at arm's length. "Sickeningly gorgeous, as ever."

"Says the woman whose bone structure sends other women straight to a plastic surgeon."

"Bones don't matter when you write like you do. I adored *Scenes From a Wedding*."

Lou pretended to clutch her heart. "You don't know how much that means to me, coming from you. I actually think it's my favorite of the bunch—but if I could write novels like yours, I'd never attempt a poem again."

"Hey, man," I said to Rob, who shook my hand.

"Is it ever good to see you," he said. He was freshly showered and shaved, but his eyes were bloodshot. "It's been a crazy couple of months."

"That bad?"

"I'm working my way up the food chain, to be sure. But I slept at the office twice last week."

Lou slid her arm around his side. "This poor man is so stressed that he refused to bring a single book to read!"

"Not even *The Grapes of Wrath*?" I deadpanned.

Lou laughed lightly, and Kathryn groaned.

"I don't want to read a single word," said Rob. "I don't want to do a damn thing but hang out with you three and sip the sweet nectar of fermented grapes."

"That's the plan," said Kathryn amiably. Dating someone involves becoming a part of their ecosystem, and I could see she was pleased that she so effortlessly blended into mine.

"Sounds like a good plan to me," said Lou.

"Where to first?" said Rob. Even in his exhausted state, he was already running down his mental checklist. When we backpacked on part of the Appalachian Trail one summer during college, I had barely been able to keep up with him—not just because he was athletic, but also because he had been so eager to reach each marker on our trail map. I, on the other hand, would have happily spent an hour examining a dappled cluster of mushrooms.

"Let's set off down Route 29 and see what we're in the mood for," suggested Kathryn.

Rob had rented a shiny silver convertible, and he drove while Kathryn navigated from the passenger seat. Lou and I sat in the back, the wind pulling our smiles taut and drowning out the sound of everything but air whooshing past us.

"Are you having fun?" I asked Kathryn later. We were at our second vineyard and I was feeling comfortable, if mildly marinated. For all my anxiety about the trip—I had not been confident that the agreeable dining experience the four of us had shared would translate into us vacationing well together—it was going swimmingly.

"I'm having the best time," she said, practically beatific. "Aren't you?"

Before I could answer, Lou called out to Kathryn and motioned for her to join her up ahead on the dusty pebbled path in the garden we were strolling through. Kathryn kissed me on the cheek and ran off to Lou.

I suppose it could have been strange being around Kathryn and Lou at the same time, but it was easier in a way. Kathryn's presence was neutralizing; she was a constant, comforting reminder that both Lou and I were otherwise occupied.

Not that Lou was concerned about whether I was occupied. If she was in love with anyone on this trip, it was Kathryn. The two of them walked with their heads bent toward each other, arms linked like schoolgirls and deep in conversation about God only knows what. (In a moment of unbridled narcissism, I found myself hoping Kathryn would tell Lou I was a literary genius, a generous lover, and any number of things that cast a flattering light on me.)

"How's the old ball and chain?" I asked Rob. Lou and Kathryn were out of earshot.

He kicked the pebbled path with his loafer. "Lou? She's amazing. She's so committed to her writing, and yet she always has some side project going on. Last month it was pottery, and now she's been bird-watching in Central Park. But . . ."

I looked ahead at Lou, whose hair glinted gold in the sunlight. "But?"

He shrugged. "We fight a lot."

"Seriously? You guys seem so solid," I said. And they did. In addition to the couch canoodling Kathryn and I had come upon earlier, Lou had been stroking the back of his head—as if he were her pet Labrador, I thought at the time—on the drive to the vineyard. He put his hand on her whenever she was within a few feet of him, like there was a magnetic charge pulling them together. It was true that Rob hadn't been emailing me about Lou so much lately, but I assumed that had more to do with his job than the state of their union.

"We are . . . I think."

Because it was Rob, and I was curious, I pried. "You *think*?"

"I mean, you know I'm working a lot. More than I even thought I would have to. Lou hates it, and she's not quiet about it. Says we need to work on our marriage, too."

I looked up ahead at Lou, who was laughing at whatever Kathryn had just said.

Rob continued. "She likes the stability of my job, but not the reality of it. I get the impression she would prefer if I were more like the last guy she dated, who was an 'artist,'" he said, using air quotes. "She says my working all the time makes her feel abandoned."

I thought of the Chekhov quote Lou had shared with me at their wedding. She probably had not anticipated how quickly it would become true. "You think this has anything to do with her child-hood?" At this point, I had begun to pick up the bread crumbs of Lou's early years—how her mother had never been around and had pushed Lou to move in with a friend while she was still in high school.

"Probably." He rubbed his forehead. "Still, you think she'd under-stand, given how important her work is to her. Right before we left, she was freaking out about being unable to complete the poem she's been working on for three weeks. As if she actually thought she would finish it while we were in the middle of Napa."

I stuck my nose into my goblet. Kathryn had instructed me to try to detect the wine's aromas, but all I could smell was alcohol-infused cat urine. I pulled my nose back out of my glass and addressed Rob. "Well, writers are all crazy. You know that."

His expression was one of pure skepticism. "Really? Because you seem pretty sane to me."

I tried not to let my face betray how insulted I was by being called the literary equivalent of a saltine cracker. I mean, sure, sanity has its perks. But at the time, I thought inspiration went hand in hand with being unhinged. Didn't you have to be a little nuts to sit at a computer day after day, struggling to wrangle sentences that may only ever reach an audience of one?

"We'll make it work," said Rob resolutely, unaware that I was still thinking about myself. He held his glass up to the sun, and a ray shot through the straw-colored liquid and hit me in the eye. "I just wish it were a little more straightforward. My parents make it look so easy."

Maybe things will improve as his job gets better, I thought as I fell back onto the feather-stuffed duvet that night and waited for Kathryn to lie beside me. I wouldn't want to be married to a workaholic, either, even if Rob's workaholism was a job requirement.

A vision of Lou, smiling at me over a glass of wine as I told her about the books I had assigned that semester, flitted through my head as the weight of Kathryn's body sent me rolling toward the center of the mattress. I pushed it aside as Kathryn's lips brushed against mine and told myself, *Give this a real chance.*

～

The following night, the four of us dined at an absurdly upscale restaurant, the kind where the meal takes hours because you can't bring yourself to rush it. After dessert, Lou told us that one of her poems had been accepted by *American Poetry Review,* and Rob ordered a bottle of champagne to celebrate, even though we were already good and toasted. Then he slipped his credit card to the waiter and told Kathryn and me that it was their treat.

"Are you sure?" I asked.

"Absolutely. In celebration of Lou's success."

Lou beamed at him. Beside me, Kathryn squeezed my thigh, then leaned in close to me. "You're next, Jim," she whispered. "Big things are going to happen for you, too."

Her words fed my hungry ego. Writing had been my lifelong dream. My grandfather had come to the United States from Puerto

Rico shortly before my father was born, and he, and later my father, had found steady work and some semblance of financial stability by working at an automotive plant. Even as a child, I understood that I was expected to follow their lead.

When I was thirteen or so, I found a copy of *The Hitchhiker's Guide to the Galaxy* in my basement—I think it was my father's, though I can't recall ever seeing him read anything but the newspaper—and I stayed up most of that night reading it, and then did the same the following night. I had already been an avid reader, but by the time I turned the last page of that book, I understood that I did not want to meander down the path that the men before me had traveled.

"You think?" I asked Kathryn. She had yet to read a single page of the novel I was working on. Her proclamation was really a bet—the kind we make on people we love.

"I know," she said.

I kissed her tenderly, even though I wasn't one for public affection, especially not in the middle of a fancy restaurant. Kathryn was good for me; I would fall in love with her. I was even falling a little bit right then.

~

Still, my gaze had lingered too long on Lou's candlelit face across the table at various points that evening. And when we all turned in for the night, I could not help but watch Lou disappear into the room she and Rob were sharing and wish that I were the one joining her.

As I stood beside Kathryn in the bathroom, each of us undertaking our various prebed grooming rituals, I found myself thinking of my mother. *"You do what you can with whatever you get,"* she used to say, shaking her finger at me and my sister, Victoria, if we had been complaining about what we didn't have. We would run off to the other room and mimic her, our hands waving wildly, until the two of us bent over crying with laughter.

My mother had died suddenly during my first year of graduate school. We had not been close, but I had foolishly believed our relationship would unfold like a novel: discord, yes, but then reconnection, followed by a satisfying conclusion. Instead, our story ended in the middle, and that was that.

Still, a parent's words have a way of leaving an indelible mark. Maybe my mother was right, I told myself. I could remain in my staid studio apartment, pining for a woman who was not mine, and never would be. Or I could move forward with what I had.

"I think," I said to Kathryn after she had removed her contacts and slipped on her glasses, "we should live together. Does that sound like a good idea to you?"

Her face was serious—though maybe it was just her horn-rims. "Yes, I want to, you know that," she told me. "I think we're perfectly suited for each other. But are you sure? Will you still think it's a good idea in a year? In a month?"

A year from then seemed like a distant planet, visible only on rare occasions and in the right light. But next month? It would be June, and my plans were few and clear. I was teaching one course that summer and hoped to spend the rest of my time working on the novel I had decided was deeply flawed, but which was perhaps fixable.

And yes, I could imagine Kathryn there through all of it. Waking up beside me, us having breakfast together before retreating to our separate spaces—her to her office, me at the kitchen table, tapping away on the used laptop I had recently purchased. We could shop for groceries together, and I would cook, because Kathryn all but swooned when I fed her. Her apartment was spacious; we could host parties and have Lou and Rob over when they were in town.

"I'm positive," I told her, and wrapped my arms around her. I marveled at our reflection in the mirror: the way she fit perfectly against my body, and how right we looked together. *Yes—positive,* I told myself.

But at two in the morning, I found myself wide awake, wondering why Kathryn had never recoded my mental data in such a way that being with her was my primary ambition. And so as I listened to her breathe deeply as she slept beside me, I wondered if I was really so positive, or if I was merely talking myself into settling.

FOUR

Fall 2000

"What's the next step for you, my friend?" Pascal observed me with a casual intensity from his office chair.

It was the last week of September, and I had again been hired as an adjunct, though my reviews from the previous semester were mixed. Some students said I was too hard, one said too easy, and many suggested that I was—to paraphrase—stunningly incompetent.

These comments cut me to the bone. I was struggling to make progress on my novel, but at least I was making strides as an instructor, or so I thought before receiving my reviews. Pascal had called me in to discuss how I could manage to not get fired, though he phrased it more delicately than that.

"I'd like to see you work at getting a short story published," he said, crossing his arms over his chest.

I frowned at him from the other side of his desk. "I'm no good at short fiction."

"So hack down some of your long fiction. If you want a real career here, or anywhere, you have to publish. And maybe take a teaching course over at Eastern."

The thought of spending even more money on schooling sounded about as appealing as taking a leisurely jog through my neighborhood sans clothing. I could ask my father for a loan, but he would cite this request as further evidence that I had chosen the wrong career and launch into yet another speech about how it was not too late to pursue an engineering degree.

At the same time, I didn't want to stop teaching—or at the very least, I didn't want to fail at it. And since I could not publish a novel or story I had not written, I would need to put even more effort into my vocation.

"Sit in on some classes with really good teachers like Lefete, or maybe Barker," Pascal said, referring to some of the professors in our department. "Go in and observe as a teacher rather than a student. See how they inspire wonder."

I laughed. "I like that you're so humble you don't mention yourself." Pascal regularly ranked as one of the university's best instructors. "But all right. I'll do that."

"Good. You have anywhere to be right now?"

I glanced at my watch; it was just after five. Kathryn was meeting a colleague after work, so I had at least an hour to kill before I needed to start on dinner. "Quick drink?"

"Just what I was thinking."

We went to a bar a block from the English building, where we wedged ourselves into a narrow, high-backed booth.

"How are things with Kathryn?" Pascal asked. Just above his head, someone had carved *Kev + Melissa 4eva* into the wood.

"Pretty good," I said. Kathryn was right: we were well suited for each other. We agreed on most things and spent long hours in each other's company without becoming claustrophobic. I was content, but as Kathryn and I read on opposite ends of the sofa or lingered over lunch on a lazy Saturday, I sometimes wondered, *Is this all there is?*

"Does she want children?" he asked.

"I'm not sure. Not yet, at least."

He nodded. "That's a plus. They get in the way, so you should be certain before you have one. But settling down, letting someone love you—that foundation makes for a healthy career."

"You say this, but you're single." Pascal had gone through a bitter divorce several years earlier.

"You'll notice I haven't published anything since."

"But you only do a book every decade," I pointed out. Unlike Kathryn, who had put out two books in four years, Pascal was slow and steady.

"Trust me, let that woman love you. Don't let perfect be the enemy of good."

I sipped my beer and said nothing.

"I would do anything to have Winnie back," he added, a faraway look in his eyes. "That woman's curry is everything."

"Do you miss your ex-wife, or her cooking?"

"One and the same." He examined me for a moment. "Do you have a plan B, James?"

"Yeah," I said, even though I wasn't sure if he was asking about my romantic life or my career. Did it matter? My whole life was a plan B. "Doesn't everyone?"

Pascal raised an eyebrow but did not respond, leaving me to wonder if I had given the wrong answer.

~

Later that evening, I stood at the stove sautéing onions for lemon chicken. I had learned to cook from my mother. This had not involved actual teaching so much as getting as close to her as possible without having my hand smacked by her wooden spoon.

There were many dishes I had not learned in time: her grandmother's pierogies, her own savory beef stew, the macaroni casserole Victoria and I begged her to make, a wish she granted every few months. Over the years, I had filled in the gaps with bastardized Julia Child recipes (so many steps, all easily reduced to a lot of butter, a little flour, and medium-low heat).

I had just topped the chicken thighs with a layer of onion and lemon when the door slammed shut. "I'm home!" called Kathryn.

"Welcome," I said as she walked into the kitchen. She was wearing a silk blouse and tailored wool pants that made her look even longer and leaner than usual. "I feel like I should have an apron on and a cocktail to hand you."

"No need." She inhaled deeply. "You don't know how good it is to come home to a house that smells like this." She wrapped her arms around my waist, put her face against my neck, and breathed in again. "And you—you smell delicious, too."

"Amazing what a shower can do for a person."

"I love it. And you."

"I love you, too." We had started saying this to each other just after Napa; I still marveled at how easily the words rolled off my tongue. I kissed the tip of her nose. "You know, Pascal says I should settle down and let you love me."

She rolled her eyes. "How is that different from now? Anyway, I've heard his theories before. You are aware he believes that the United States should split into three separate countries, and that children are the death of one's writing career?"

"And you don't?"

"No on both counts," she said, laughing. "Unless he's telling you how to construct a story, don't listen to the man. Speaking of which, how's the book coming along?"

"Oh, you know. It's coming."

Kathryn ran her hand up and down my arm. "If you're not into it, it's okay to move on to another one."

"I'm into it."

"You do remember I wrote three novels before my debut was published."

"You do remember I have written zero novels before this one. It would behoove me to get to the end of this draft before moving on." It was a shame that getting to the end involved writing the other half of the book. I tugged at the enormous bow hanging from the neck of her blouse, and the two silk ties came apart, revealing her elegant neck. "That's better."

"Are you trying to change the subject?"

"*Me?*" I said in a high-pitched voice. "I would never do that. But let me tell you about the chicken I just made for you . . ."

I was relieved when she didn't bring it up again. Kathryn wanted so very much for me to succeed. She seemed to view my success as inevitable, really, and most of the time this felt like standing in the sunlight. But every once in a while it seemed that her expectations shone a spotlight on the deficit of my dreams.

~

A month or so later, the phone rang, rousing me from a deep sleep. I didn't have to answer to know it was Rob. It was the end of the workday in Hong Kong, which was usually when he called. I tiptoed out of the bedroom so I would not wake Kathryn. The scrubbed light of morning streamed in through the windows, and I squinted as I made my way to the other side of the apartment. "That you, dong nugget?" I said when I reached the kitchen.

"*Soy yo*, ass hat. How's it goin'?"

"You blasted?" I rubbed the sleep from my eyes with my knuckles, then reached into the cupboard for a canister of coffee.

"Little bit. It's the only way to get through here." He and Lou had been living abroad for three months. Already, it felt like a year. "Listen, James. You're an emotionally intelligent person."

I laughed and poured ground coffee into a measuring cup, then transferred that into the filter. Kathryn always laughed at me for being so precise about it. "Am I?"

"You're a novelist, for cripes' sake."

"Am I?" I said again. At first, I had blown off Kathryn's suggestion to abandon my work in progress and begin a new draft. But when I still had not returned to my story weeks later, I began spinning a new one in my head about an average man living in an average town who begins to suspect that his beautiful, above-average wife has a secret identity. A cautious optimism had begun to blossom in me: this novel, I felt, had real potential. Now all I had to do was write it.

"Stop," said Rob.

"Fine, fine. So what's up?" I was guessing what was up was that Lou was miserable; Rob mentioned this every time we chatted. But maybe things had changed.

Or not. "Lou hates it here," he said. "She's lonely and feels cooped up. She's lost ten pounds, and she didn't have two to spare. She wants to go home, and when she gets there, she wants to get a job. It helps her think more clearly, she says."

"You have to be in Hong Kong until . . . next June. Right?"

He sighed. "Yeah. But they're already talking about extending my contract through the following year."

"Dude, you can't."

"I know. But it would be such a huge win for me. A career-maker, even. I'm raking in nearly twice as much for the company here as I was in the States." He paused. "Maybe I can ask them about putting in an extra six months instead of another year."

"Is that your only option?"

"I guess I could wait it out, see if Lou gets better before I commit to anything. But she wants to go back to New York. Now. Without me."

"So let her."

"Come on, James. I don't want to be without Lou for a week, let alone six months. You can't possibly think that's a good idea."

I hadn't been thinking anything when I said it; it just kind of fell out. But now that I was giving it more than a half second of consideration, I did think it was a good idea. Yes, Rob financed their lives. But Lou didn't need him, at least not in the short term. "She's a fully capable adult who has taken care of herself nearly as long as she's been alive. You have the rest of forever to be together," I told him.

"I don't know. That doesn't sound so hot for our marriage. I want her here with me. But I also want her to be happy."

The coffee had just begun brewing. I pulled a mug from the cupboard and swapped it with the glass carafe. When it was a third of the way full, I put the carafe back. Then I poured cream into the mug and watched it billow from the center of the coffee in white clouds.

"Well, is she still writing? That makes her happy, doesn't it?" A horn honked in the distance, and it sounded like Rob was standing in a wind tunnel. "Where are you, anyway?"

"At a bar in a neighborhood that makes Manhattan look calm. And no, she's not really writing. She did get a couple of older poems published, though."

I took a sip of coffee and sighed: for all Kathryn's teasing, it came out right every time. "That's great. You know where?"

"Um. *Blue Press* or something like that? And the *North American Review*."

I had never heard of the former, but the latter was a big deal. I felt a swell of pride for Lou and wondered if I should email her a congratulatory note or send my congrats via Kathryn. "So what does she do all day if she's not writing?"

"Hell if I know! I keep telling her this is such a great opportunity to take her career to the next level, but I come home and find her scrubbing the grout with a toothbrush, even though we have a cleaning service. I mean, seriously—you could eat raw fish off the floors. But mostly she hates that I'm gone all the time."

"So what are you doing at the bar right now?"

"Networking is half the job! You know that." He exhaled loudly. "If she's lonely, she sure as hell doesn't act like it when I come home at night, if you know what I mean. I have certain . . . needs. That aren't being met."

Thank God we were on the phone, because I actually cringed. It was like hearing someone talk about your sister. Or, you know, the woman you love. "Hang in there," I said to Rob. "It's going to get better."

"How?" He sounded kind of hopeless, which was not something I was at all used to.

So I lied. "It just will."

I heard him take a sip of something. Then he said, "Well, that's a relief. You have a sense of these things."

"I do," I said, lying again.

"Listen, I have to run—my coworker just showed up. But thanks, man. Let's talk soon, yeah?"

"Definitely," I said. "Say hey to Lou for us."

"You got it. Tell Kathryn we said hi, too."

Our apartment was on the second floor of a large house facing a city park. I poured myself more coffee and stared out the window at the treetops, which had recently turned saffron and umber and cadmium yellow, thinking about what Rob had just told me. When my mug was empty, I returned to bed.

"Was that Rob?" Kathryn murmured when I slid beside her. She was sprawled out luxuriously; she liked to stay up late and sleep in, as did I. When our schedules allowed, we would remain beneath the sheets until close to noon.

"Yeah. He and Lou are having a tough time."

"I know. Lou emailed."

"Really?"

"Yes," said Kathryn, rolling onto her side. She propped herself up on an elbow. "Don't worry, every couple goes through it. And she's so young."

"She's only three years younger than me."

"*You're* so young," said Kathryn, who was thirty-three at the time—an age that now seems as fresh as spring, but which held a sort of gravitas when I was in my twenties.

"Do you think they're doomed?"

"Doomed? No, I think they're two humans. Love is hard."

"And that is why you're the successful writer."

She didn't argue. "Come here, you," she said.

Not even yet November, it was already frigid. I burrowed beneath the quilt and warmed myself against her and thought about how good we were together. Our life was not perfect, if there's even a version of existence that remotely fits that definition. My writing was stalled, and teaching felt as though it was getting harder rather than easier. Kathryn's last book had not sold as well as she and her publisher hoped it would. Though she believed the novel she was currently writing was her best yet, she still fretted about her career. That distress spawned other anxieties. Was she only a so-so novelist? she would wonder aloud. A subpar instructor?

Her personal worries, which sometimes spilled out after we had split a bottle of wine in the evening, were harder for me to field. Were we serious about each other? Did I really love her? Really *really*? Kathryn didn't use the *M* word, and when we talked about children, it was to comment on how harried our friends with kids seemed to be. Yet I suspected that her desire for a baby would emerge soon, just as a shadow rises on a wall as the sun sets. After all, my sister, Victoria, and her husband went from not wanting children to having two within a span of three years. And Victoria was a year younger than Kathryn.

As I watched Kathryn's face twitch as she drifted off, I thought, *Yes, this is good, and it is easy.* Easier than anything I'd ever known as an adult, and maybe would again. Of course, I didn't know or appreciate that then because I had no point of reference. In your twenties, it's easy to think most of your better days are still up ahead. But sometime around the point at which you find yourself in a face-off with forty, time does a peculiar thing and unfolds at once, almost like a map, so that while you can see that you are no longer truly young and you are not yet old, it's quite clear that you will be very soon—if you're lucky.

So, writing this to you from that precipice, I will simply say this: If you find yourself in an effortless position in life, as I did beside Kathryn in bed that fall morning, enjoy it, but don't stop there. When something comes to you so easily, it may leave that same way, and you'll be left wondering if it ever was at all.

FIVE

2001–2002

Lou and Rob returned to New York together in the spring of 2001. They had a massive fight about it; in the end, she had been unwilling to stay, and he had been unwilling to let her go home alone. "I love my job, but I love Lou more," he told me. "What can I do?"

Worried about the repercussions of leaving Hong Kong before his company wanted him to, Rob began working longer hours than ever and was rewarded with yet another promotion. Lou got a job as a part-time copyeditor at an architectural magazine and went back to writing in coffee shops, as she claimed the loft they had rented in Tribeca was too eerily quiet for her to concentrate.

Through Rob, I knew that their social life largely centered around his career. They went to dinners with his clients, attended events with his colleagues, and even went on vacation with his supervisor. "Lou got a whole new wardrobe of stuff that she wouldn't normally wear, and she ends up talking to my colleagues' wives, half of who are about as interesting as empty cardboard boxes," Rob confessed. "I worry she feels like she has to play a part for me."

I, too, often felt like I was playing a part, at least when it came to being a grown-up. Humdrum acts, like negotiating the rate on my credit card or buying and applying shower caulk, seemed novel—almost as though I was trying them out once, when in fact they were things I would do again and again over the course of my life.

~

Then one bright September morning, four planes crashed into two towers, an open field, and the Pentagon, and at once none of us were playing at being adults anymore.

Kathryn and I were at our offices when the news came through via a university email. I had never received such a message before. Even absent the word *terrorism*—which, if you can believe it, was not a term most Americans used before that day—the only way to interpret it was seriously.

I immediately called Rob and Lou's apartment, which was entirely too close to the World Trade Center. When no one answered, I called Rob's office in Midtown. Nothing.

Then Wisnewski called me, and for a moment I thought maybe he had heard from them. But he was only checking to see if I knew whether Rob and Lou were okay.

"I'm sure they're fine," I told him, though I was sure of no such thing. "I'll let you know the minute I hear more."

Classes were cancelled soon after I got the email, and I ran through the halls of the English building to Kathryn's office. She rushed at me as soon as she saw me. "I can't believe it," she said as we clutched each other.

"Me neither."

"Lou—she was probably home. God. This feels like the end of everything."

"I know," I said, because it did. I could not imagine what the next hour would be like, let alone the following day.

When we got home, there was a voicemail from Lou on our answering machine (for your reference, that was a plastic box that recorded voice messages for one's home phone, which used to be a stationary device that was typically attached to the wall). "Hi. It's Lou. We're okay. We're at Rob's coworker's place on the Upper West Side. People are saying it's not safe to be in the city, but we don't have a car and there really isn't a way out. Phone lines are spotty, but we'll call you as soon as we have a plan. We—we love you guys."

"Thank God," I said after we had played it twice.

Kathryn's eyes were filled with tears. "They could have died," she whispered.

"But they didn't." *Though they still could,* I added mentally. It seemed that it was probably only a matter of time before there was another attack, and this fear hung in the air between us. I took Kathryn in my arms. "They're okay. They're going to be okay. We all will."

~

"James," said Kathryn later that evening.

We had slept through much of the afternoon and had only just woken up. After switching on the radio and hearing the latest, we were on the sofa having dinner for the devastated—chocolate ice cream directly from the tub.

"Yes, sweetie?" I said, and stuck an enormous spoonful into my mouth. Though I knew what to do with various cutlery and mostly did not chew with my mouth open, I had a pig's appetite and could not seem to stop myself from shoveling food down my gullet with abandon. It was one of the only things Kathryn nagged me about, and I assumed she was about to tell me that I might consider limiting mouthfuls to half-cup portions.

Instead she said, "I want to have a baby."

My head shot up. "That's a common response to trauma, isn't it?"

She crossed her legs, then uncrossed them and smoothed the front of her shirt. It was like watching a panther cower. Anxious? Often. Fretful? Very. But Kathryn was almost never truly nervous.

"No, that's not it," she said. "This is what I've wanted for a while now, and . . . I guess I've been waiting to tell you. Now seems like the right time."

"Oh. Wow." I was looking straight at her, but in my mind's eye I saw myself in up to my elbows in crap, a diaper bag digging into my shoulder. I saw myself trying to write through a colicky clamor in the background. I saw my silver coupe with a *For Sale* sign on its windshield, and me behind the wheel of a minivan. You'll notice a theme: I was the infant in these scenarios. I was not at all prepared to have a child.

"I'm not saying we have to get married," said Kathryn quickly. "I don't really care too much about that."

"Okay," I said. While I was not averse to it, marriage was barely north of children on my mental map. Which is to say very, very far away.

"I know you're halfway through your book, too, and you're focused on finishing," she said.

The novel I was working on—the one about the man whose wife may or may not be a spy—had been stunted by my self-consciousness over my previous inability to write an entire book. In fact, I was only a quarter of the way through the first draft, though I did not correct Kathryn.

"And maybe you just aren't thinking about kids yet. But you just turned twenty-nine, and I'm almost thirty-five, which is supposedly when eggs stop being . . . robust. And it's not going to happen overnight, so . . ."

"I see," I said, though I did not, really. "Do you think I might have time to think about it?"

"Of course. It's not a decision I expect you to make on the spot." She sounded relieved, though something in her eyes told me she would have loved nothing more than a resounding *yes* from me at that exact moment.

So think I did, though not about having a baby. I didn't want to think about that, because I already knew my answer: it was no.

Instead, I thought about Kathryn and how we could continue to be content together, if only she didn't expect things to change.

But beyond this—deep in that hidden place that even I was only able to access on occasion—there was another issue. And that was that I craved fireworks, shortness of breath, that whole-body tingle. I wanted to be with a woman whom I loved so much that I was nervous when she was near. If I were to start a family and spend the rest of my life with someone, I wanted her to give me the same feeling I had around Lou.

~

Kathryn and I didn't hear from Rob and Lou again for a few days. When they called, we learned that they couldn't return to their apartment, which was coated with ash and dust. (In fact, they would not be able to go back for months, and when they did, it was only to collect a few belongings.) They stayed at Rob's colleague's pied-à-terre on the Upper West Side for several weeks, then moved into a rental in Brooklyn, where Lou had found them a flat.

Mid-October, I told Kathryn that I was not ready for a baby, and that I wasn't sure when I would be. She cried but said she understood. Yet my confession ruptured something between us (as I write this, I find myself thinking that maybe that ruptured thing was hope). By December, I had moved out.

There's no such thing as a clean break in a college town, and Kathryn and I ran into each other more frequently than either of us would have preferred. At first, she would glance away when she saw me. But several months passed, and when we crossed paths on campus or on the street, she met my gaze and sometimes even gave a little wave.

The first few times this happened, I thought maybe she was giving me a return-to-me look. But one day I was shuffling across the Diag, a pile of papers in one hand and a travel mug of coffee in the other, when I looked up and saw Kathryn leaving the library. As our eyes met, it occurred to me at once that her expression wasn't desire at all. No—it was pity.

~

In the spring of 2002, I was informed that the university would not be rehiring me the following fall. Maybe it was because I was no longer tied to one of their star professors. The school had a formal employment system in place, of course. But then, and probably now, a strong suggestion from those who mattered—such as a good number of our colleagues, who greeted me with skeptical looks or outright frowns when I ran into them in the halls or lounge—counted for a lot.

More likely, my separation from Kathryn was a tart cherry on the dirt pie that was my career. I was neither a standout teacher nor a published author. The dean of the department, who had been the one to deliver the news, said something along the lines of *it's a competitive field, you do have promise, you can apply again in the future, blah blah blah.* And yet as soon as I sat down in front of him, I had already decided that my short and unspectacular career in academia had come to a definitive end; I had absolutely no interest in continuing to humiliate myself by being subpar.

"I'm sorry, James," said Pascal, who had stopped by as I was packing up the contents of my small shared office.

"Yeah," I said. I had just found a framed photo of Kathryn in a drawer, where I had shoved it months ago, and I set it facedown on top of a stack of reference books.

"Listen, I know someone high up in development at the business school. They're hiring a writer."

"What kind of writer?"

"The kind who is paid to string words together in a coherent fashion," he retorted. "Does it matter? The salary is probably twice what you make now. You can actually live and write fiction on the side, as surely you know this starving-artist crap is overrated. Apply and I'll put in a good word for you. It's that or try to find another teaching job making even less money in the middle of South Dakota."

"I'm glad you have faith in me."

He raised an eyebrow. "It's not *you* I don't have faith in. It's the system."

"I don't know a thing about business." Further, I did not want to take a job at which I would, well, suck.

"Obviously, or you wouldn't be making peanuts at a public institution. Come on, James. Don't be a dunce. I get it if you want to move to LA or New York. But correct me if I'm wrong: you don't actually want to live anywhere else, no?"

In the future, sure. But pack up the apartment I had just settled into? Find a new bagel place, a new dry cleaner, a new set of friends? "No," I admitted.

He clapped me on the back. "Then thank me and apply."

I did, and I got the job—not so much because of my interview, said Craig, the rangy, energetic man who was to become my new boss. Instead, they chose me because I had aced the writing test, and because Craig's supervisor's boss had known Pascal for years and trusted his recommendation. I began in mid-July.

~

"A businessman," my father said with approval when I had dinner with him that August. We were at his favorite Cuban place, which was not as good as a real Puerto Rican joint, he claimed, but which served a decent *ropa vieja* and a flan he spoke about in a way that he had never spoken about my mother.

I leaned back in my chair. "Not exactly, Pops. I'm still writing."

In reality, I had set aside the spy novel and was tossing around an idea about an ill-fated pair of lovers—except I wasn't sure I had it in me to start another book. And the fund-raising materials I spent the better part of most days drafting were less like writing and more like patching a wall with a bunch of wet plaster that was routinely thrown at me over the course of two-hour meetings (which were inevitably ninety minutes longer than necessary). Really, the closest I had come to artful prose was in a three-paragraph-long brochure detailing design plans for a new wing of the school.

My father speared a stringy piece of beef and pointed it in my direction. "When are you going to learn, James?"

How's never for you? I thought. I was almost thirty years old, but when it came to my father, I may as well have been thirteen. The lessons he wanted to teach me were not the kind I was even remotely interested in. "Learn what?" I said, draining my soda.

"Doesn't matter what something is. It's what you *call it* that counts." He stuck the beef in his mouth, then sat back in his chair, pleased with himself.

"Is that so."

"It's so." As he lifted his chin proudly, I was deeply sad to the point of wanting to weep or smash something. In that moment, my father looked ancient, and I felt that surely he would die seeing the world in his own set way.

And within that particular version of reality, I would remain defined not by who I was, but by what I was not.

SIX

2003

"You're too close to the eighth hole, James!" hollered Rob.

"Good God!" I ducked to avoid the golf ball vaulting through the air toward me.

"You're not *that* close!" He motioned for me to move toward where he and his friends were standing. "Get over here, whack job!"

I stood slowly as the ball landed with a thud approximately half a mile from my person. "Right," I muttered. Whose stupid idea was it to go golfing?

It was Rob's, and it was my stupid idea to agree. It was his thirty-first birthday, and apparently using titanium rods to hit resin-covered rubber spheres across a grassy knoll was what men who had amassed great fortunes early in life did to celebrate the passage from one gilded year to the next.

Well, at least I was able to afford it. I hated that this was what cheered me as I wheeled my borrowed bag across the green. Pascal had been right: it *was* good to be making a living wage. My wardrobe was now less sloppy scribe and more business casual. My savings account had gone from malnourished to pleasantly plump. (My ego had fattened a bit, too; being good at my job had erased some of the shame I had experienced from failing as a teacher.) And when Rob called to see if I might want to fly to New York to join him, Aidan, and Max on a golf outing in Hastings-on-Hudson, and stay in the city for a weekend, I was able to say yes without having to calculate what it would cost.

I didn't need years of psychoanalysis to understand why padded biweekly paychecks were of such comfort. My parents didn't fight often, probably because it might have required my father to speak to my mother in full sentences. But when they did, it was about money. I vividly recall him, red-faced, holding up a grocery store receipt. "We don't have this kind of cash to blow on food!"

My mother was crying, and she motioned to where I was sitting at the kitchen table. "How do you expect me to feed two men and a little girl on what you give me?"

I was in grade school then, and under different circumstances would have been thrilled to be identified as something other than a child. Instead, all I could think about was how I was responsible for their rift. For days afterward, I ate half of what my mother served me to demonstrate that I didn't need much, until she pinched the back of my arm and told me to stop being wasteful.

A few years later, my father became a supervisor at his factory. Our rusty station wagon was traded for a new sedan, and our bland green kitchen doubled in size and was painted pale yellow. My father subdued his complaints about my mother's spending habits, and he continued to move up the ladder right up until his retirement. But like my mother, I never stopped double-checking price tags and receipts, tallying up totals, wondering if the money I had would be enough—and if so, for how long.

Maybe that was why I preferred Rob's house. It was larger than mine, and nicer, too. But it was the *feel* of the Logans' that I loved. They were just regular old middle class (which, at the time, did not often require racking up credit card debt to stay afloat). There were always freshly baked cookies or brownies on the counter, though. Nancy bought extras of everything, so if we emptied a bag of chips or box of cereal, it didn't matter. Like Rob, they were generous and secure, and being with them made me feel that way.

"*There* you are," said Rob as I rejoined their group. "See how easy it is to be in the right place?"

"I resent you mocking me. And I resent that your birthday outing may result in my needing dentures."

"Stop wandering around like you're tripping on shrooms and you won't lose any teeth."

"Boys!" said Aidan. "Let's move."

Rob had been playing golf for a good long while and was able to expertly swing and send the ball swiftly toward the hole for which it was intended.

Not so for me. My father had urged me to learn the game so I might better network and seal deals in my imagined career in the automotive industry. I had played a few times over the years and was always left with the impression that I had just wasted several valuable hours of reading time. Now I regretted not at least visiting a driving range near home before I showed up in New York to make a fool of myself.

I brought my iron to the ball with little conviction and watched it lift weakly into the air and land entirely too close to where I was standing. I turned to Rob. "You were saying?"

He rubbed his forehead. "I'm worried. I think Lou is unhappy."

"Okay, why?" I asked.

He looked at me like I was a dolt. "Because of me. I work too much, and she cries too much. And so on and so forth."

"Eesh, that's not good. You talk to her about it yet?"

"Have you ever tried to tell someone who's unhappy that you think they should cheer up?" He squinted from behind his aviators. "You get one of two reactions: 'Yes, and water is wet, now leave me alone,' or 'I'm not unhappy, I'm psychotic; move before I stab you.'"

"Maybe she's depressed. My mother was depressed," I said, thinking aloud. It was true, though this was not usually what I focused on when I thought of her. When I was young, she cried a lot—while watching TV, when her friends asked her how she was doing, sometimes even in the middle of the store for no apparent reason—until my father made her see a doctor. An orange bottle of pills appeared on the kitchen counter, which was emptied, then replaced each month, and while she never really seemed happy, neither did she continue to burst into tears at random.

"Really?" Rob said, incredulous. "She was always so . . . perky."

"I guess." My mother thought Rob was a good influence on me, so she was pleasant when he came around. In fact, she was most genial when she was around people who weren't her relatives (as we all are, I suppose).

But domestic life disappointed her; I knew this even as a child. She sometimes told Victoria and me what a fast typist she was, and how she would have made a good secretary. She and my father had a deal, though: he worked, she took care of our home, and so it went for the rest of her days.

"Maybe Lou would be better off getting a full-time job?" I speculated. The magazine where she had been working had been shuttered a few months earlier, and she had not yet found another part-time gig. "Maybe that's why she's down in the mouth."

Rob frowned. "She doesn't need it, and it's not like she has nothing to do. She volunteers at a center in the city, teaching kids how to write poetry."

"How often?" I asked as I watched Max nail his shot.

Rob, Aidan, and Max all hooted. Rob turned to me, still grinning at Max's success. "I don't know. Maybe once a week? I'm usually working when she's there."

I was surprised he didn't know how often Lou volunteered, though I said nothing to this effect. "She's probably lonely," I told him. "And bored."

"But she has her writing! Don't writers *like* to keep to themselves?"

"Yes, well, a certain degree of solitude is required for writing. But that doesn't mean it's a good way for her to spend every single day."

"She sees her friends," he insisted. "Elyse, Renee, Jennifer One, Jennifer Two."

I looked at him questioningly.

"You can't possibly expect me to remember their last names. Jennifer Two's the one who's a drunk. When she and Lou go out, the next day neither of them remembers what happened at the end of the night."

"That's not ideal."

"Nope. And of course, she's always even bluer afterward. You're up, by the way."

I walked over to where my ball was, and this time my halfhearted attempt landed my ball beside the hole. "And you guys?" I ventured when Rob rejoined me. "Are things better? She's not saying stuff like she wants a baby, right?"

He gave me a strange look. "I'm over thirty. Lou and I will have been married five years in November. We're going to start procreating at some point in the future."

"Oh. I thought you didn't want kids until after forty?"

"I once wanted to hop in a tin can and head to the moon if I could get a ticket. Now, staying alive sounds more interesting than space travel." He surveyed the course. "Things change."

"All you, birthday boy," Aidan said to Rob.

"You'll see," said Rob. He walked forward, lifted his putter ever so slightly, and sent his ball rolling. He turned back to me before it had even dropped into the hole. "You'll be in my shoes one day, and what you thought you wanted won't sound so good anymore."

~

I was staying at a hotel in Union Square, not far from where Lou was throwing Rob's birthday dinner. After showering off the layer of sweat and defeat I had accrued during the golf outing, I headed out.

The restaurant was tucked into one of those blink-and-you'll-miss-it West Village blocks. It was a swanky place flanked by enormous ceramic planters in the shape of Buddha with bright foliage sprouting from their heads. There were floor-to-ceiling glass panels on either side of the restaurant door, and through one of these I spotted Rob and Lou. Her chin was lifted—she had to look up to make eye contact with him—but he was staring off to the side, scowling. She put a hand on his arm in what looked like a peacemaking move, but he shook his head and she took her hand back. I saw his lips form a single word: "No."

I had no idea what they were arguing about. But my pulse was a staccato in my throat, and I had already jumped to all sorts of conclusions, which could best be boiled down to *No wonder Lou is blue. Rob is a jerk.*

"Hello!" I said loudly, even though I had not fully made it through the door; I wanted to jar Rob right out of his dickishness.

Mission accomplished. "James?" said Rob, visibly surprised. He collected himself. "Early like a good Michigander should be." He offered his hand, and I shook it firmly, then turned to kiss Lou on the cheek.

"Jim!" she said with glee. "I'm so happy to see you. Next time you skip golf and come hang out with me, okay?"

"I take it Rob told you about my performance."

"I may have," said Rob.

Already they seemed more relaxed; my decision to subtly insert myself into their squabble had been the right one, or so I told myself.

"Was this joint your idea?" I asked Lou as we walked into the restaurant. There was a waterfall in the center of the dining room, pouring into a fountain filled with fish. The tables were made to look like cabanas, and the waiters appeared to be killing time between modeling gigs.

She laughed. "Of course not. Rob loves this place."

I examined her for what I hoped was a quick minute and came to the conclusion that she looked different. Not visibly depressed, but different. She was wearing diamond earrings—big ones. Her nails were still too short, but they wore a fresh coat of pale pink polish. Everything about her was polished, in fact, except her hair, which had grown long and was sticking out all over the place.

"You channeling Samuel Clemens?" I asked, motioning to her curls.

"You channeling Truman Capote? That's some suit you've got," she shot back.

I fingered the edge of my charcoal jacket. I bought the suit shortly after I was hired at the business school, and though I had purchased several others since, it remained my favorite. "You like? It really doesn't look as spiffy without the bow tie."

"Come here," she said, grinning, and opened her arms to me.

Even through the layers of linen she was draped in, I felt her rib cage against my forearms. "Is that lug of a husband still stealing food from your plate?" I said, only half joking.

She blushed. "I just get so wrapped up . . ."

I did not get a chance to inquire what, exactly, she got wrapped up in because in walked the rest of our party: Max and his wife, Lubna, Aidan and his girlfriend—a cheerful redhead whose name has gone missing in my mind—and Lou's friend Elyse.

"You remember Elyse from our wedding, right, Jim?" Lou said.

I did not, but I nodded.

"So nice to see you again," murmured Elyse, who had no doubt been forewarned about our setup. She was a song—tall and tan and young and lovely. I leaned forward to kiss her cheek, which she coolly accepted.

The minute Elyse turned to greet Lubna, I narrowed my eyes at Lou.

She smiled sweetly in response, then whispered, "Don't get all worked up. Odd numbers are no good, and you deserve a nice dining companion."

"Thanks, I think," I whispered back.

Our party was seated at one of the dining cabanas. Elyse was to my left, and Lou was to my right. The two of them yapped back and forth, doing their best to include me in their discussion, but I ended up talking to Rob over Lou's head.

Sometime after drinks were served, a waiter set a small white plate in front of each of us—compliments of the chef, she said. Lou sniffed at her plate, which held a paper-thin wafer topped with tiny green leaves and what appeared to be miniature tadpoles. "Think it's still alive?" she said, then laughed.

"Like you're not used to this kind of stuff," I said.

"I don't think I'll ever get used to it. It all seems so over the top sometimes."

I eyed her twinkling diamond studs. "Over the top, huh?"

"You *know* what I mean," she said, swatting me. "My mom used to have a saying: 'If you don't remember what's not yours, life will remind you right quick.'" She laughed into her drink. "Then again, she used to beat the crap out of me. So screw her Podunk idioms."

She was tipsy. Maybe even on her way to being blitzed. But I had never before heard her speak at length about her childhood, and I lapped it up like a man who just went days without water. "My God, Lou. That's terrible."

"So says my therapist. But a bad childhood beats a rotten adulthood. Ha, *beats*."

We both snorted.

"Do you ever wonder how you ended up—well, you know." I gestured around us. *"Here?"*

"One tiny stroke of kindness after another, I guess." She drained her drink and gave me a sad smile. "When I was really little, the family next door basically took care of me. In middle school, I had a teacher who helped me see that I wasn't as stupid as my mother and her roving troupe of boyfriends claimed I was. At sixteen, I moved in with a friend whose parents had both gone to college. They encouraged me to go to school and make something of myself. The rest is ancient history."

"You ever write about this?" I had a hard time keeping up with the poems Lou published. Most literary magazines were print-only then, and personal websites weren't the norm among the poetry crowd.

"No, I don't like to look back in that direction if I don't have to. Maybe *you* can write about it, though." She laughed again. "Put it in one of your novels and call me Lorraine."

"Putting you in one of my novels would require me to write said novel."

"You stalled?"

"Not so much stalled as in need of a new transmission."

She touched my arm. "I know the feeling. Why not go back to that novel about the spy wife? That was a great idea, and you could pull it off."

Elyse, who had just finished talking to Lubna, leaned toward us. "What are you two yapping about? Sounds juicy!"

I was not about to brief Elyse on our actual conversation. *"Very,"* I said, wiggling my eyebrows. "I was just telling Lou here how I recently began performing with the Cirque du Soleil."

"Really?" she said, eyes wide.

"Alas, no."

Both Lou and Elyse laughed, and I found myself laughing, too. If Lou was polished, Elyse was coated in varnish: her skin was bronzed, her bob was cut just so at the chin, and there was not a single thing about her that had not been preconsidered. She was not at all my type. But there she was, giving me an interested look.

"She likes you," said Lou when Elyse went to the restroom. We had almost finished the succession of artful, tiny plates that comprised our dinner, and she seemed to have sobered up a bit. "And she could use a distraction. She just went through an awful breakup."

"I'm nothing if not distracting."

She looked wounded. "Don't be like that, Jim."

"Like what?"

"I'm trying to be helpful."

"So am I."

She frowned at me, and even though I knew I had upset her, I said nothing in response.

After dinner, we went down the street for drinks. Aidan and his girlfriend left first; then Max and Lubna departed. Around midnight, Elyse put a long, thin hand on my arm. "Want to split a cab back?" she asked.

Lou was huddled against Rob, their bickering from earlier in the evening already in the distant past. Now they looked like a perfume ad: the newly graying, suit-clad hunk; the wispy, slightly disheveled beauty on his arm. They kissed, then turned toward me and smiled.

"Will we see you tomorrow, Jim?" said Lou.

"Sure." My response came out cold and flat, and yet I did not apologize or smooth it over by saying more. No, I'm sorry to report that I actually felt a little pleased when Lou frowned at me.

"Shall we?" I said to Elyse.

"We shall." She laughed and slipped her arm around my waist.

And off into the night we went, two people doing our damnedest to move forward with what we had.

SEVEN

Winter 2004–Summer 2005

Wisnewski got sick at the end of 2004. He was still living in Oakwood, the suburb where we had grown up, and was working in sales at Chrysler. He had inherited his parents' brick ranch and married a woman named Jen, who had been a few years behind us in school. They had two kids and a nice life.

Wisnewski and I were lazy in that way people who know they'll always be friends can be. Even though it was all of forty minutes away, he didn't like coming out to Ann Arbor—too little parking, too many liberals—and I didn't drive to Oakwood all that often, either. When I did, I felt like I had to stop by my father's, and I didn't really want to do that. But when I skipped it, I felt guilty, which was just as bad. So Wisnewski and I mostly saw each other around the holidays and in the fall, when he was willing to momentarily cast aside his feelings about the hippie socialists I lived among while we went to see the Wolverines play football.

Anyway, he called me that December and said, "Well, Hernandez, the bad news is I have cancer. The good news is it's the kind that's curable."

It was lymphoma, which has a high survival rate. But by the following spring, it was clear that Wisnewski was on the wrong side of statistics; one treatment had failed, and the next one wasn't working a whole lot better. This was made known to me when Jen called me one morning and said, "Listen, James, Jason's doing badly. I think you and Rob should come see him."

A few days later, I picked Rob up from the airport, and we headed straight to Oakwood. I had been hoping to catch up with him—maybe have him help me shore up my courage before we arrived—but he spent the ride sending missives from his cell phone.

"Sorry," he said when he caught me scowling in his direction. "Work's nuts and I wasn't exactly planning on this trip."

"No worries," I said, even though I was, in fact, annoyed. I hadn't heard from him all that much lately, and when I called or emailed him, it was often a week or more before he finally got back to me. "At least you came."

I had been to Wisnewski's several times since he and Jen had moved in, but it was still strange to walk into his childhood home and find it nothing like I remembered it. His dad had been a hoarder, back before there was a term for that, and there used to be piles of stuff—newspapers, plastic tubs, you name it—everywhere. But after Wisnewski's dad died and his mom moved to Florida, Jen emptied the place out. The dirty walls had been painted in autumnal colors, and the musty odor had been replaced with the scent of overbaked pumpkin pie. Everything was tidy and matching and suburban.

"Hey, assholes," said Wisnewski, who was waiting for us at the door. He had always been a big guy—not especially tall, but well over two hundred pounds. Now his skin hung on him like a costume meant for someone larger, and he hobbled into the living room and kind of threw himself down on the sofa.

"I bet it's good to be out of the hospital, right?" I said, settling into a deep leather recliner.

"Yeah, I'm taking a break." He grimaced. "It's—it's in my liver."

"Shit," said Rob, who was next to Wisnewski.

"Shit," I echoed.

"Yeah," said Wisnewski. He put up his hands. "What can you do?"

"Hey, guys," said Jen, sticking her head into the room. "Can I get you anything? How about a beer?" She had gotten heavier, like she was absorbing Wisnewski's loss.

Rob looked at Wisnewski. "You gonna have one?"

"Always. Three brewskis, hon," he said to Jen.

"You got it."

"Man, I love you," said Wisnewski to Jen when she returned with an uncapped beer for each of us. He turned to us. "It's good of you guys to come."

"I'm only sorry it's been so long," said Rob.

"Don't even mention it. I know you're busy, businessman. How's Lou?"

"She's good. She's in Tucson right now. Where are your kids, anyway?"

"They're at Jen's mom's for the afternoon. I didn't want them running in circles around you."

Rob smiled. "I don't mind that. I'd love to see them the next time I'm here."

"Sure, sure." Wisnewski's eyes were somewhere far off. Then he grinned. "Hey, you remember when we left Helmer's car in the middle of the football field?"

I hadn't thought about Barry Helmer in a while, let alone spoken with him. Last I had heard, he was still in the navy and stationed in Spain.

Rob laughed. "Oh man, he was so pissed. That was the best."

"And remember how James lost the bet about Helmer and had to write our English papers for us?"

"And then you got caught!" said Rob to me, laughing even harder.

"*Almost* caught," I corrected. "I just about wet myself when I had to convince Mrs. Lafferty that I had only coached you guys through them. I was sure I was a second away from getting my college admission revoked and ruining my entire future."

"Man, you were always a tool," said Wisnewski affectionately. He had yet to take a sip of his beer.

"Remember that time we stripped your clothes off and kicked you out of my house?" Rob said to Wisnewski. "We were expecting you to wig out, but there you were, sitting on the deck as calm as can be. Nothing gets to you."

"Except cancer," said Wisnewski, and we were all quiet for a minute.

Then we went back to talking about the past. High school was fifteen years behind us—a lifetime ago, but like yesterday, too. That's how it goes; so much disappears, but the memories that remain are often so vivid they might as well have just happened.

Eventually, Wisnewski started to fade, so we clapped him on the back, but not too hard, and promised to come again soon.

"Well, that was terrifying," said Rob once we were back in my car. "He doesn't look good."

"No," I said. "But it's not over just yet."

Regret ran through my mind like an old film reel as we pulled away from Wisnewski's house. Why hadn't I made more of an effort to see him? And what about our other friends—Helmer, Carl White, Joe Phelps? What about Heather Ballard, or Carrie Krefbaum, whom I had taken to prom—or her best friend, Tiffany, whom I had made out with instead of Carrie? Had these people fallen out of my life for good reason?

I turned to Rob, who was already retethered to his phone. "You have anywhere to be?"

He looked up. "Yeah, I have a hot date at the Olive Garden."

"Well, I don't know. Maybe you wanted to see your folks."

"Not this time, unless I want to extend my stay by three weeks."

"So can we swing by my dad's?"

"Of course. Do you need to let him know we're coming?"

"No," I said, turning onto the street where I had spent the first eighteen years of my life. "He'll be there."

And he was. We found him in the garage, puttering beneath the hood of a circa '70s Mustang. He looked irritated to see me, but then he spotted Rob and perked up. He didn't ask why were there. Like us appearing on a random Saturday afternoon was what he had been expecting all along.

"Whose car is that, Pops?" I asked.

"A neighbor's. I'm fixing up cars in my spare time." He scowled at my Toyota, which was in the driveway. "Not the commie kind."

"You are aware that Japan is a constitutional monarchy, yes?"

He ignored me. "Rob, how are you?"

"Not too bad. You look good, Javier. How's life been treating you?"

"Eh," said my father, sounding exactly like my grandfather. "I go to the bar to watch fights, I work on cars." He paused. "I made a new friend."

"A friend, huh?" I said.

"If it's something to tell you about, I'll tell you." He wiped his brow with his forearm. "I'm taking it slow."

When my mother died, I half expected my father to, too. The man had not known how to make a doctor's appointment or locate his own socks and underwear, let alone feed himself. But life had marched on, and he with it. And now he had a girlfriend.

"Can't you find James a nice woman to settle down with?" said my father to Rob. "I'm waiting for grandkids."

"You have two," I reminded him.

"I want some that have my last name. Can't Rob here get you a good job in finance? Rob, couldn't James take a few courses, switch gears?"

Of course he had used an auto metaphor. And of course I did not remind him that most of the time he told people I already worked in finance. "Pops. I'm happy doing what I do."

This was mostly true. I continued to excel at my job; as it happens, a basic proficiency in the English language holds actual value outside of the field of literature. There were times when I contemplated driving a pair of scissors directly into my skull, sure. But I liked being good at something, and as I was discovering, the better I was, the more effort I wanted to put into my work.

"Javier, a chimp could do what I do," Rob told my father. "Run the numbers, move the numbers, figure out what works, press the same button over and over, inform people you have pressed that button. James here has actual talent."

Like Kathryn's praise, Rob's statement was based in faith, not fact; he had not read my work since I was in graduate school.

"I don't know about that," I said.

"If you didn't, why would you still be doing it? I'm not saying someone should hand you a Pulitzer for your unfinished novel. But there's a reason you haven't quit yet."

"Just talk to him," my father said to Rob, like I wasn't standing right next to him. The minute we got back in the car, Rob was on his phone, muttering as his thumbs tapped out one email after the next.

"This bad, even on a Saturday?" I asked.

"Yeah." He sighed deeply. "Clients want to know what I'm going to do with their millions before Monday comes, even though they know the market's closed. My boss wants to know what I'm going to do about my clients. My team wants to know what I'm going to do about the boss." He dropped the phone into his lap and looked out the window.

Past him, the trees and grass along the highway formed a long green blur. "Sometimes I wonder what it's all about. I wish I had something like you and Lou have."

For a split second I thought he was implying that Lou and I had a romantic connection, and my heart immediately began to pound against my rib cage. Then it occurred to me that he was talking about writing. "No, you don't," I finally said. "Trust me. Like every writer knows, if there were anything else we could do, that's what we would be doing."

In fact, my very first creative writing professor had used a variation on this line—*If there's anything you can do other than write, save yourself the heartbreak and go do that*—and I remember thinking it was arrogant, and maybe even intended to preemptively eliminate his competition. I had never repeated it when I was an instructor, so I wasn't sure why I had just used it on Rob.

"How is Lou, anyway?" I asked. "Are you guys still having trouble?"

"Not as much. She seems better lately; she's really wrapped up in her writing. She's at a poetry retreat right now, actually. And she found a literary agent last month."

"That's great. And you?"

"I'm good," he said, and picked up his phone again.

It's funny—an incident that feels like a massive misstep as it's happening often ends up as a footnote in your personal history, if you remember it at all. But a seemingly insignificant "should have" can turn out to be one of your biggest regrets.

Rob did not volunteer any additional information about his career or how his marriage was faring. But I suppose I understood—in the way that humans who have spent large, formative chunks of their life together can—that he was unhappy, and he and Lou weren't doing so well, either. Yet I said nothing; I did nothing. The next morning, he was on a plane back to New York.

EIGHT

Winter 2006

Lou published her first book of poetry, *You Are Here*, when she was thirty-one. I was thrilled for her, even if her success was a fresh reminder of my own failure. I had not finished the so-I-married-a-spy novel, even though Pascal had encouraging things to say about the first half. For all my quoting Didion, I knew how the story would end (sorry to spoil it for you, but everyone dies) yet could not figure out what to do with the middle. Right after the average man learns the terrible truth, my motivation disappeared along with the protagonist's mole of a wife. One day of not writing became two, then twenty, and before long I only looked at my draft when the mood struck, which was less often than a full moon rising in the sky.

There is something about leaving things undone that wears away your confidence, and when I arrived in New York on the evening of Lou's book launch, I felt bared to the bone, all my live wires exposed.

Who goes to poetry readings? I wondered as I walked into the bookstore. Half the city, by the look of the crowd that had gathered. I didn't see Rob but quickly located Lou, who was standing in the center of the room. She was wearing an ivory wool dress and a huge smile.

Lou's editor introduced her, and then she took the stage. She was nervous at first, and her voice broke several times. But poem by poem she unwound, until she was expansive and at ease, delivering each verse with emotion. She was on one of the last poems when she spotted me. She leaned into the microphone. "Hi, Jim," she murmured, then smiled at the crowd. "Jim's an old friend of mine."

I don't remember much about what happened after that. She read again, there was applause, then a brief question and answer, and more clapping.

She called me out, I thought, an electric current shooting through my body. *Me, me, me.*

Lou was surrounded by people afterward. I was too jittery to talk to her, anyway, so I went to find Rob. I found him chatting with a couple in the corner. As the three of them turned to greet me, I realized the couple was Kathryn and the man I sometimes saw her around campus with. I suppose I knew in a roundabout way that Lou and Kathryn had kept in touch. Still, seeing her there was a knee to the nuts.

"Hello, James," she said pleasantly. "You flew in, too?"

"Yes, just tonight," I said, as though the ratty college-era duffel I was toting around hadn't indicated as much. Work had been hectic for weeks as the business school prepared for the end-of-year fund drive, and I had taken a late-afternoon flight and cabbed from the airport directly to the bookstore.

Kathryn gestured to the man beside her. "James, this is Christopher Bucknell."

"James Hernandez," I said.

"Christopher is a physicist," said Kathryn as Christopher nodded in the smug way that someone who has put in the time to become a physicist has earned the right to do. "And my husband," she added, as if the previous title had not been enough rope to hang me.

"How lovely," I said as Rob stuck his elbow into my side. "I am a hack at the business school, and Kathryn's ex."

Kathryn glowered, and for good reason; I had no cause to be a prick, particularly to a person with whom I had once occasionally shared a toothbrush.

Then I noticed it. The dress she was wearing, which dropped like a curtain from her bust, made it hard to tell. She was glowing a bit, but she had always been radiant. But as Kathryn shifted toward Christopher, I saw the unmistakable swell of new life.

"Oh," I said.

Kathryn's eyes met mine. "I'm due in May."

"That's wonderful," I said, and mostly meant it, but I also sort of wanted to crawl into a deep hole, or maybe even a cave with a bear who had just awoken after a very long winter.

"Thanks," she said.

"Well," I said, and cleared my throat. "Lou was great, wasn't she?"

"Yeah, she was," said Rob. "You're coming over tonight, right?"

"Definitely," I said. I was hit with a sudden urge to flee, which I opted to heed. "You know, I should really get going if I'm going to make it to the after-party. I need to drop my bag at the hotel, and then I'll see you guys back at your place."

"Great. So we'll see you soon," said Rob.

"Absolutely," I said. "Kathryn, Christopher Bucknell, so long."

~

Rob and Lou lived in a brownstone apartment in Cobble Hill, Brooklyn. It was a movie set of a place, narrow but well lit and decorated with Swedish furniture and Moroccan rugs. When I arrived, the party was already in full swing, so I grabbed a glass of champagne from a table and jammed my way through well-dressed revelers, feeling every bit the unsophisticated Midwesterner that I was. I was working on my second glass when I found Lou in the dining room.

She gave me a sideways hug. "It is *so* good of you to come."

"Wouldn't have missed it for the world. Congrats, Lou. I'm thrilled for you. The poems are great, and"—I grabbed a copy of her book from the credenza—"I mean, you have a *book*! And you're practically a teenager!"

She scrunched up her nose. "Thank God I'm not; those were the worst years of my life. But thank you, Jim. I'm really thrilled. Honestly, I'm still pinching myself."

"Lou!" said a leather-skinned man dressed in jeans and a Rolling Stones t-shirt.

"My publisher," she whispered. "Come find me later," she called over her shoulder as the man whisked her off into another conversation.

Kathryn and Christopher were on the other side of the apartment. Attempting to maintain that distance between us landed me directly in front of Elyse, whom I had not spoken with since that one night in 2003. She and I made small talk, but I couldn't stop staring at the man she had come with, who was wearing a gold-buttoned blazer and was so high I was sure he was going to float off right in front of me.

Eventually Elyse and Captain Coke-face headed elsewhere, but in the interim Kathryn and Christopher had drifted closer to where I was standing. I fled to the kitchen, but they continued their oblivious trek toward me, so I quietly let myself out onto the patio.

It was cold, and two smokers huddled together, puffing with fervor. They crushed the last of their cigarettes beneath their heels, nodded at me, then hustled back inside.

The sky was lit with industry and overpopulation, and it was hard to see the stars. I was counting airplanes when Lou came up behind me.

"What are you doing out here?" she asked.

I made a face. "Oh, you know. Crowd control for introverts. But what about you? Why are you not enjoying your own party?"

"I needed a second to collect my thoughts."

"I can go," I said, already starting for the door.

"Don't you dare," she scolded, and I returned to my place beside her. "I can think just fine with you here. Though brrr! It's freezing."

I handed her my sport coat. "Here. I hope it doesn't reek of social anxiety."

She laughed and slipped the jacket over her shoulders. "Thank you. So was it okay, seeing Kathryn? I couldn't not invite her."

"I wouldn't have wanted you not to. And yeah, it was fine." I considered it for a moment, then added, "It was tough. She's probably a lot happier and better off now. But I . . ." *Eh,* I thought. *What's the point in not telling Lou what's on my mind?* "I miss her a little, you know?"

"Oh, Jim," she said wistfully. "Things between you two didn't work out for a reason, don't you think?"

"Sure," I said, though I was beginning to suspect that the reason was, in fact, me.

The second floor of the brownstone behind Lou and Rob's was dimly lit. Through the windows, I watched a man take an infant from a woman's arms and begin to pace back and forth.

"So has Rob told you?" said Lou after a moment.

"Told me what?" I had been thinking about the baby across the way, and probably about Kathryn's pregnancy, too. As such, my immediate assumption was that Lou was going to tell me she and Rob were planning to have a child. My next thought was less a coherent idea than a flash of jealousy. When two people become three, they stop being fellow citizens and form their own nation, one that is largely impervious to foreigners.

Lou was gnawing on her lower lip, which was threatening to bleed. "We . . . we're having trouble."

"That's normal, right? You've been married eight years," I said, like I knew a damn thing about marriage.

"I think there's someone else."

A storm of emotions tore through me. Repulsion and anger, yes. But curiosity, too, and if I'm totally honest, the smallest bit of excitement. "That can't possibly be true," I said at last. "He works too much."

"Yes, he does. And so does his supervisor. *Andrea,*" she said, like a curse. "I used to call her his work wife, but it's not so funny these days."

For all of Rob's girlfriends and one-nighters before Lou, I had never known him to be unfaithful. Maybe he was getting his midlife crisis out of the way early—though that didn't seem right, either. "Are you sure? That's out of character for him."

"I'm not sure, actually," she admitted, pulling my jacket tighter around her. "But whether or not he's actually cheating isn't the point, is it? Doubt's a symptom, not the disease. Something's broken between us."

I hesitated. Was I being disloyal to Rob by talking to Lou about this? Probably. As pleased as I was that Lou was confiding in me, I was disappointed that Rob hadn't come to me first.

Then again, perhaps he had tried to, and I had been so busy registering his small complaints about Lou that I had ignored the bigger picture. And why? Because I hadn't wanted to hear anything negative about her? Or because I had wanted them to fall apart?

I settled on a feeble statement that allowed Lou and me both to opt out of the conversation: "You don't have to tell me about it if you don't want to."

"I do want to. Who else understands?" Lou's eyes were moonlit as she looked at me—or maybe that's just my memory making too much of the incandescent bulbs over the back door. "Rob thinks we should have a baby. Like that will fix everything."

So I hadn't been completely off base about them procreating. My breath formed tiny clouds in front of my face. "What do *you* think?"

"I think it's lousy timing. He's spent years on his career, and instead of putting equal time into our relationship, he wants to plow forward and have a kid." She shook her head, sending her hair bouncing off her shoulders. "I mean, we're talking about adding a whole other human being to the planet!"

"And everyone knows humans are the worst," I said gravely. "You'd be *way* better off getting a dog."

She broke into a smile. As we looked at each other, there it was again—that terrible, wonderful feeling, pulling me under.

"You're great, Jim," she said after a moment. "Maybe I should have married someone like you."

I froze, trying to figure out how to respond, but it didn't matter; the back door opened and out popped another smoker, who immediately began chatting with Lou. By that point, I had lost circulation in my digits and was fairly certain my nose was frostbitten. Also, there was the issue of my attempting to get over Lou having just been undone with one offhand comment. "I'm going to head in," I told her.

"I'll be right behind you. Do you want your jacket?"

"No, you keep it."

Maybe I should have married someone like you, I heard her say at two in the morning, and at four. Those ruinous words rattled around in my mind again at six when the cabs on Seventh Avenue began to bleat below my hotel window, and I gave up and got out of bed.

She couldn't have meant it, I decided as I showered. It's not that I thought I had no merit as a potential partner. Yes, I was occasionally introverted and often awkward. But I was usually kind and typically competent, and my life was humming along. I was soon to receive a third promotion at work and had even saved up a down payment for a house.

Still. What would Lou ever see in a man like *me*? For all my longing, my actual appeal was not something I had put much thought into. (When you're wondering what you'd do with the megamillions jackpot, you try not to ruin the fantasy by calculating your odds of winning.) That morning, though, I considered the possibility that maybe—just maybe—she had said that about marrying me because she, too, felt that same strike of lightning when we were together.

I took a brief nap, then rode the train into Brooklyn. I had more than an hour to kill before I was supposed to be at Rob and Lou's, so I stopped at a bistro for a bite.

Back then, Brooklyn wasn't quite the breeder Mecca it has since become. But there was a tiny, dimple-faced child at the table to my right who looked a lot like you (or at least that's how I remember her). She was giving me a gummy smile, so I smiled back and wondered what it would be like to have a child of my own and whether I had made a mistake in ending things with Kathryn. She had not been making that terrible pitying face at me, but seeing her had stung all the same. When we mutually decided to end our relationship, I was certain we had made the right decision. The last thing I had expected to feel all these years later was regret.

I pulled Lorrie Moore's *Self-Help* out of my backpack. My coworker Nessa—herself an academic expat, and my closest friend at the office—had pressed it into my hands like a door-to-door missionary with free copies of the Bible. As I began to read, I understood why. Moore's stories were sharp, concise portraits of everyday life. I had always found the old adage "Write what you know" to be rather ridiculous. Then again, spinning tales about apocalyptic doom and gloom and married folks wasn't working out so well for me. Perhaps I would be wise to rip a page from Moore and begin to chronicle something that looked more like my own existence.

Halfway through my meal, the sweet baby at the table next to me began bawling. Then the table to my left was seated with two children, who started banging fork upon spoon upon table, and screeching in response to what I gathered was the wrong kind of bread in the wire basket that the waitress had placed before them. Their mother had the terse smile of someone running on goodwill and caffeine, while their father looked like he would rather be, say, face-to-face with a gladiator in a colosseum in ancient Rome. I wolfed down my food, paid my bill, and headed to Rob and Lou's.

"Want a cup of coffee, Jim?" Lou asked as she let me in. Their apartment was littered with the remnants of the previous evening—lipstick-smudged glasses on the credenza, appetizer plates piled high in the sink.

"Sounds great," I told her. "Thanks."

Rob was at the dining room table. "Hey, douche nozzle," he said, stretching his long legs onto a second dining chair.

"Hey yourself, dong nugget. That was some party. What time did everyone leave?"

"The last of the stragglers took off around one."

My whistle echoed off the tin ceiling. "Lou," I called, "did you have a good time?"

"Of course," she called back from the kitchen. "But did *you*?"

"I wouldn't call concurrent encounters with past partners *fun*. But the reading and party were great," I said as she walked back into the dining room. "And like I said, I'm really happy for you."

She handed me a mug of coffee, and I thanked her. Then she handed Rob a mug, and he said, "Do we have anything to eat?"

"No, because you didn't go out for pastries like I asked you to," Lou said in a voice that had nothing to do with croissants. She walked to the credenza and began gathering wineglasses, while Rob remained at the table, sipping his coffee.

"How's work going, Rob?" I asked, hoping to lighten the mood. "Greenspan's departure still denting the market?"

He grunted. "How could it not? You can't expect Oz to keep humming along after the little man disappears from behind the curtain."

"Fair enough." I thought about what Lou had said about Rob working all the time. Maybe they were overdue for a getaway. "You two have any vacations planned?"

"Yeah, I have a trip to London coming up."

"That's a work trip," said Lou, gathering another round of glasses from the credenza. "Not a vacation."

"I'm sorry my company doesn't meet shareholders in Bora Bora," he said without turning to her.

"Forget it."

"Happy to."

As embarrassed as I was to find myself in the middle of Rob and Lou's spat, the insults they were lobbing at each other only solidified my suspicion that perhaps they were not so well suited for each other, after all. Yes, they loved each other—or so they said—but was this ugly fight not evidence that their love was not as deep as they claimed, or even the wrong sort of love? I again thought of Kathryn, who had never spoken to me that way, nor I to her. If we had stayed together, maybe we, too, would have succumbed to the same fate.

Lou sighed in defeat. "Fine. Why don't you two go out? Go get a bite to eat, then walk to the Promenade or something." She turned to address me. "He'll spend all of Sunday at the office, and probably tonight, too. Might as well enjoy him while you can."

"A bite to eat sounds good," I said. Yes, I had just come from lunch, but did it matter? Their sparring made Lou's comment about marrying someone like me that much worse. I was ready to get out of there.

"Agreed," said Rob. "When do you take off again, James?"

"I fly out tomorrow at one," I said. *And not a moment too soon.*

"Boo, that was too short," said Lou. "Have you ever thought about moving here? You'd love it. A single successful guy like you in the city—you'd have your pick of the litter."

I laughed. "Successful? You must have me confused with someone else."

"Do I?" She was standing behind Rob and winked at me over his head.

And I thought, *No, I can't move to New York.* In fact, by the time Rob and I set out, I had decided it would probably be best if I did not visit again for quite some time.

NINE

November 2007

Wisnewski died, as I had known he would from the moment I got that first call from Jen. What I didn't know was how awful it would feel to lose him. After all, my own mother had died. What could be worse?

But here, I thought as I looked into the open casket—here was the deflated shell of the boy with whom I had biked through our neighborhood, summer after summer. Here was the middle schooler who had howled with laughter when I began to go through puberty, then primed me on birth control in a way my father and health teacher had failed to. Here was the teen who, after I downed vodka like it was water (never do that—never drink alcohol faster or in larger quantities than you would a piping hot espresso), pried the cup from my hand and made sure I didn't drown in my own vomit. Here was the man who had been my lifelong friend.

And now he was dead.

I began to cry as soon as I saw him laid out at the front of the funeral home, then transitioned to what I hoped was a more subdued form of weeping as the funeral service began.

By the time Wisnewski's nine-year-old daughter stood before his casket and sang the first few lines of "Amazing Grace," I was back to blubbering and no longer cared what Rob thought, or Lou, or anyone.

No, the only person I cared about was Wisnewski—man, Wisnewski, how could he possibly be gone? All the tears I had not shed for my own mother came pouring out of me that morning. But that's a funeral for you; every lost life of your brief existence washes over you anew, with a fresh wave of loss added to that terrible sea of grief.

After the funeral, Lou, Rob, and I drove to Wisnewski's house, which was no longer actually his, I realized as we pulled up. The place was packed with relatives, coworkers, and dozens of high school classmates Wisnewski had kept up with over the years. I had mostly avoided everyone at the funeral home, but now I found myself in the unfortunate position of having to chitchat over plates of crusted deviled eggs and tiny ham sandwiches slathered with ungodly amounts of mayonnaise. I had just finished catching up with Helmer, who was back in the States for a stint and thinking about leaving the navy for good, when Lou sidled up next to me at the buffet.

Her nose was red and her eyes were swollen. "How's the punch?" she asked.

"If you like extra-strength cough syrup, then you'll love this," I said, ladling dayglow liquid into a plastic cup for her.

She took the cup from me. "This is hard on you."

"The funeral was a good hard. This," I said, motioning around, "is unearthing my latent agoraphobia at a frightening speed. I can't think of a worse time to discuss life's minutiae."

"You getting the old 'What do you do?' Or worse, the dreaded empty question 'How are you?'"

"How *are* you, anyway?" I said.

She socked me in the bicep with surprising strength. "Not so hot, Jim. Not so hot at all. The funeral was a little too close for comfort."

My expression must have indicated I had no idea what she was talking about, because she said, "My mother?" When I gave her another blank look, she shook her head in frustration. "Let me guess: Rob didn't tell you that my mom died."

"What? No. I'm so sorry." I had not seen Lou since a few months after her book party, when she and Rob had come in for Nancy's birthday. I hadn't heard from Rob that much lately, either, and when I did, all he talked about was his career. Not that I was doing such a bang-up job of reaching out to him. It wasn't intentional, necessarily, but I had grown tired of his never-changing narrative of how he was working too much yet was allegedly unable to do anything about it. The last time I had spoken to him, he had not asked me a single question—not one!—about my life. And so I mimicked him and put our friendship on the back burner.

"Thanks," said Lou. "It was about four months ago. There wasn't much to it. She had a stroke, and my uncle had her cremated before he even called to tell me she was dead. End of story."

"I am so sorry," I said again. "I know how terrible it is to lose your mother."

"I suppose. I've more or less been motherless as long as I can remember."

"And yet."

"And yet." She stuck a finger in her mouth to gnaw on a nail, then yanked it out self-consciously. "I always hoped she would become someone else—someone who loved me more, I guess. Now that she's gone, that hope is, too. It's stupid, but it's still what hurts the most."

I nodded. Part of me despaired that my mother and I had never mended our relationship. But as I recalled Wisnewski's sunken face, I found myself wondering if maybe it wasn't for the best. If we had been closer, it only would have hurt more to lose her.

It was good to catch up with Lou, especially since enough time had passed that I no longer felt quite so awkward about her comment at the book party. Still, the afternoon was slow. As I watched Jen press yet another plate of food into someone's hands, I thought about what would follow for her. My father had been stoic at my mother's funeral— quiet, occasionally weepy, but mostly unemotional. But for months afterward, he drank too much, ate too little, and holed up in his house. If you didn't know better, you would have thought my mother was the love of his life.

Jen would probably react differently; after all, she had loved Wisnewski deeply, and moreover, she had two kids to care for. But the day might still be one of the best she would have for a long time. And the one person who could help her through it now happened to be unavailable for the rest of time.

I was just coming back from a trip to the bathroom when I ran into Rob in the hallway. He was talking low on his phone. "Yeah," he said into the receiver. "Call you later . . . You, too."

There's a cadence to conversations you have with your significant other, a tone that you don't use with anyone, no matter how familiar, but a person you have known in the biblical sense. As such, I instantly assumed Rob was talking to Lou, even though I hadn't seen her leave the house.

Then she walked up behind him. "Let me guess," she said sharply.

He slipped the phone into his pants pocket. "Don't, Lou. Just—don't."

She narrowed her eyes. "I *don't* intend to do whatever you're referring to, since that would involve staying here. I'm going to your parents'."

I had already started walking in the opposite direction when Lou called after me. "Jim? Will you please give Rob a ride? I'm going to head out."

Rob's parents lived half a mile away; he was perfectly capable of walking himself home. "Of course," I said.

"Thank you. I'll see you soon."

"Dude, what's going on?" I asked Rob as I watched Lou hug Jen good-bye.

He kicked at the ground with his loafer. "What's going on is that Wisnewski was too young."

"I'd argue that anyone under ninety-eight is too young to die, no?"

"But *thirty-five?*" he said. "People in the 1800s could reasonably expect to live longer than that."

"I see your point. What is going on with you and Lou, though?"

He shrugged. "We're not okay."

"You want to talk about it?"

"No, I want to go get drunk. You up for a trip to the bar?"

It was not so much a question as a declaration of intent. If Rob wanted me to go to the bar with him to deal with whatever it was he had going on, then it was my obligation to take him. "Sure," I said.

We said good-bye to Jen and the rest of Wisnewski's family, then headed to O'Grady's, a place Wisnewski had loved. The air was thick with smoke—perhaps impossible to believe, but it was once legal to boost everyone else's odds of lung cancer as well as your own—and I sat there gasping and thinking that I was too old for smoky bars. As if Wisnewski's death had not been enough to remind me that we humans would inevitably deteriorate at a rapid rate, I had found several gray hairs a few days earlier.

"Work still bad?" I asked Rob after a waiter had brought us two tumblers of scotch.

"As usual. There's some bad stuff going down that I'm supposed to keep from getting worse."

"That mean you're sleeping at the office again?"

He looked sheepish. "Sometimes. And Lou . . . I mean, she just doesn't get it."

"How so?"

"This is the life I signed up for. And she signed up for it with me when we got married."

"You guys were really young, though," I argued. "Maybe she didn't understand."

"Still, it shouldn't come as a surprise. And the more she calls, the more I want to stay at the office. When I come home, all I hear is how I'm making her feel bad. There's . . . this woman at work." He said it casually, but I knew—I just *knew*—that it was his way of easing me in. Testing me, even.

"Rob. Come on."

"It's—" He downed his drink and motioned for the waiter to bring two more, even though I hadn't touched mine yet. "We're close, is all. She knows the pressure I'm under because she's under it with me. I don't have to explain everything to her."

Given that I knew what it felt like to be shut out when Rob let work swallow him whole, it was hard not to sympathize with Lou. "So she's a psychic," I said.

"You're going to nag me, too?"

The plastic back of my chair squeaked as I leaned into it. "This woman—"

"Andrea Jones."

"Fine, Andrea Jones. The reason she doesn't nag you is because she's not your wife. Good God, Rob. You got a full ride to undergrad—let's not pretend you're stupid. Greener grass, all that glitters. You know the drill."

"James Hernandez, walking compendium of clichés. And for the record, your perfectly green grass is now married to another guy."

"Damn," I said, but he just shrugged. "Listen, let's say you and Andrea get married. You have this big wedding—"

"I'd elope."

I snorted. "It's like you've thought this through."

"When you're married, you run through all the scenarios. Trust me." He glanced up from his glass, which he had been staring into as if it were some sort of high-octane wishing well. "Hey, do *not* look at me that way, okay? You don't know what marriage is like."

I know what loyalty is like, I thought, the irony lost on me. "So let's say you get married at city hall," I said. "Then what? Doesn't Andrea Jones get tired of you working all the time, too?"

"I doubt it, since she works even more."

"What's her middle name?" I asked. This was a litmus test of mine—a weird one, I'll admit, but I felt it demonstrated whether you were really nuts about a woman or whether she was just window dressing for your ego. For example, I had not been even the slightest bit curious about Elyse's middle name. I had been dating Kathryn for six months before I learned that her mother's maiden name, Salter, was her middle name; I still felt guilty for not asking sooner. Lou told me that her name, Louisa Astrid, means "famous warrior with divine strength" at the bar the first night I met her. If she had not, I probably would have inquired before the weekend was through.

Rob's face was wooden. He would probably never learn what went between Andrea and Jones. He had a nickname for her, though: "Andie's a great woman. If I was single, she's the kind of woman I would want to marry."

Finally, a topic on which I had firsthand knowledge. "That sounds like the words of a man who's in love with the wrong person," I said.

"Who said anything about love? I'm just at a crossroads. Andie makes me feel smart and capable. But Lou . . ." He drained his second drink. "In her eyes, I screw everything up. And now she doesn't think she wants to have kids. She thinks she'll end up being the kind of mother her mother was. Who, may she rest in peace, was an awful person. Yet Lou—who puts spiders outside instead of crushing them, and can't even admit to her narcissistic, energy-sucking friend Jeremy that he is the worst poet that ever picked up a pen—has decided that having children will somehow turn her into someone else."

On this count, it was hard not to feel bad for him. Yes, he worked too much, and yes, he could be surprisingly dense for someone who managed other people's millions. But I could see him teaching a daughter to ride a bike. I could imagine him casting a line off a dock with a son.

"Kids—that's a deal breaker for you?" I asked.

"If it were the only issue? Maybe not. But there are others." He exhaled. "I know you and Lou are friends, so I don't want to say too much."

Were Lou and I friends to the point that he could not tell me the truth? Regardless, weren't he and I *better* friends—or was I officially getting the brush-off? It was impossible to tell whether he was being disingenuous. "I don't know, man. I think you should find a way to work it out. If it's important, you can make it work, just like you've made everything else work," I said, even though I was not at all convinced that effort was what was going to solve their relationship woes.

His phone buzzed on the table. He turned it over to see who was calling, then flipped it again quickly, making me wonder if it had been Andrea Jones.

"Make it work," I said again.

~

When I got home, I poured myself some whiskey from the bottle my father had brought over after I bought my house. Glass in hand, I wandered over to the bookshelves in the living room and grabbed *The Great Gatsby* from the top shelf. It's a dazzling book, to be certain, but I've always found it kind of soulless at its core. I had chosen it because I wanted to go back to the place and time when I first read it.

I had just graduated from high school, and Rob, Wisnewski, Barry Helmer, and I were at Rob's aunt's cabin in Grand Marais, in Michigan's Upper Peninsula. As I opened the paperback, I could almost hear the guys taunting me about my unrelenting nerdiness and all the fun I was missing out on while they were boating and fishing and four-wheeling.

Goading aside, it was a good week. Every night, the four of us would go out on the dock with a twelve-pack or three and make blissfully oblivious predictions about our future. Rob had made almost as much money as he said he would, but he hadn't taken inflation into account, which might explain why he hadn't yet bedded a swimsuit model or purchased a Lamborghini. I, alas, had not become the next Stephen King. And while Helmer had done well for himself in the navy, he had confessed at the wake that he didn't like it all that much. Of the four of us, it was really Wisnewski who had come closest to living his dreams, and that's because all he had wanted was a little more money than he needed, a good woman who loved him, and a couple of kids.

Maybe that was what it was all about, I thought as my eyes blurred the words on the page. Maybe Wisnewski had figured out the secret to everything.

I read until I was too drowsy and bereft to stay awake any longer. I must have been in bed for an hour or so when my doorbell rang. I assumed it was a drunken coed; I lived close enough to campus that late-night high jinks had been known to happen in my neighborhood.

But when I looked through the heavy leaded-glass panels of the front door, Lou was staring back at me.

I blinked and looked again.

Still her.

She was bundled in a coat that made it look as though she had been swallowed by a large animal, and part of her face was hidden behind a cashmere scarf. I threw the door open. Winter had come early that year, and snow circled her on the porch.

"What are you doing here?" I asked. "How did you even know where I lived?"

She yanked the scarf down. "I have your address, so I located a map on this weird thing called the interwebs. Are you going to invite me in?"

I glanced behind me. The living room wall was coated with various paint swatches I had put up months ago; I had yet to decide which shade of gray was best. I had last vacuumed, oh, approximately never. "Won't you please be my guest?" I said, pretending to remove a top hat from my head.

"Ever the smart-ass, huh?"

"Always," I said, hoping she didn't notice that my hands were trembling.

She slipped off her boots. She wasn't wearing socks, and her toenails were small pink shells. Her face was blotchy, and somehow this seemed charming. "I know it's weird that I'm here. I can go if you want," she said.

"No," I said. In Mandarin, the word *ma* can mean five different things, depending on the tone you use. English isn't a whole lot better; based on the speed of my one-syllable response, Lou and I both knew she would not be going anywhere, at least not on my account. "Let me take your coat," I said. "You want a cup of tea, or a drink?"

"Tea would be nice."

I indicated that she should head to the living room, but she padded behind me into the kitchen. "Please don't look around," I said, only half joking.

"I already guessed that you lived in a charming house with a filthy kitchen," she said, helping herself to a paper towel.

I laughed, though another part of me was thinking, *She thought about what my house looks like?* "Well, you were right," I said, and began to fill the kettle.

She sat on one of the stools at the small kitchen island and wiped her nose with the paper towel. Then she looked at me and said, "I'm leaving Rob. I didn't know where else to go."

A hotel? I thought, vacillating between horror and elation. I wasn't sure how to respond, so I pulled out my cliché handbook. "You're not really leaving him. It's just the funeral. These things have a way of reopening old wounds. Sleep on it. You'll be less sad tomorrow."

Lou looked at me with enormous, sorrowful eyes. "I'm inherently sad, Jim. I have a feeling you understand that about me."

As she said this, it occurred to me that I did, in fact, know this. But how?

"We can talk more about that some other time," she said, and I thought, *Yes, but how about you tell me right now? Tell me everything and I will bear it with you and make it my own.*

But some other rational part of me—which was, alas, quickly disintegrating—thought, *James, you horrible turd, this is the wife of your best friend, and you can no more have her than you can chip off one of the faces on Mount Rushmore and declare it yours.*

"Rob is my friend," I said limply.

She looked at her hands. "I know. This is awkward."

"No," I said, this time with a shred of dignity. "What's awkward is you and Rob not trying harder to fix things. Don't you think you can fight your way out of it?"

"I have been trying to claw my way out of this hole for more than two years, but it wasn't until today, seeing Jason in the funeral home, that I realized that I can't keep trying." She started to cry softly. "Do you know who Rob was on the phone with for half an hour today? It wasn't me, and it wasn't you."

"Oh no. I'm sorry." And I was. But I was angry, too. What was *wrong* with Rob? Had a parasite meandered into his cerebral cortex? Even if he was not having a physical relationship with his supervisor— and based on our conversation at the bar, I was fairly certain that if he wasn't already, he would be soon—why would he choose her over his wife? I didn't have to meet Andrea Jones to know that she was no Lou.

The kettle began to whistle. I poured a cup of tea for Lou, which I set on the island in front of her.

She curled her hands around the mug and shivered. "I know this makes things hard for you, but I honestly wasn't sure who else to turn to. We have a connection, don't we, Jim?"

Well, yes: if we had not had a connection, this story would end here. But I didn't want to oversell it or reveal just how dumbly in love with her I was. So I just nodded and asked if she wanted to head to the living room.

We took opposite ends of the sofa. Lou tucked her feet under her comfortably; I sat too stiffly for a man in his own home.

"So," I said.

"So."

I sighed, suddenly feeling the full weight of my shortcomings, and at the same time, acutely aware that I was fortunate to have these short-comings (see: death of childhood friend). "You can't really think there's no hope. Rob's a good guy. He loves you." I cringed as I heard how dim I sounded. I mean, someone must have said this same thing to Anne Boleyn at some point.

"Jim," said Lou, and inched down the sofa, closer to me.

I don't know why we do the things we do. Sometimes it's as if we already know everything is about to change, and we can't wait another moment to begin. And so I made what some might call a stupid choice.

I reached out for Lou.

Ralph Waldo Emerson said that you must do the thing you are most afraid to do, and I was terrified when Lou gave me her hand. Even more than I was afraid of ruining everything between me and Lou—or Rob and Lou, or me and Rob—I think I was ultimately afraid of missing my chance. After all, wasn't poor Wisnewski proof that it could all be over as quickly as it began?

Before I joined Wisnewski and the great majority, I wanted to wrap my arms around Lou. I wanted to feel her lips on my own and give myself over to the illusion that she was mine, as much as any of us can make such an outrageous claim about another person.

I didn't kiss her, though. Her fingers grew warm in my hand, and we looked at each other while a hundred unsaid things passed between us. By the time we broke apart, something between us had shifted, maybe forever, even though things between us would go no further that night—and also maybe forever.

"What will you do next?" I asked Lou as I showed her to the door.

She stepped onto my snow-covered porch and looked up at me with a sad smile. "Oh, you know. I'm thinking I might just go and ruin everything."

TEN

January 3, 2008
TO: James J. Hernandez
FROM: Louisa Bell
SUBJECT: Hello

Dear Jim:

I'm sorry I didn't write sooner to thank you for taking care of me after Jason's funeral in November. As you probably know, I moved out of our apartment at the beginning of last month. Rob and I haven't spoken since. It pains me to admit it, but I think it's for the best.

I am as lonely as I've ever been, and that's saying a lot (do you remember the Chekhov quote I once shared with you?). Yet I take comfort in the fact that solitary periods tend to lead to solid work, at least for me. Writing has been my lifeboat; my oar;

my compass. If I continue in my current state, I will have a dazzling new collection of poems to submit in short order.

How's your writing going? Are you still working on the book about the couple with secrets? Now there's a topic with universal appeal! (So says the woman who may or may not be getting divorced, ha.)

I've rented a studio in Clinton Hill, and Elyse helped me land a job as a freelance copyeditor at a magazine that advises young women on the countless ways they are inadequate, then offers a dizzying array of solutions for said inadequacies, each of which is only effective until the next issue arrives. I work roughly two weeks out of the month. When I'm not at the office, I try to work on my own writing, but spend many days staring through the leaded windows of my apartment as the dull, prom-iseless part of winter sets in. At least the holidays are over. Forget Eliot's opinion of April; December has always been the cruelest month for me, and this past one was particularly sadistic.

Anyway, I'm just writing to check in, with a heavy dose of gratitude. Happy 2008, my friend. I hope this year is your best yet.

Always,

Lou

January 4, 2008
TO: Louisa Bell
FROM: James J. Hernandez
DRAFT: Re: Hello

Lou,

~~Happily surprised to hear from you. Glad writing is coming along. I'm here if you need me.~~

January 4, 2008
TO: Louisa Bell
FROM: James J. Hernandez
DRAFT: Re: Hello

~~Lou,~~

~~It's so nice to hear from you. I've been worried.~~

January 4, 2008
TO: Louisa Bell
FROM: James J. Hernandez
SUBJECT: Re: Hello

Lou,

Happy New Year to you, too. I was wondering how you were doing. Glad you're getting settled in a new place, and that you made it through December. (Personally, I hate the holidays. As you might imagine, I try not to advertise this, as it only solidifies my image as a misanthropic weirdo—so please keep it close to your vest.) Doubly glad to hear your writing is fast, furious, and sustaining. Ride that wave as long as you can.

As for me, I'm not really working on the novel so much these days. I was recently promoted—I'm now a senior communications officer at the B-school, responsible not just for written materials, but also for direct correspondence with multimillionaires who pass out large endowments to the university the way one might toss bread crumbs to sparrows. As such, my hours have increased, and I often work until six or seven. Were I a more inspired, industrious person, this wouldn't interfere with my ability to write fiction. But as I am who I am, I'm in a holding pattern: unable to start a new book, and unwilling to return to the unfinished one. (Yet I've managed to turn this email into a novel.)

It was nice to see you in November. I hope you're doing well—or at least well-ish. Let me know if you need anything.

All my best,

James

January 31, 2008
TO: James J. Hernandez
FROM: Louisa Bell
SUBJECT: Star stuff

Dear Jim:

Did you know the word *disaster* means "bad star"? It's derived from Greek; ancient Greeks (along with most of the civilizations that predate ours) believed that ill-placed planets were responsible for catastrophe. I've always been fond of Jupiter myself; she is said to bring good fortune, and like me, she has a solid core beneath her unstable surface. These days, though, I feel I am an exploding star, pieces of me vaulting through the air without aim.

I left Rob; I do acknowledge my role in that disaster. And at heart I feel it is—well, without getting too much into it, I think this is good for him. For us. Or maybe I just have to believe that in order to get through it.

My purpose in writing, however, is not to brief you on the heavens or mortal me, but to see how you're doing, particularly regarding Jason. I forgot to tell you the last time I wrote how terribly sorry I am for your loss. This must be so hard for you. It was for me, and I barely knew him. I was thinking about what you said about my mom, how isolating it is to be without a mother. I had convinced myself that her death didn't affect me, since she and I were essentially estranged. But the more I think about it, the more I suspect that you were right. It is almost impossible to wrap your mind around the permanence of the whole thing, isn't it?

Anyway, I hope you are well. And if you're not, know that at the very least, you are not alone in that.

Always,

Lou

February 2, 2008
TO: Louisa Bell
FROM: James J. Hernandez
SUBJECT: Re: Star stuff

Lou,

You're not wrong about mothers, or lack thereof. I think about Wisnewski a lot, and like you, he makes me think about my mother. Two chunks of my childhood—poof! Gone. How can that possibly be?

Are you still finding solace in writing? Hope so. I wish I could say I am, too; but alas—I remain "between projects," which is a corporate euphemism for laziness.

Hang in there,

Jim

February 27, 2008
TO: James J. Hernandez
FROM: Louisa Bell
SUBJECT: Re: Star stuff

Jim,

I'm hanging. When do I get to return to solid ground?

Rob has said no to couples counseling. He said *I* left *him*, and, to quote: "I am better now than I have been in a good long time." I suppose I shouldn't be telling you this, but I also suppose you already know how he feels. And so—again, no surprise to you—we are moving forward with the divorce. I can hardly believe it.

He is seeing that woman outside of work (I probably shouldn't bring this up, either, but my well of self-pity is pretty darn deep right now, and the delete key and I aren't on great terms). Jennifer ran into them in a bakery in Long Island City last weekend. If ever you want to know what your soon-to-be ex-spouse is doing, leave no borough unturned.

Always,

L

February 28, 2008
TO: Louisa Bell
FROM: James J. Hernandez
SUBJECT: Re: Star stuff

Yes, Rob told me about hiring a divorce lawyer. I'm so sorry, Lou. I'm not sure what else to say, except I hope you're doing as well as can be expected.

—J

March 3, 2008
TO: James J. Hernandez
FROM: Louisa Bell
SUBJECT: Re: Star stuff

If by "as well as can be expected" you mean drinking copious amounts of vodka, and not the good kind; eschewing the company of every human who is not a stranger; and staying up until three a.m. in my hovel to write poems that seem like they came from a madwoman, then yes! I am the very picture of impending-divorce success.

In truth, I'm sorry I mentioned the stuff about the man soon to be known as my ex-husband. I'm sure that puts you in a bad position, but of course, you're too kind to say so. I do hope you'll forgive me.

Always,

L

March 10, 2008
TO: Louisa Bell
FROM: James J. Hernandez
SUBJECT: Re: Star stuff

No need to apologize, Lou. It's okay. I only wish things were different.

—J

P.S. Madwomen are said to write well. Keep at it.

March 10, 2008
TO: James J. Hernandez
FROM: Louisa Bell
SUBJECT: Re: Star stuff

You're a dear, Jim. Thank you. Hope I'll see you again sometime this century.

Always,

L

May 7, 2008
TO: Louisa Bell
FROM: James J. Hernandez
SUBJECT: In New York next week

Lou,

I'll be in the city next week. I've decided to take part of my four years of unused vacation* and attend one of these conferences where you speed-date a bunch of literary agents in hopes that somehow your written communication skills translate into the ability to verbally convey (in less than three minutes) the brilliance that is your work in progress. It's short notice, but think you might want to have lunch while I'm in town?

Best,

Jim

*Only a slight exaggeration

May 7, 2008
TO: James J. Hernandez
FROM: Louisa Bell
SUBJECT: Re: In New York next week

Jim, yes! I'm not at the magazine next week, so tell me when and I'll pick where. It'll be really great to properly catch up—can't wait.

Always,

L

ELEVEN

May 2008

I didn't set out to secure a spot among history's most irrational lovers. But neither can I claim that it "just happened." In truth, it was a small series of choices that snowballed into a much bigger decision, which then became an outcome that none of us saw coming.

Let me back up. Before I asked Lou to get together in New York, I had mostly been able to rationalize our emailing back and forth. After all, I couldn't control what she told me, could I? And I wasn't about to tell her *not* to email me. That, I thought, seemed rude and insensitive in light of what she was dealing with.

So I did my best to keep my messages cordial, kind, and brief. I even told Rob at one point that Lou and I had been in touch. "I don't expect you not to talk to her just because we've separated," he said, almost offhand, and then began yapping about mortgage-backed securities, only to hang up two minutes later so he could take a work-related call.

Yet I knew—I *knew*—that each message Lou and I exchanged heightened my feelings for her, which I had mostly tamped down. But those feelings only reemerged stronger the night of Wisnewski's funeral. To be honest, I don't think I would have asked to see her in New York were it not for a particularly frustrating conversation with Rob. I don't offer this by way of an excuse; it's simply what occurred.

As soon as I registered for the writing conference, which Pascal had urged me to attend, I called Rob to see if we could hang out while I was in the city. I hadn't seen him since the funeral. Since he and Lou had split up, I thought he would need to lean on me more. Instead, their separation had the opposite effect: he called even less often and emailed only in response to emails I sent him. Most of these messages were so brief they may as well have been telegrams (or text messages, though back then—and this may blow your mind—none of us texted).

In this way, I learned that Lou had moved out and was pushing for mediation, while Rob had kept the apartment and hired a divorce lawyer. When I encouraged him to wait on the divorce, he quickly shut me down; he was sure I meant well, he said, but he didn't want to talk about it.

So I wasn't entirely surprised that before I even had a chance to tell him when I would be in town, he said, "I'm swamped."

"Well, I'll be around for three days," I said. "We could just grab a quick drink. Or whatever."

"Things are really bad," he said. When I did not respond, he added, "When are you here?"

"I get in on the twelfth."

"Yeah, that's definitely not going to work for me."

Ouch, I thought, then reminded myself that he was hurting. On top of the mess with Lou, there was no way he wasn't still dealing with the impact of Wisnewski's death. After all, they had been friends longer than any of us and had even attended the same nursery school.

"Bummer," I said, hoping I didn't sound irritated. "You doing okay, though? You know, with the separation?"

"Yeah."

"Really?"

"Honestly? It's the last thing on my mind right now. Work is—well, I'm basically trying to turn around the *Titanic* before it hits an iceberg."

There was laughter in the background; I was sure of it. "Who was that?" I asked.

"No one," he said.

I swear I heard him shush someone, but there was no point in making a big production out of it, even if that someone was probably not a slaphappy secretary, but Andrea Jones. "What do you mean about the *Titanic*?" I asked.

"I can't say much more than it's not good."

"Okay. So—"

"Listen, buddy, I've gotta run. I have a meeting in five."

Over the years, Rob had called me countless names, many of which aren't fit to print. But *buddy*? This was how you greeted the guy you saw at the gym most days but had never actually introduced yourself to. It was something you named your dog. "Okay," I said.

"Talk soon," he said, and hung up.

I stared at the phone, *buddy* still ringing in my ears. Our friendship was not as strong as it had been at other times in our lives, but until that point, I had been under the assumption we were just on the down cycle of a natural ebb and flow. Now I was beginning to develop another theory, and that was that Rob had begun to think of me the way he thought of Lou. That is, I was someone on the outside, someone who didn't understand what he was going through and was therefore to be shut out.

I thought about Andrea Jones laughing in the background, and how little impulse control Rob seemed to be exhibiting lately. This did nothing to strengthen my willpower. Instead, I sat down at my computer and gave in to my own impulse—which was to see if Lou wanted to have lunch with me.

After all, if I was going to be on the outside with Rob's almost-ex-wife, I saw no reason why I shouldn't see her. And it was just lunch, I told myself. Was anything more harmless?

The minute I clicked the "Send" button, it seemed to me that I had just slipped down a very deep rabbit hole. Harmless? Who was I kidding? This was Lou we were talking about.

Who was now practically single.

Who was still, for all intents and purposes, my best friend's wife.

Oh God, I thought with horror. *Maybe she'll laugh at me—that would probably be for the best. Or maybe she'll have the good sense to pretend to be out of town.*

But when she emailed to say yes, she would love to get together, I did not cancel or admit that I wasn't actually sure us getting together was a good idea. Instead, I took it as confirmation that I was overthinking an innocuous meal between friends.

~

Lou called an hour before we were supposed to meet. "Jim?" She sounded a bit frantic.

"I'm here. You okay?"

"Yes, yes, totally fine. I'm calling because I'm at my agent's office and I got myself in a situation where I accidentally agreed to have lunch with her and her team and—well, I'm so sorry, I should have said no but it was all in motion before I had a chance to."

I was at once disappointed and relieved. "That's totally fine," I told her. In the floor-length mirror in my hotel room, my skin was less olive and more jaundiced, and my hair looked as though I had recently stuck one of my digits directly into a light socket. Now I would have time to get a haircut and work on the pitch I was slated to give literary agents at the conference the following morning.

"Do you have plans tonight?" she asked.

I did, in fact. Nessa had set me up on a blind date with her college roommate, a supposedly lovely woman who lived in the city but was considering moving back to the Midwest. I had a built-in excuse to say no to Lou, but instead of using it, I again allowed impulse to guide me. "Nothing firm," I said.

"Great! There's a Korean barbecue on the Lower East Side that's fantastic." She rattled off the address. "Seven okay?"

If we met at seven, I would definitely have to cancel my date. Nessa would not be pleased. "Perfect," I said.

It's only dinner, I told myself. And sure enough, when I saw Lou skipping down Rivington Street smiling at me, everything seemed normal—though for a split second I expected Rob to be with her. *Well, he could have been; his loss,* I thought with so much vitriol that I surprised myself.

"Hey, you," I said, pushing Rob from my mind as I hugged Lou. "You look great."

She stepped back to look at me. "So do you, Jim."

Stray snips of hair from my barber visit pricked the back of my neck, and I touched my collar self-consciously. "Not really, but thanks."

"Oh, stop it, you know you do. Shall we sit by the window?" she asked as we stepped into the restaurant. It was not yet truly warm, but the promise of heat hung in the air. I nodded.

"Sorry again about lunch," said Lou as the hostess seated us. "But thank you for being so flexible."

"No worries. Actually, let me rephrase: I'm happy to make the change."

"Come again?"

"One of the things I've learned as a semicorporate scribe is that when you use a phrase like 'no rush' or 'no problem,' all people hear or read is 'rush' or 'problem.'"

She made a disgusted face. "Don't you dare use that rule in your fiction."

I laughed, instantly at ease; she had that effect on me. "That's simple enough, because using it would require writing fiction."

"And you're not?"

I shrugged.

"Maybe you're doing it Hemingway-style!" she said, and pointed her menu at my chest. "Gathering up rich life experiences before you write about them."

"Yes, rich experiences," I droned. "Saving lives by securing funding for executive education. Foraging for sustenance at Kroger. Macheteing through the overgrown jungle of my backyard."

"Oh, Jim. You're not actually unhappy, are you?"

That was the thing: I wasn't. On the whole, I was actually quite content. But we humans aren't too good at stasis, are we? No—we like to throw a wrench into something the minute it starts running smoothly. We throw ourselves over the ledge reaching for the big, shiny object, when the smaller, duller version would do just fine.

"No, I guess I'm not," I told her. "Though at this point in life, I'm fairly certain meaning is more important than happiness."

"Aren't they one and the same?"

"Maybe. But more importantly, what about you? How the heck are you holding up?"

She gave me a crooked smile, and for a second I wondered if she was going to cry. Then she waved down the waiter. "Let's get drinks before we get into that."

We ordered, but instead of talking about the separation, Lou told me about a series of poems she was writing—a nautilus in verse, she described it. In return, I told her about the pitch I had prepared for the agents I would be meeting at the conference. She shot the pitch down, then promptly helped me rebuild it. By the time we had finished the meal, I was no longer deflated but instead brimming with possibility, which is one of the very best feelings there is to have. It had been a good idea to have dinner after all, I decided as the waiter handed me the check.

Lou let me buy dinner on the condition that she would buy me a drink at the bar just down the street. I agreed, ignoring the nagging little voice in my head saying that drinks were a far worse idea than lunch. *What would Rob say if he saw you?* I thought. Yet it was such a languorous, lovely evening, and Lou seemed so casual about the whole thing that I again assured myself that it was no big deal.

At the bar, Lou immediately launched into a series of questions: Had I seen Kathryn around Ann Arbor? (Yes.) With her new baby? (No.) Did it bother me? (A little, I admitted.) What was my long-term career plan? (What was a long-term career? I said laughingly.) And who was my dream publisher? (Any of them, I said, dead serious.)

We were drinking champagne—I don't remember why, maybe because Lou loved it, and I loved making her happy. "Lou," I said, watching bubbles rise from the bottom of the flute, "are we going to talk about that other thing?"

Her expression was fierce as she addressed me. "And what's that, Jim? That I pushed Rob away?"

"Who pushed who?" I asked, direct in the way it's easiest to be after several drinks.

She raised a fist. "Life with Rob included: Love," she said, flicking out her pointer finger. "Stability." Another finger came out, and another. "Affection and adoration—which, by the way, are not the same thing as love. So being there wasn't his thing," she said, wiggling her pinky. "He was gone a lot. But was it worth it to destroy the whole thing because of that?" she said, mimicking an explosion.

"He was the one who moved forward with the divorce," I said.

"But *I* left *him*. And when I did, I knew that a permanent separation was a possibility."

"So why did you do it?"

We were again seated at a window. I watched a group of teen boys in baggy jeans stroll past, and an elderly woman wheel a wire cart filled with laundry. A small child tugged a weary middle-aged man down the street. "I have a tendency to rush ahead," said Lou. "To preempt the end, like it'll somehow make it hurt less. I think that's why I barely called my mom."

"You really felt it would end with Rob, though?"

Her smile was tight. "It seemed inevitable to me. I couldn't help him get unstuck, and he wouldn't make me a priority. I didn't want to wait around to see just how much he was willing to hurt me before he decided to call it off himself."

My head was awash in champagne. "Can I ask you something?"

"Anything."

"Did you only say that to me at the book party because you thought Rob was cheating?"

"He *was* cheating." Her cheeks flushed. "I don't know if they were sleeping together before we split up, but it sure as hell was an emotional affair."

"How can you be certain?" I asked, like I hadn't overheard the way Rob was speaking to Andrea Jones at Wisnewski's house.

Lou drained her glass and looked away. "This is awful to admit, but I went through his email. I had to know what I was dealing with. And he left his computer wide open one night, almost like he wanted me to find out. I don't know if he loves her, but she loves him; that's for sure." Now she turned to me, her eyes flashing. "God, I'd met her half a dozen times before this all started and always thought she was a nonentity! Why would Rob go for the buttoned-up corporate type? When lo and behold, I should have known all along that he would want someone who's the exact opposite of me."

My heart was pounding. Why was she telling me this? Was it a confession—or a preemptive absolution? "That's almost impossible to

understand," I said at last. "But how is that any different from you saying you wish you had married someone like me?"

"That was different," she said, "because I adore you for *you*, Jim—
not for who you're not. And I get the feeling you would never hurt me."

"No," I said quietly. "Even if I wanted to, I don't think I could."

Neither of us spoke another word to each other—not after the bill
had been paid, or when we went out onto the street, or when I hailed a
cab and we both climbed into it. Adrenaline shot through my veins as
we crossed the Manhattan Bridge and headed through Brooklyn. I had
to remind myself to breathe, and just about ran out of air when Lou slid
across the leather seat halfway through the ride, so our arms and thighs
were pressed against each other. *You wouldn't hurt her, but you'll crush
your own best friend?* I thought, even as another part of me argued, *You
haven't done anything yet. And you don't have to. Drop her off and go back
to your hotel. Let it go.*

"Is this really a good idea?" I finally said as she unlocked the door
to her apartment. But instead of answering, her lips were on mine, and
she tasted like lip gloss and champagne and ten years of longing.

I once read that the only thing that separates humans from other
primates is less body hair and the ability to write. Chimpanzees, it
seems, are frighteningly skilled at deceiving their fellow animal, and
many a gorilla has fought for his family. Even monkeys show compas-
sion when there is no clear reward. But when it comes to mating, we're
all animals, our impulses swiftly shutting down the rational regions of
our brains. And so on that evening, the logical notions that should have
sent me in an ethical direction were replaced with animal instincts—
and yes, a handful of stupid human justifications.

I had waited so long, I told myself as Lou's hair fell around my face
like a veil, shrouding us from the rest of the world. It was just one night,
and I would never have this chance again.

Rob never, ever had to know.

TWELVE

I awoke disoriented, unsure of where I was or even whose body was beside me; after all, the last person I had actually slept with, in the literal sense of the phrase, was Kathryn. (None of the few women I had dated since had been interested enough to stick around to see if I snored.)

Then I looked beside me, where Lou was still blissfully unconscious, and the previous evening came rushing back. Part of me wanted to die on the spot. Another part had hit pause on my internal panic button while taking note of the fact that Lou's eyelids were not lavender or pale pink, as I had once imagined, but ivory with blue marbling. As I stared her, she began to rouse.

"Love is an atrocity," she said, her voice raspy.

"Good morning to you, too."

She pulled the sheet over her face. After a moment, she lowered it, looked at me, and whispered, "What have we done, Jim?"

"Would you like me to debrief you?" I was flooded with dread and guilt and even horror, but I was kind of hoping that Lou would reassure me that it was all going to be fine.

"Rob can never know about this. *God!*" she said, nearly shouting. "I cannot *believe* I'm even hearing myself say that. Screw Rob."

"I agree about him not finding out, but can we maybe not talk about him for a while?" I said feebly.

She yanked the sheet back over her head. "I need time to process."

"Is that your way of saying take a hike?" (I will admit, as awful as I felt, even saying this hypothetically split my heart in half.)

Even then, she couldn't help but be kind. "No, no, I didn't mean that at all," she said, sitting up. "Let me make you a cup of coffee."

"You don't have to," I said, but she was already padding across the apartment. She was wearing the plain white t-shirt I had been wearing under my button-down the night before, and a lump formed in my throat. Though I had only just begun to wrap my mind around what we had done, at a base level I understood that Lou and I had crossed a threshold, and our relationship would never again have the lightness it had before we slept together.

Button-down, I thought suddenly. *Clothes. Conference . . . crap.*

"What time is it?" I said to Lou. My phone had died, and I had not brought a charger.

"Noon."

"You're kidding, right?"

"Of course I am. It's almost nine."

"I have to go. I've already missed check-in for my conference, and I'll be lucky if I make my first agent meeting. Is it hard to get a cab from here?"

"Next to impossible. I'll call a car service for you."

The driver honked before I had taken a second sip of my coffee. I looked at Lou, who was sitting cross-legged on the counter with a mug of coffee in her hands.

"Go," she said. "It's okay."

I was reaching for the doorknob when I turned and looked back at her. "Lou? What do we do?"

She was still in my t-shirt, and she looked so, well, perfect sitting there that I wanted to ditch the conference, and maybe my job and all other aspects of life that did not center around her.

"Can I answer that later?" she said with a sad smile.

I let go of the doorknob and ran to her. Then I kissed her once, twice, and again for good measure and left before I could change my mind. Bad enough that I had just ruined everything. Worse was that I was tempted to do it again immediately.

~

To this day, I remember next to nothing about the writing conference, though suffice it to say I did not come away from it with a literary agent or renewed hope in my so-called fiction career. And what did I care? Writing a book was ridiculously insignificant in light of what had just transpired.

"How are you feeling?" I asked Lou that afternoon. We had met just outside my hotel and had wandered a few blocks over to Central Park. As we escaped the shadow of dull high-rises for a canopy of trees, I kept glancing around nervously. It was unlikely that we would see Rob, given that he was chained to his desk until long after sunset. This did nothing to quell my paranoia.

Lou didn't seem so poised herself. "I don't know, maybe we should go somewhere," she said as we began down a paved path.

"Like a museum?" I said.

"Like Key West. Or maybe Vermont. We could rent a car and go away for the next couple of days."

I'd be lying if I said I wasn't thrilled that she had just admitted she wasn't through with me. "Is that not the literal interpretation of running away from it all?" I asked. Again I thought of the night before, which had been amazing. Everything I had ever imagined, really—except the guilt. The guilt I had not fully considered. Certainly I had not anticipated that it would feel like a thousand pounds of sadness on my heart.

"I guess it is," she confessed. "But running away seems slightly more palatable than reality right now."

We sat on a low stone wall on the park's south side, watching children chase each other in the afternoon sunlight. "So you feel pretty awful, too?" I asked.

"Like the worst person ever. Well," she said, managing a small smile, "maybe the second worst."

"You're telling me. But seriously, why did we do it?"

She pursed her lips. "That was stupid of us. Really, really stupid. But I've had what you might call feelings for you for a long time."

I stared at her. "You have?"

"Come on, Jim. You didn't think I became attracted to you in two hours' time."

"I suppose not."

"And I knew you had feelings for me, too."

My ears grew hot. Of course she had known. But had Rob? He couldn't have. Or maybe he did, and he had simply trusted me. Now my whole face was burning.

"Until last night, I never in a million years thought I would actually *act* on those feelings," she said. "It was like something crazy came over me."

"So I was an itch that you scratched? A mental lapse?"

She touched my arm lightly. "If we were both single and we had just met, I would want to be with you."

This was not a direct answer to my question, but I felt slightly less defeated. "We were good together, weren't we?" she added.

I could still feel her soft lips on mine, the way she fit into my arms just so. Guilt or no guilt, it had been thrilling to act on something that I had wanted for so long.

Yet there had been something familiar about being with her, too—and not because we had known each other for a decade. To be honest, Lou had reminded me of Kathryn. I tried to push this thought out of my head. To admit that it had been even a little like anything I had experienced before seemed akin to declaring it a mistake.

"We were amazing," I told Lou. "But now that we've opened Pandora's box, what do we do with that?"

"We go back to your hotel, Jim," she said.

~

I had barely closed the door to my room when Lou fell against me. The motions were the same as those of the night before: mouth upon mouth, my hands in her hair, hers tugging at my shirt to close the nonexistent gap between us. But this time our kiss was more bitter than sweet.

We did a tortured sort of tango across the room and ended up on the bed. Instead of continuing to kiss, though, we lay side by side on our backs. Her hand found mine, which made me think of a story I recently read in the paper about an elderly man who had passed away in his sleep. When his wife awoke to find him, she stayed where she was. According to the report, her heart gave out within an hour; their daughter discovered them later that day, hand in hand, heads turned toward each other.

The back of my throat tightened, and there was a familiar tingle behind my eyes. But I refused to let myself cry, because to do so would be to end up weeping beside Lou, and that was not how I wanted to leave her.

I don't know how long we remained that way; it must have been awhile. "Do you think this will be enough?" I finally asked.

"It will have to be," she said softly. "What we've done is terrible, but we can't tell Rob—that would be even more selfish than us having slept together. I don't know." She sighed deeply. "Maybe it's out of our systems now. Maybe you'll go back to Michigan and find a life partner and I can . . . figure out how to navigate the world as a young soon-to-be divorcée."

"Do you even *believe* in life partners?" I asked. It seemed to me that the previous night had diminished, if not completely obliterated, the odds of my finding a woman to spend the rest of my life with. And even if I did, would I be able to recognize her before it was too late?

"Sure I do," said Lou. "Swans mate for life. So do eagles."

"Even the bees in the trees do it," I sang.

She laughed. (Was there a better sound? I thought not.)

But the relief was short-lived because my thoughts immediately returned to Rob. He was probably two-thirds of the way through his twelve-hour workday, stressing about a market shift that meant nothing to the majority of the world, even though it would later have at least an indirect effect on their bank accounts. I prayed to God that the economy would remain the worst of his worries for a very long time.

"I should probably go," said Lou as she sat up. "I'll miss you terribly, Jim."

I pushed myself into a sitting position and looked at her. "I already miss you. You know I'm in love with you." The minute I said this, I wanted to pull the words out of the air and shove them back in my mouth. It was true, but my confession did nothing but add another tangle to our mess. After all, we had already learned that you should not do at night what you cannot manage in the bright, revealing light of day.

Lou leaned forward and hugged me tight. "Do your best not to be, okay? Not just for yourself . . ."

But also for Rob. We both knew what she meant. "I'll try," I told her. There was a small scar just above her eyebrow. I ran my finger over it. "There's so much I still don't know about you."

"The less we know about each other, the better. But before I go, what's your middle name?"

My eyes smarted.

"What is it?" she asked. "Too much? You don't have to tell me."

I blinked hard. "My middle name is Javier, for my father."

"James Javier Hernandez," she said quietly. "That's very nice. But you know, I think I prefer Jim."

"Me, too," I said.

She kissed me lightly, then took her purse and slipped out the door. I lay back on the bed, thinking about how, save for a few letters, the difference between love and loss was so slight it was almost impossible to perceive.

THIRTEEN

June–August 2008

"You have gone and lost your mind!" Pascal stared at me, his eyes bulging. Then he stabbed his falafel with his knife, raised it, and took a bite, still looking at me as though I had sprouted a horn in the center of my forehead.

Several weeks had passed since I returned from New York, and I had not heard from Lou. I don't know what I had been expecting—after all, we had agreed that it was over for us, almost as fast as it began—but it wasn't radio silence.

I craved her. Not just physically. Even to hear her voice, to have her reassure me that what we had done was necessary and inevitable, would have been almost enough.

Yet the emails I wrote her sat unsent in my draft folder. My finger hovered over her number on my cell phone, but I never pressed "Dial."

It was remorse that kept me away. Rob's shadow followed me throughout the day; his ghost haunted me at night. As often as I thought about Lou, I thought about Rob even more, and how he, like an invisible hand, had guided me through some of the most pivotal points of my life.

Like our freshman year of high school, when he had gone up to a beefy senior who had been taunting me, said a few words, and I was never again jeered—by anyone. Or just before my sophomore year of college, when Rob filched my university password, logged into my account, and changed my major from engineering to English literature. "Someone had to," he said, ignoring my protests after he smugly informed me of what he had done. "Your father can't take calculus for you. Start making yourself happy before your grades plummet and you flunk out."

My oldest and closest friend. And here I had gone and pulled a Brutus to his Caesar.

The consequence of this was that I was losing my mind, and not in a leisurely fashion. I forgot to pay my electricity bill. I blanked on an interview with a celebrated professor whom I was supposed to profile for the school's website; I realized this only when she contacted me to say her next availability was approximately never. Sometimes I *pretended* to forget meetings because I couldn't bring myself to show up and act normal. Each time the phone rang or someone knocked on the door to the broom closet I called my office, I jumped, as though it might be Rob. Deep sleep, appetite, pleasure in mundane things like showering and sunshine: these were all distant memories.

Talking about it was the only way out of my mental straitjacket. But Wisnewski was no longer available to chat, and even if he were, we had never been in the habit of discussing emotional issues the way Rob and I had always been able to.

Obviously, Rob was out of the question—not that he had been calling or emailing me. Over the past few years I had accepted his long hours as the cause of the growing hole in our friendship; I had grown used to hearing from him infrequently, and largely at his convenience. After I slept with Lou, though, his being out of touch no longer seemed work related. No, it felt like a sign that he had sensed a shift in the universe and was hiding from the flaming comet heading his way.

Desperate to talk through my distress, or at least distill part of my paranoia, I asked Pascal to lunch.

"I know I'm a fool," I told him. "If Rob ever finds out . . ."

Pascal shook his head. "Rob. Rob. *Now* you think of Rob! And what will Kathryn say?"

I looked down at my plate. "Right, since she and Lou are still friends."

"Yes," he said dryly. "Or they were. I mean, of all the women."

"Listen, you can't tell anyone. Ever. Especially not Kathryn, but . . . no one."

"Who would I tell?" Pascal leaned back in his chair, looking at me with bewilderment. "My God, if you aren't the human condition in a nutshell I don't know who is. You've likely read a library's worth of novels illustrating why affairs are a terrible idea, and then you go and pull an Anna Karenina."

"An affair." Up until that point, I had not used that term, let alone considered it, and it sounded like Farsi on my tongue. Not only had I had an affair, but I had done so with my best friend's wife. It was the stuff of soap operas. It was a plotline I would never have used in my own fiction. Yet there I was, living it out.

Pascal sighed from low in his chest. "You've got to pull yourself together. Do you want to end up like me?"

"Last I checked, you were doing okay."

"Eh," he said with that melodic lilt of his. "It is my experience that by and large, women undervalue being alone, and men overvalue it. I'm lonely, and the future's not looking so bright for me. Ladies aren't so interested in a fellow with a potbelly who's recently joined the AARP."

I took a bite of rice, but it stuck to the roof of my mouth, so I washed it down with a swig of tepid, bitter tea. "Who's to say I'll end up alone?"

"You think there's no cost for giving your heart to someone who can't really take it? But who knows," he added. "The wonder of life is that almost anything can happen."

Back at my desk, I stared at my computer screen as one asinine message after another rose to the top of my inbox. What *was* the cost of giving my heart to Lou, anyway? Would I end up alone, as Pascal implied? I checked my voicemail, but the only call I had received that wasn't from Pascal, Victoria, or my father was from a woman named Jessica, with whom I had gone on a date several months earlier; she had apparently decided to scrape the bottom of her barrel.

I redirected my attention to work. I was supposed to draft a press release announcing a major educational collaboration with a university in India. *The Spice Is Nice*, I had written on the top of my document. I shook my head in disgust and erased the text, grateful that none of my coworkers had a chance to witness my culturally insensitive stupidity.

What was happening to me? The sunlight streaming through my office window stung my eyes, but when I squeezed my lids closed, there was Lou, her head resting on her pillow as she looked up at me tenderly. I would have given anything to go back to that exact moment in time.

In an instant, Rob's face replaced Lou's. Acid burned my throat as I thought about how my fling—my *affair*—would raze him. Even if he never learned about it, how could I ever resume our relationship? Every sentence that came before my confession would be a lie of omission.

Yes, after years of self-deception, my culpability was suddenly screamingly obvious. The minute I realized I had feelings for Lou, I should have made every attempt to *not* be close to her. We should not have struck up a friendship; we should not have had conversations as intimate as we did. And we never, ever, should have had dinner alone.

In my own half-assed fashion, I had orchestrated this, I realized with horror. And like the drafts I abandoned before writing the end, I had not been able to see past the middle of my own story. Why had I not had the foresight to see the ruin on the other side of this affair?

As I forced my eyes open, it occurred to me that what I should really be wishing for was not to go back to that moment with Lou, but for it to never have happened at all. Because I was not sure a short stay in paradise had been worth an extended stint in purgatory.

~

The longer I went without hearing from Lou, the more I felt that there was no doubt she regretted everything and never wanted to speak with me again. We were not going to be together—but could we not still be friends? Or had I now lost two of the people most important to me in one fell swoop?

In response, I doubled down on my reclusiveness. "Why don't you take some time off?" said Craig, who had surmised that I was on the verge of a breakdown. "Go hiking, go to the beach, whatever you need. We can function without you for a week."

I thanked him and promptly returned to work. At another point in life I would have used such an opportunity to write fiction. But I could barely manage to put together an email, and the evenings and weekends stretched endlessly. My usual nightcap had turned into two, sometimes three, which would facilitate sleep only to wake me several hours later. My requisite morning cup of coffee had become a full pot, and I was constantly wired and tired. A full week without supervisor-dictated, deadline-enforced aim wasn't a vacation. It was a prison sentence.

~

One night in July, I was sitting on the deck, staring up at the glittering sky and contemplating the position I was in—not specific to Lou and Rob, for a change, but in a more global sense.

Most of the people I knew in their mid and late thirties had lives, capital *L*: committed relationships, children, careers that they truly cared about. At nearly thirty-six, I was batting zero on almost all of these counts. It was true that my career was going well, but it was not at all the career I had dreamed of. And yes, I had not wanted children up until that point; but even that I wasn't so sure about anymore. I again thought of Wisnewski. What fatal flaw did I possess that kept me from embracing his good-enough approach to living?

Such was the potholed mental road I was moseying down when my phone rang. It was probably Victoria, who had deduced that something was not right and had been calling every few days to check on me. I sighed, pushed myself up onto my feet, and let myself in through the sliding doors. But when I looked at the caller ID, it was not my sister, but Lou. She had finally reached out. Was this good? Bad? Did it even matter?

"Lou, hello!" I said, entirely too chipper. "How are you?"

"I'm okay. You?"

"I—you—it's really good to hear from you."

I was sort of hoping she would respond, "It's so good to hear from you, too!" Instead, she said, "I'm sorry I haven't been in touch sooner; I needed time to think. I feel pretty terrible, Jim."

"About what we've done."

"Yes."

"Me, too," I admitted.

"I'd like to see you," she said, which I immediately interpreted as "Us being together is still the worst idea, but I would like at least another night or seven with you." *Yes, I could find a way to spend a week together,* I thought, like I hadn't just spent weeks drowning in remorse. *A day, even, would do just fine.*

"Great. But when?"

"I thought I might fly in to Detroit tomorrow. Would that be okay?"

I was so excited by this turn of events that it didn't occur to me to question her haste. "Yes, sure, absolutely." It was hovering around ninety degrees, even at nine at night, and a trickle of sweat slid down the side of my face. I wiped it on the arm of my t-shirt. "Do you want to stay with me?"

She hesitated. "If it's all right with you."

"Of course."

"I'm looking at a flight that gets in at eleven in the morning. Would that work?"

I did not ask how long she would be staying. Instead, I looked at the glass doors, which were smudged with hundreds of fingerprints, all of them mine. Behind me, the plates piled in the sink might as well have been petri dishes; I would have to start cleaning immediately. "Absolutely," I said.

"Thanks, Jim. It'll be good to . . . talk through everything."

Yes, I thought with relief. It would be good to talk through it with the only person who might actually have some idea what I was going through, since she was in a near-identical position. "I'm looking forward to it."

"Me, too," she said, more brightly this time. "I'll see you soon."

~

Lou broke into a smile when she saw me pull up outside arrivals at the airport.

"How was your flight?" I said as she hugged me. She smelled like she was wearing a new perfume, or maybe she had changed her shampoo.

"Fine," she said. She was pulling a small suitcase behind her, which I took from her.

"You staying awhile?" I asked.

"Maybe I will," she said, hoisting her leather tote up on her shoulder. I gestured that I could take that, too, but she shook her head and climbed into the front seat.

As I looked at her again as I got in the car, I realized she was, well, kind of gray. Not that she was any less beautiful; when someone is significant to you in the way Lou was to me, a change in their appearance just doesn't matter that much because they are already imprinted on your brain in such a way that automatically triggers affection and attraction.

Even so, I was a little rattled, both by her appearance and by how quiet she was being. I reacted by prattling about Neruda's *Memoirs*, which I had just finished reading. I was merging onto the highway when she interrupted me: "Jim."

"Yes?" I said, my head still halfway in Chile.

"I'm pregnant."

On instinct, my foot pressed on the brake, and I jerked the wheel to the right as I looked at her with disbelief. Behind us, a driver laid on his horn.

"Please don't kill us," she said calmly, and placed a hand on my shoulder.

"Oh my God. Oh my God," I said because it was basically the only thing I was able to manage. "Is it—"

"It's yours."

"Are you sure?"

"Good Lord, Jim. Of course I'm sure."

"Oh my." My throat was closing in, and my hands were shaking so hard it was difficult to grip the steering wheel. "How is that even possible? I thought you were—"

"I was on birth control, yes. Unfortunately, it seems the pill's not quite as effective if you take antibiotics, and I was just finishing a course when you and I slept together." She peered at me. "Are you sure you can drive?"

"Yes," I squeaked. "Though maybe the next time you have big news, maybe don't tell me in the car, okay?"

She squeezed my shoulder lightly. "I'm really sorry. I just couldn't wait another second."

"So you're—it's what—two months? Three?"

"Nine weeks."

"When did you figure it out?"

"About three or four weeks ago."

"What!" I hollered. "No wonder you couldn't wait. Why didn't you say something sooner?"

"Well, I had to go to the doctor to be certain, and to find out how far along I was." She took her hand off my shoulder and added quietly, "I really am sorry. I haven't been in a very good place since you were in New York, and this was—well—unexpected. It was almost like I was waiting for it to go away. It's going to kill Rob."

Would it ever. Lou had refused to have a child with him. I had refused to have one with Kathryn. But in a single night, the two of us had unknowingly secured one tie, and in doing so, completely severed several others. I felt sick. I had damaged my friendship with Rob in an irreparable way, even if he was still blissfully ignorant of this fact. "Have you told him about us?" I asked.

She shook her head vigorously. "We've talked a little bit, but only about the divorce. That's part of why I'm here. I wanted to tell you in person, and I was hoping we could decide together. About the baby . . . and what to do about Rob."

I had no idea if I was ready to be a father—is anyone ever, really? But could I say no to a life that already existed, when that life was half of Lou?

"You're going to keep it?" *It* sounded wrong. "The baby," I corrected myself.

"I don't know," she said. "You know, most of my friends have been pregnant before. Some wanted to, obviously, but for a lot of them it just happened. Rob and I—we've had accidents, but I never got pregnant. Not once. I don't know, Jim. I feel so awful about Rob finding out that I want to vomit every other minute, and that has nothing to do with morning sickness. But I wonder, too, if this isn't meant to be. If it isn't, why did I get pregnant now? This has to be for a reason, right?"

My mind hadn't gotten as far as reasons; I was still more or less at the *we are having a child* part of it all. But I nodded because her words seemed to make some sense.

"You know," Lou continued, "my mother used to tell me she almost got rid of me when she was pregnant. That's how she put it, if you can believe it. I don't know, as insane as this is, I don't want to have an abortion. It affects both of us, though. What do you think?"

Outside, cars whizzed past us, and we past them; seedy motels and office buildings and trees blurred together. "I think that it would probably be best to move forward. To not terminate the pregnancy right now."

"Okay," she said. "Then that's our plan."

~

At dinnertime, I knocked on the door of the guest bedroom, where Lou had been napping. "You hungry?" I asked. "I made spinach pasta with chicken."

She stuck her head out the door, and I pretended not to notice that her eyes were bloodshot. "No, everything tastes like cardboard right now. But I'll join you."

We sat across from each other at the table. I had just begun grating Parmesan over my pasta when she said, "This feels all wrong."

My stomach lurched, but then she walked around the table and sat next to me. "That's better. What are you thinking about?"

I put the hunk of cheese on the table and stared at her. "I'm thinking I'm terrified."

She put her head on my shoulder. "Me, too. But eyes on the prize, right? We've made a human."

"That's right." I wasn't thinking about the miracle of life, though. I was focused on the mess we were in, and how my desire and greed had set this all in motion. Why couldn't I have left well enough alone?

But it wasn't just me who screwed up, I thought as I looked at Lou's stomach, which showed no signs of harboring a tiny life-form. It was Rob, too—with his foolish fling and stubborn headfirst plunge into divorce. If he had said yes to mediation or reconciliation, would Lou ever have invited me into her bed? As much as I hated to admit it, it seemed highly unlikely.

Yes, I blamed Rob, too. I needed to.

FOURTEEN

"Jim? Are you okay?" asked Lou. She was sitting on the edge of an exam table, her hands tucked under her thighs while we waited for the ultrasound tech. As she had gathered, my mind was elsewhere. Specifically, I was thinking back to one afternoon when Rob and I were kids.

"What's it like having a sister?" Rob asked me. We were in his basement playing Donkey Kong and working our way through a box of pizza.

I shrugged. "You know. Annoying."

"But you have someone to talk to," he said. "Someone other than your parents to keep you company on, like, vacation and when you go out to dinner."

The only vacations I went on were with Rob, and if my family ate out, it was at Taco Bell—not exactly a hot spot for conversation. I wasn't going to point this out to Rob, however, even if he already knew it. "More like you have someone to get you in trouble all the time," I retorted, trying to figure out if I should make Mario climb a ladder. As soon as I decided to send him up, a barrel came tumbling down, and my turn ended. I tossed my remote beside me on the sofa. "Vic slaps me, but if I even *look* at her, she starts bawling and my dad hollers at me. You're lucky."

"I don't think so," said Rob, who had started his turn and was staring intently at the flashing screen as he pressed the controller. "If you have a brother or sister, you don't get lonely—everyone knows that. I don't want to have kids until I'm super old. But when I do, I'm going to have a whole bunch. Dude, like three sets of twins. I'll have so many you can borrow one and I won't notice."

Maybe Rob would be right, I thought as I looked at Lou. Maybe he and Andrea would fall deeply in love and have a gaggle of children like he had predicted all those years ago. Maybe they were even expecting at that very moment, and this would soften the blow that Lou was having my child.

None of this was remotely reassuring. "I think I'm okay," I told Lou. "Or at least okay-ish. You?"

"Nervous, obviously. I . . . I don't even know what to hope for right now."

Before I could respond, the tech knocked and let herself into the room. "Ready?" she chirped, then instructed Lou to lie back and pull her gown up and her skirt down. Once Lou's stomach was bare, she spread gel over it and began pressing the wand below Lou's navel.

I held my breath, waiting to see a tiny person or maybe hear a heartbeat. But there was nothing but blackness and silence.

"Hmm," said the tech.

"Is everything okay?" I asked.

"One second," she said cheerfully.

The fear in Lou's eyes suggested that she now knew what to hope for. I offered her my hand, which she grasped tightly.

"Tilt up," the tech said as she put a small towel under Lou's hips. She began to move the wand around again.

For the longest minute in history, we saw nothing. Then a fast flutter appeared on the screen. "That's your baby's heart!" announced the tech. "Yes, that's exactly what we want to see. And there's its head, and its spine . . ."

Sure enough, there you were—a wiggling little skeleton who seemed to be waving right at us. *We're having a child,* I thought with wonder. True, I understood this in the way that one understands the earth is constantly rotating without feeling its spin. But for the first time, this all had a purpose.

"Right now this baby is nice and healthy," said the tech. "Mom and Dad, you've got a good-looking kid here."

When I looked at Lou, she was crying. She squeezed my hand again. "She's perfect, Jim."

"She?" I asked Lou later as I examined the ultrasound pictures the tech had given us. It was too early for a gender scan, but maybe I had missed some crucial clue. "How can you tell it's a girl?"

Lou glanced down at her stomach. "I can't. I just have a feeling."

I thought of what Rob had told me about her being afraid she would become her mother. "Are you feeling okay about becoming a mom?" I asked.

She tugged her shirt down. "I think so. And I have almost five more months to get used to the idea. But yes, I'm thrilled. I can't wait to meet this baby of ours."

But on the way home, she stared out the window, dazed. "This is so strange," she said at one point. "I can't believe I'm in Michigan right now, and we're going to have a child."

What she did not say—which I had heard all the same—was that what was truly so strange and heartbreakingly sad was that she wasn't making this life-altering journey with the man she loved. She was making it with me.

FIFTEEN

September 2008

Rob called me a week or so after Lou's ultrasound. It was a Monday, I think, or maybe a Tuesday; I was rushing around in the kitchen, trying to put together a sandwich to take for lunch.

When I saw his name flash across the phone screen, I wanted to lick the peanut butter–coated knife I had just used at the exact moment I developed a deadly nut allergy. Then I wanted to impale myself on said knife, just in case someone produced an EpiPen too soon. *Even slow death by cyanide,* I thought, *would be preferable to talking to him.* We had not spoken in nearly two months, which had suited my guilty mental state just fine. I was going to call, I told myself—just as soon as I figured out what to say.

Lou was sitting at the table with a mug of tea, reading the newspaper. We had been living together for more than six weeks, and though I struggled with our platonic arrangement—guilt had not fully quashed my desire—I had accepted that for the time being, we were essentially roommates who were collaborating on a significant science experiment. "It's Rob," I said to her.

She looked up from her paper with dread. "Oh crap. What are you going to do?"

I grimaced. "Answer, I guess. I can't avoid him forever, can I?"

"I don't know, Jim. Be careful."

My heart was pounding as I walked into the living room. "Hey, man. Long time no talk. What's up?" My voice was thin and reedy, but Rob didn't notice.

"There's trouble, dude," he said. "A whole ton of trouble."

I swallowed. "This about Lou?"

"Lou?" Rob said, almost like he didn't know who I was talking about. "I wish."

"What's the trouble, then? Are you back in the city?" The last time he had emailed, he said he was ping-ponging between London and New York.

"Yeah, I'm home now. At my apartment. The company . . ." He exhaled loudly. "It's folding. I mean, it's fold*ed*. Done deal. I'm toast, James."

"Wait, what?" I was having a hard time wrapping my mind around what he was trying to tell me. "What does that even mean?"

"We've—they've—declared bankruptcy. It'll be all over the news by noon. The whole operation is a house of cards, and the Fed figured it out."

I had heard my coworkers talking about Rob's company—how it had recently shut down an entire division dedicated to subprime mortgages and laid off more than a thousand people. But I had been so wrapped up in Lou's pregnancy that I had missed the part about bunk investments foreshadowing the company's bankruptcy and the collapse of the financial market. My wish about the economy being the worst of his worries came ricocheting back to me. Each thing Rob said was more damning than the last.

"So you're out of a job?" I asked after he had finished.

"Uh, *yeah*. Another bank is in talks to buy some of the company's divisions, and some employees will be moved over." He paused. "I won't be one of them."

He said it in a way that suggested the rest was going to have to be coaxed out of him. "And?" I asked.

"I'm basically number five in command in the division where the most shit is hitting the fan. Which means I'm going to be unemployed indefinitely. And that's if I don't . . . God, I can't even say it."

"Wait, wait, wait," I said. "That Andrea woman—she's your supervisor."

"Was," he corrected.

"That makes her the number four in your division, then?"

"Technically number three."

I let out a low whistle.

"Yeah, it's not good. There's a chance she's going to face indictment. Or worse. No one really knows right now."

"She with you now?"

"No, she's on her way home."

I wondered if by home, he meant to his apartment. I kind of hoped so. "Did you know that this was going to happen? With the bank, I mean? Argh, should I even be *asking* you this?"

"Probably not," he admitted. "I just—I don't even know what to do, James."

He had not come to me for advice in a good long while. I would have been flattered if I weren't so busy thinking about how I was not just the scum of the earth, I was also the grime stuck to the gum attached to the bottom of the shoe that the scum of the earth was wearing on his filthy foot. "You have money in the bank, right?" I said.

"Yep."

"A lot of it, if I'm not mistaken?"

"I guess so."

"Is the government going to come after it?"

"I don't know. I doubt it—it's not like it's in an offshore account, and I paid taxes on everything."

"There's that, at least. Well . . . I don't know, man. I'm really sorry about this." *I'm especially sorry because your not-yet-ex-wife is sitting in the other room, and, oh yeah—she's having my kid.*

"Me, too. I'm in a deep, deep hole." He didn't ask how I was doing, and I didn't volunteer this information. Honestly, I wanted to get off the phone as soon as possible, before I gave some indication that I had rigged a trapdoor at the bottom of the hole he had just mentioned.

I heard a click. "There's Andie on the other line," he said. "I've gotta go."

"Keep me posted, okay?"

"I will," he said. "James?"

"Yeah?"

"Thanks," he said.

"Don't mention it," I said. *No, really—don't.*

I stood there for a few minutes, phone in hand, thinking about what a horrible human I was. Then I went to my computer and opened the front page of the *New York Times*. It confirmed everything Rob had said, and worse. The *Washington Post* and Reuters offered more of the same.

Even if Rob had not been directly involved—and that seemed unlikely—why had he stayed on at his company? When he was in London in May to "turn the *Titanic* around," as he had described it, he must have known. He could have walked away then. I mean, Rob had taught me how to unravel a quadratic equation when our algebra teacher could not. He had later advised that I drop statistics when I was struggling to do even the most basic problem set. "James, give it up," he had said. "You don't need it anyway, unless you go into engineering, which you're not going to. You're a writer, so go write."

He had risen through the ranks of his company faster than any of his colleagues. How could the smartest guy I knew get tangled in such a sticky web?

Then again, I thought as I turned off my computer, *this was the same guy who trusted me.*

~

The week was endless. I could not stop thinking about what Rob had told me and how at some point in the near future it was only going to get worse for him. At least there would be time between now and then, I told myself.

When Saturday finally arrived, Lou was craving cider doughnuts, so we made plans to visit an apple orchard just outside of town. We were about to pull out of the driveway when a car parked in front of my house. It was a sedan, the same color and model as Rob's mom's car.

That was because it *was* Rob's mom's car. And Rob was behind the wheel.

"Oh my God," I said. When I was a kid, my mother caught me stealing a pack of gum from the checkout aisle at the grocery store. She didn't make me return it or even confess. Instead, she just *looked* at me, leaving me to panic about what she was waiting for and what was going to happen to me. Each second was more gut-wrenching than the last, and when we finally got home, I threw up all over the lawn. This feeling was a lot like that. Only worse.

Lou began to laugh.

"Why are you laughing?" I snapped. "This is the least funny thing I can think of."

"Obviously," she said, still sputtering a bit. "I can't help it. I'm afraid, and sometimes this is how I react when I'm uncomfortable."

I was the most annoyed with her I had ever been, but her laughter was the least of my worries. What were we going to do? I considered fleeing, but that would be just as fishy.

Maybe Rob's visit was fortuitous, I reasoned. Maybe it was a sign that now was the time for us to reckon with the truth. I took a deep breath and let myself out of my car.

"Hey!" I said, sounding awfully prepubescent for a man who was just a few years from forty. "You didn't tell me you were flying in."

Rob was slouching like he had just suffered a career-ending defeat, which I suppose he had. "I hope you don't mind that I didn't call. I, uh, switched off my phone. Too many reporters trying to get in touch." His eyes shifted toward my car. "Is that . . . Lou?"

Lou had just climbed out of the passenger side of my car. "Hello." She said this coolly, the way you would greet an acquaintance whose company you didn't particularly enjoy. But her eyes told a different story; the sight of him clearly pained her. "I'm staying with Jim for a bit. I needed to get out of the city."

"You what?" Rob hadn't shaved in several days and probably hadn't showered all that recently, either. To tell you the truth, he looked kind of wild-eyed and unstable. "What the . . ." He looked at Lou, and back at me. "Can someone please tell me what is happening here?"

Neither Lou nor I responded. Honestly, I didn't trust myself to open my mouth for fear my breakfast would find its way to the grass, just as it had that day my mother caught me pocketing the gum.

"You have *got* to be kidding me," he said, and let out a string of expletives. "As if things weren't bad enough already. Please," he said, looking at me with those same savage eyes, "for the love of all that is good and holy, tell me this is not what it looks like."

I could not seem to get my brain and mouth to collaborate. "You—we—" I sputtered.

Lou stepped forward. Her smile was forced. "I don't know what you're thinking, but whatever it is, it's not that," she told him.

"*Lou.*" I said her name too harshly, and she looked at me, furious and wounded. I opened my eyes wide, trying to convey that there was no backing down now. Running from the firing squad did not prevent you from getting shot.

"Trust me, Jim," Lou said in a low voice.

She was right, of course, but it was already too late; Rob's face was twisted with pain. I had known all along that Lou and I had done a terrible thing to him, but it was not until that very moment that I was able to appreciate just how appalling it was. My instinct—and this is atrocious, I'm aware—was to do something horrible to myself, like scale a tree and throw myself from it in such a way that resulted in my femur poking through the center of my thigh. Anything to make his pain seem less terrible, or at least give him something else to focus on. Even now, I cannot recall a time when I felt more wretched than I did as Rob pulled at his face with his hands. "This is over right now," he said.

I had no idea what he meant, but before I could ask, Lou said quietly, "But it's not over between you and Andrea, is it?"

"It's over between *all of us!*" Rob shouted.

"Rob, come on. Can't we talk about this?" I said to him.

He looked at me with disgust. "*Talk?* Absolutely not." He turned toward his car and muttered to no one in particular, "I've got to get out of here."

"Where are you going?" I called.

"To find a very tall bridge," he hollered.

He wasn't serious. Was he? Oh God. I began running toward him. "Rob!" I yelled, but he was already in the car. He revved the engine and took off down the street, tearing through the stop sign at the end of the block.

At once Lou was at my side. She put her hand out. "Keys."

"What are you going to do?"

"I don't know, but I've got to go after him."

"No, you don't. That's my job."

"Yes, I do. Keys, please," she said again. "He's still my husband, Jim."

When I hesitated, she looked at me fiercely. "Trust me on this one. I know Rob. He can't go this alone."

Her words led me to believe that unlike my halfhearted thoughts about self-harm, Rob was actually tempted to hurt himself. Maybe because of this, I handed her the keys. She took them from me and got into my car without saying good-bye.

As I stood in my driveway and watched her drive away, I was as alone as I had ever been in my life.

~

Lou called just before dinnertime. I was in the kitchen, staring at the chicken breast I had just cooked and could not bring myself to eat.

"Is Rob okay?" I asked, sounding a little hysterical because, well, I was. I had spent the day pacing my house, asphyxiating on anxiety. "Are *you*?"

"Yes," she said quietly.

"Thank God," I said, pushing my plate away. "I've been trying to call you. Why did you wait so long to tell me what was going on?"

"I was helping him."

"Did you tell him about . . . the baby?"

"I did."

I had to remind myself to breathe. *"And?"*

"He didn't seem all that surprised. It was almost like he knew."

"So did he take it okay?"

She let out a bitter laugh. "Oh, I wouldn't say that. Safe to say he took it very badly. But I think it'll work out."

Were Rob only dealing with a professional catastrophe, I might have been inclined to believe her. But I had just obliterated his personal life, too. "And how's that?"

"It just will," she said.

I opened the trash and threw the chicken in it; what was the point? "Well, what did you say? How did you calm him down?"

"When you have spent a third of your life with another person, you tend to figure out the best way to deal with them in any given situation."

I had spent more than half of my life with Rob and had not managed a single reassuring word. "Right," I said.

"I have to go back to New York, Jim," Lou said softly.

I slammed the trash lid shut. "What do you mean, you have to go back to New York? What about our baby?"

"I'm not going to cut you out of her life. I just need some time to figure out what's right for us. What's right for *me*."

"What does *that* mean?"

"I don't know. This past month, it's been like a vacation. A fugue, even," she said. "We've both been in denial about what we've done to Rob. We shouldn't be together."

"We are *not* together," I said sharply.

She ignored this comment. "I'm going to go back to Brooklyn for a bit. I still have the apartment, and I have a doctor there. Maybe I'll come back at some point, but . . ."

"Maybe?" I said. The kitchen was starting to fade on me, and my heartbeat was deafening in my ears. "*Maybe?* You can't do this, Lou."

"Do what, exactly?"

"Leave!" I exploded. "We may have wrecked almost everything, but at least we have us!"

"I don't know why you're yelling at me like that. It's not like you, Jim."

"I'm sorry," I muttered. "But you can't expect me to be okay with you going back to Rob."

"I'm not going *back* to anyone, Jim. My focus is entirely on our baby."

Our baby: these two words managed to calm me. "Okay . . . so now what?"

"I'm going to fly back to New York as soon as I'm sure Rob is okay. Would it be all right if I left your car at the Logans'? Maybe your father could come get you, or you could take a cab here?"

"What do you mean about Rob being okay?" I asked.

"Just trust me," she said vaguely.

"And your stuff?" I argued. She had been wearing her purse when she left, but what about her clothing, her laptop, the various creams and lotions she had littered the bathroom counter with?

"I'll come back for the computer at some point, or maybe you can FedEx it to me." She paused. "Everything I really need is already with me."

Right, because you're with Rob, I thought. My mouth was dry. "Keep me posted," I finally managed to say.

"Of course." She sounded relieved. "Don't despair, Jim. I'm trying my best, and I know you are, too. I'll talk to you soon, okay?"

Beneath my feet, the floor appeared to sway. "Okay," I said.

~

I waited until morning to call my father. He picked up on the first ring. "Hello?" he said, sounding awfully sprightly for that hour of the day.

"Pops?" When I was a kid, he had asked Victoria and me to call him Papi, which was what he had called his own father, a man he had both respected and loathed. I must have called him that when I was very young, but by elementary school I realized none of the other kids—who were white or Lebanese or Iraqi or even Vietnamese, but not Latino, not a single one of them—addressed their fathers as "Papi." So I started calling him Pops, which I had heard on television, and Victoria did, too, and that was that.

"What's wrong, son?" he asked.

I furrowed my brow. "Nothing. I was wondering if you might have some time today to come get me."

"Come get you? What's going on?"

"My car is at the Logans'. It's a long story."

I was grateful that he didn't ask for the short version. "Okay," he said. "I'll be there in half an hour."

It was a forty-minute trip, longer if traffic was bad. But he was at my door thirty minutes later, just as he said he would be.

"You need anything?" he asked, looking me up and down. I hadn't showered and was wearing track pants, a t-shirt, and a hooded sweatshirt that looked as though it had recently fed an eclipse of moths.

I grabbed my wallet and keys from the table in the entryway. "I'm good," I said.

He didn't say anything for most of the drive, but for my father, that wasn't so strange. And just as well; my mind was elsewhere.

"This about the woman?" he finally asked as we were pulling off the exit ramp to Oakwood.

"What woman?"

"Rob's wife."

"How—"

"I called your house a few weeks ago. She picked up. I've been alive long enough to know how these things work." He shook his head, still staring at the road.

"They're getting a divorce."

"And?"

"And Lou is going to have my child. *Our* child," I said.

He whistled.

"I'm pretty sure this is the part where you tell me congratulations."

"Congratulations, then. Whooo boy," he said, shaking his head again.

"You said you wanted to have more grandkids."

"Still true."

I slumped in my seat, instantly regressing to my teenage self. "I thought you'd be happy for me."

"I will be, just as soon as you're happy about it."

"I *am* happy about it."

"Okay," he said.

We rode the rest of the way in silence, my grief muddled with the anger I was feeling toward my father. When we pulled into the subdivision where my father and the Logans lived, he glanced my way. "Why don't you come over to my place first? I'll make you a cup of coffee."

"Thanks, but I should get going."

"The woman? Where is she now?"

"Lou," I said tersely. "And she's in New York." Or at the Logans'; I wasn't really sure.

"All right." He drove past his street and continued on toward Rob's parents' house. "Here you go," he said as he pulled into their driveway.

What a mess it was, to have and maintain a family. I stepped out of the truck and shut the door behind me.

As I was walking away, my father rolled down the passenger-side window. "James," he called.

"What is it, Pops?"

"Life breaks everyone."

The sun was shining bright, and I squinted at him. "Is that Hemingway?"

"No, it's Hernandez," he said, pushing his index finger into his chest. "You might be broken now, but you'll put yourself back together."

A sudden chill came over me. Part of me wanted to shout, "Screw you, old man, you don't know anything about my life!" But another part wanted to cry out, "How?"

"You call me if you need anything," my father said, then rolled up the window and drove off.

I was hoping Lou would greet me, but instead, Nancy met me at the side door. "Come in, come in!" she said. Her hair was a shade of yellow not found in nature, and she looked like she had aged half a decade since I'd seen her the year before. She added in a whisper, "Lou left for New York this morning, and Rob's in a bad way. Maybe you can help him feel better."

Oh, I highly doubt that, I thought. "Where is he?"

"In the basement."

We'll face this like men, I told myself as I walked down the stairs. *No,* I corrected myself, *we'll face this like two men who have been friends for the better part of their lives. People work through difficult things all the time, and I can't not say anything. Talking to Rob about it is the right thing to do. It's the only thing to do.*

He hit me before I even saw him, shoving me with his full weight and sending my backbone into the edge of the stairs. Pain shot up my spine, setting off fireworks behind my retinas, and I moaned.

"I suggest you get out of this house before I put you in a wheel-chair," he growled.

My back hurt so much I could barely speak. "Can't. We—"

"Talk about this?" His face came into focus. "What is there to say? You're sorry you ruined my life?"

"Don't you think that's a bit harsh?" I croaked.

He stood over me, glowering, and I'll admit I was about as afraid then as I had ever been. "You're about to find out what harsh feels like," he spat.

As the stabbing feeling in my back gave way to a warm, throbbing sensation, I started to get angry. I had screwed up. More than a little. But how dare he act like this was all my fault? "*You* were the one who let Lou go!" I yelled.

"I was in the middle of a breakdown, you asshole! And just when I was starting to put myself back together so I could get her back, I find out that *you* got there before me!"

"Is that why you were begging her to sign the divorce papers?"

"She is still my wife!" he roared. "And you! You—" He stumbled backward, like I had struck him. When he finally spoke, his voice was garbled. "You were my friend."

SIXTEEN

Late 2008–Early 2009

What had I been expecting, exactly? For Lou to stay forever? For Rob to forgive me on the spot? For the three (soon to be four) of us, and maybe even Andrea, to laugh over dinner and stay in each other's lives after subtracting and then adding and multiplying ourselves in a way that bore little resemblance to the figures in which we began?

No, Lou was right. The two of us *had* been living in a fugue—a daydream state free of consequences. Now we had been thrust back into real life, and it was simply not possible to get back to where we had been before.

The only other thing Rob said to me before I left his house was that we would never speak again. I wanted to believe it was his anger talking, but his were the words of a man as stubborn as he was smart. They were intended not only as a warning for me, but as a resolution for himself.

Yet I was almost surprised when Rob refused to pick up when I called, and even more so when a robotic voice informed me that his number had been disconnected. So I sent him an email:

Rob,

There are no words that can adequately express how incredibly sorry I am. As Lou told you, we're not together—we never will be. It was a onetime thing, a terrible mistake. Please, Rob. I know it's going to take time, but at least try to forgive me.

James

The next morning, he responded:

NO.

No signature. No nuance. No possibility of reconciliation. Just—no.

As I awoke to a hollow house each morning, I was again reminded that my fool's math had left me at net zero. I was without my oldest friend. I was without Lou, whom I still loved, even though I knew I shouldn't. I was without my child. And this was all my own doing.

I told no one but Pascal about Lou's pregnancy. ("Oh, you've done it now!" he said. "You've done it now!") His reaction, like my father's, solidified my shame. I spent most days with a deep, aching pain radiating in my stomach, as though my actions were a cancer spreading from my core.

As she had promised, Lou emailed updates about her pregnancy and sent me ultrasounds, and we spoke on the phone a few times a week. When I asked how she was feeling, she was vague; when I asked if she had seen Rob and if he was in the city, she changed the subject. The only thing she wanted to talk about was you.

You were often awake at night, she told me, and would surface below her taut skin like a whale rising for air. Sometimes you would dive deep after pressing your foot or hand against her belly, sending pain shooting down her back. Other times you would hiccup, she said, making her abdomen bounce for the better part of an hour.

When Lou told me that her twenty-week ultrasound scans revealed that you were a girl, just as she predicted, I cheered on the phone, overcome with the joy of you being you. Then I hung up and cried, overcome with the sorrow of both of you being so very far away.

~

Lou and I had discussed the possibility of my coming to visit. She wanted to give me a chance to experience part of her pregnancy, while what I wanted—though I did not come out and admit this—was to not feel so damn alone. I flew to New York at the beginning of December, two months before you were due to be born.

When Lou opened the door to her apartment, I was relieved to see she was no longer gray-tinged, but instead pink all over, and swollen in places where she had once been gaunt. She greeted me as though I had been away by choice and she had been waiting to welcome me back.

Yet things between us were awkward. Tense, truly, as though my physical presence reminded her of how we had hurt Rob. "I've only talked to him twice since I left Michigan, and that was to finalize our divorce," she said when I brought it up the first night.

So again we focused on her pregnancy. I felt like a prying friend, requesting information that was perhaps not mine to know: Was she still tired all the time? (No, she had a newfound energy until nine at night, at which point she passed out no matter what the setting, only to be awoken a few hours later by you breaststroking through her womb.) What was she craving? (Thai food and Swedish fish.) Was she nervous about the birth? (No, she had been taking classes with one of the Jennifers and felt prepared to deal with multiple birthing scenarios and drop-kick any doctor who pushed her into having a C-section.)

And what, what—what?!—would happen after the baby was born?

On this last question, Lou remained vague. When I reminded her what she had said about coming to Ann Arbor, she sighed and said it was no longer that simple. "My life is here," she explained, one hand roving over her belly.

No, I thought, *Rob is here.* She wasn't working, after all, and she didn't even like her rental. "Won't you need help with the baby?" I asked.

"I'll be fine," she insisted. Her eyes widened. "She's kicking. Do you want to feel?"

I nodded and put my hand gingerly on her stomach, afraid to hurt her. But Lou put her hand on top of my own, so that it was spread across her flesh, and directed me toward a lump that she said was your foot. You pressed into my palm, then retreated, and I thought of how interesting this was without fully registering that I was feeling my own child.

On my last day in town, we took a walk through Lou's neighborhood. People nodded and smiled at Lou. One man shouted, "Any day now!" to which Lou replied, "Only if I want a baby in an incubator!" An elderly woman congratulated us, and I thanked her on behalf of the three of us.

We had just stopped at a children's shop when I mentioned Ann Arbor again.

"I don't know, Jim. I have a network here," Lou said, running her fingers across a large egg-shaped contraption with wheels, which looked like some sort of incubator-stroller hybrid. "I don't know anyone there."

"You know me, and I'm her father," I said as we continued through the store.

"Yes, you are, and that won't change." She held up a tiny sleeping bag with a hood, frowned, and put it back on the table where she had found it. "But I'm finding it hard to imagine me and the baby forging a life in Michigan, and you're not going to come here."

"I could," I said as we stepped back out onto the street.

We had just started across an intersection when a sedan came speeding toward us. I held my hand out like a school crossing guard, as Lou, unfazed, continued to walk at the same pace she always had; even pregnancy couldn't slow her down.

"And give up your home and a good job?" she said as we reached the other side. "Even if you found a position here, you'd never make enough money. It's not like it used to be in New York. You have to sell a kidney to afford even a cockroach-infested hole-in-the-wall."

Or be an investment banker like Rob, I thought. "I only need one kidney, and you're going to need help."

"I promise you'll know the minute I do," she said.

She was equally elusive about the birth and whether I would or should be present for it. As she pointed out, there was at least a monthlong period in which she could go into labor. "What are you going to do, take an indefinite leave from work?" she asked. "I think it's better for you to plan on being here to spend time with the baby after she's born."

Lou and I had no romantic future together—we had agreed on that. But why should we not try to build some sort of life out of the wreckage? Why not start over in a way that would at least salvage what we had left? Divorce or no divorce, I could not help but wonder if she was holding out hope that she and Rob would reunite. And if they did, did that mean I could not be a part of her life, which would in turn cut me out of your life, too? I left New York feeling deeply despondent.

$\sim$

Since I was back to being alone, I had gotten into the habit of grocery shopping at night. I went frequently, buying only what I intended to eat over the course of the next day or two. There were other things I could have done with my evenings, sure. I considered writing a new novel, or even returning to the last one, which was still only half completed. But the truth was, my eyes glazed over when I tried to even *read* a book; writing was out of the question. Shopping served as a nonwork activity that put me in contact with people but did not require extended interaction.

One of these evenings, I believe it was in late December, I was perusing the dry-goods bins at Kroger—would I be in the mood for chocolate-covered pretzels the following day or Spanish peanuts?—when I looked up and saw Kathryn.

Me being me, I was ready to rush off in the other direction, but she wheeled her cart straight at me. "Well?" she asked, looking at me in a way that suggested she already knew the answer to the question she was about to ask. "How are you?"

Her cart was filled with various brightly colored produce and a jumbo-size box of diapers, presumably for the same child she had been pregnant with when I had seen her at Lou's book party. It occurred to me that enough time had passed that she could have already had another baby.

"Oh, you know. Peachy," I said.

"Are you still writing?" she asked.

"No," I said, because what was the point in lying? "How about you? How's family life?"

"Hard. Great, but really hard."

"I'm sorry," I said, though I wasn't, really. I didn't want Kathryn to be miserable, but neither did I want her life with Christopher Bucknell, PhD to be a perpetual picnic.

"I hear you're having a child," she said, and another woman pushing her cart past us turned to look at us, then scurried on her way.

I decided that I would take both the peanuts and the pretzels and tore a couple of clear plastic bags off the rotating rod. "Says who?" I asked, scooping peanuts from a large plastic bin.

"Says Lou."

I felt my ears get hot. So Lou had told Kathryn herself. I supposed someone had to. I wondered if it had been awkward, and whether they would remain friends. "Oh." I dropped the peanuts into my shopping basket, which I had set on the floor. I arranged another bag beneath another dispenser and pulled the lever, unloading four times as many chocolate-covered pretzels as I'd intended to purchase. Had Kathryn not been there, I would have left the overstuffed bag beneath the dispenser and started over with a new bag, but her presence made me acutely aware that discarding the pretzels wasn't the most ethical move. I dropped the bag of pretzels next to the peanuts in my basket. "Yes. We are. I'm very excited."

"James," she said.

I didn't really want to hear it. Certainly not beneath the bright, artificial lights of my preferred supermarket—but not ever, really. "Yes, Kathryn?" I asked wearily.

"I always knew."

"That we would meet again in the bulk-food aisle?" I said, in a last-ditch attempt to redirect our conversation.

"That you were in love with her," she said, too loud. "I always knew, deep down, that Lou was your idea of the perfect woman."

I was expecting it, I think, but I winced all the same.

"You tried to fight it; I'll give you that," continued Kathryn. "And I wasn't really concerned when we were together because I assumed Lou being with you was about as likely as you being struck by lightning. Then again, it never occurred to me that Rob might cheat on Lou. That kind of grief makes people do crazy things."

That's not what it's about. The man Kathryn had dated before me had cheated on her, more than once. Her frame of reference was different from mine, or so I told myself. "Are you angry?" I asked.

She answered in interrogatives that made it clear she thought this was an inane question. "At Lou? For wanting a child? And keeping it? Even if that child happens to be *yours*?"

"Well, yes. But I mean at me."

She pulled her chin back. "God, no. I mean, yes, it stings. But I feel way worse for Rob than I do for myself."

I startled. Of course, she was right; it was Rob who had fared the most poorly in all this.

"Anyway, I'm not thrilled about it, but Lou and I haven't been close since she split with Rob. I thought she just needed space, but now I wonder if that space had something to do with you. Maybe none of this is actually so sudden and surprising." Kathryn eyed me warily. "As for you, not all relationships are meant to last. My life worked out as it should have." She glanced at the scant contents of my basket, and back at me. "Though I guess you don't ever really stop loving someone, do you?"

"What do you mean?" I asked. Let's be honest: I wanted to hear her come out and say, *Of course I still love you, James.* Because as I regarded her—her face scrubbed bare, clad in a t-shirt with a crusted, unidentifiable orange smear across the chest, in the middle of one of life's truly tedious tasks—it hit me quite suddenly that I had loved her, far more than I had known or been able to admit. As she had just said, I always would.

Kathryn put her hands on her cart, ready to return to her shopping. "I don't know. But for your sake, as well as Lou's and your child's, I hope you're able to enjoy what's next." She looked down at a beautiful gold watch on her wrist, which I had never seen before. "I need to get going; Isla gets up at the crack of dawn every morning." She sighed. "Listen— as Christopher often says, parenting makes quantum mechanics look simple. I really do wish you and Lou the best."

"Thank you," I mumbled.

She began to wheel away but then turned back to me. "James?"

"Yes?"

She gave me a smile so small it could have passed for a frown. "It was good to see you."

Our run-in gnawed at me for days afterward. I thought about what she said about being able to enjoy what was next and tried to convince myself that clearly—clearly!—I would be able to.

Mostly, though, I considered what she had said about Lou. I *had* held Lou up as the perfect woman—the ideal love, really. And I was only beginning to understand the consequences of that.

SEVENTEEN

January 2009

You were born on an unseasonably warm day in late January, shortly after five in the morning. I wish I could tell you about your birth, but at that particular moment I was driving through the middle of rural Pennsylvania, not far from where Lou had once lived as a child, completely unaware that you had just come into the world.

I had been granted a leave of absence from work, but I hadn't planned to go to New York until the week of Lou's due date. After all, she told me, most first births are late.

But most is not all, and Lou went into labor two weeks early. And rather than the long, unmedicated labor she had been bracing herself for, her contractions had barely begun when you began to show signs of distress on a fetal monitor. She was promptly whisked into the operating room, where you were delivered not by her midwife, but by a surgeon she had never met.

I arrived at the hospital around nine, dazed with sleeplessness and anxiety. Lou was fast asleep, tethered to a hospital bed with IVs. Jennifer—the one I danced with at Lou and Rob's wedding—was slouched in an armchair at Lou's side. When she saw me, she stood and whisked me into the hall.

The air smelled of bleach and metal. Across the way, a woman groaned. "How are they doing?" I asked Jennifer.

She was biting her bottom lip so hard I wanted to tell her to stop. "The surgery was scary," she finally said. "One minute Lou was in labor and the next she was in the ER. But she was such a champ. She went into it with her chin up, even though she was terrified. I mean, you know how she feels about needles."

I didn't, in fact, and yet another wave of guilt came crashing over me. Why did I listen to Lou? I should have come to New York at the beginning of January and waited it out. I should have been there. "And the baby?" I asked. "How is she?"

Jennifer's face lit up. "Gorgeous, and as healthy as a horse. She's in the nursery. You can ask them to bring her in to see you."

Lou was just beginning to wake up when a nurse wheeled you into the room. Her face was puffy, and her slim limbs were swollen from the fluids they had been pumping in through her IVs.

"There's our girl," she said as the nurse placed you in my arms. "Isn't she wonderful?"

As I stared down at you, my first thought was *Yes, she's the most wonderful thing that's ever happened to me.*

My second: *Don't drop her.*

Oh, but you were a glorious little thing. Your skin was the same caramel of my father's; your eyes were bright and almond shaped, like Lou's, but gray at that point, rather than the hazel they would later become.

I hadn't spent much time around infants, and certainly not newborns. Even though I had seen you jump and swim in Lou's womb, I still couldn't believe how animated, how very alive you were in my arms. You lifted an impossibly small hand up to your face. Myopic and curious, you examined me, and I prayed some part of you recognized me as your father.

"Did you name her?" I asked Lou. We had discussed a few names the last time I was in New York, but none had seemed right.

"I was waiting for you." She gave me a funny smile. "What do you think about Emerson Bell?"

My heart seized, thinking of the Emerson quote about doing the thing you are most afraid of. "Emerson Bell Hernandez," I said to you softly. "It's perfect. *You're* perfect."

If my love for Lou had been tangled up in indecision and regret, what I felt for you was pure and inevitable. I've never been one for organized religion, but on that morning I thanked God, and the universe, and every unseen force that had contributed to you being there in my arms. My actions had caused so much pain; they had brought me so much pain. But as I held you, all the pain fell away. What remained, Emerson, was you.

EIGHTEEN

Early 2009

I stayed in New York for three weeks after your birth. I mostly remember feelings and fragments from that time. Joy, as I cradled you in my arms and sang every lullaby I knew, and a few I didn't really know, too.

Despair, when I couldn't calm you in the middle of the night and had to wake Lou, who desperately needed sleep, so she could nurse you.

Hope—that temporary balm, that ephemeral elixir—after Lou promised we would find a way for me to remain in your life.

But the most pervasive of these was grief. Many a night, I found Lou sobbing in bed, only to have her send me away, reminding me that Rob was probably who she longed to have comfort her.

Not that I could fault her, since my own instinct was to pick up the phone and call Rob, too. I wanted to share the news and show you off (Look! I've made a real, live human!). And each time I had this urge, I was reminded that he was no longer a part of my life and never would be again. I had recently overheard Lou tell a friend that divorce was worse than death because it came with all of the pain and none of the resolution. I knew just what she meant.

I missed my mother, too, which caught me by surprise. She had treated tenderness as though it were ill timed, if not downright inappropriate. She didn't really hug; if she kissed you, it was with her lips pulled so tight you could feel her teeth behind them. Reassuring words were reserved for friends and neighbors—not her children.

But all the same, she was my mother, and she would have been thrilled to have a granddaughter. Maybe you would have even bridged the gap between us.

Now the gap I faced was six hundred miles wide. When the day came for me to return to Michigan, I wanted to yell and kick and refuse to leave. But I didn't break down in front of Lou. (And why? What cool-guy facade was I trying to uphold? I had no game, and we both knew it.) Instead, I kissed your wrinkled forehead and hugged Lou and made her swear she would let me know if she needed anything. I drove home mournful and spent.

There is even less about the next month that remains in my mind. Did I fall behind at work? Probably. I seem to recall my colleagues looking at me questioningly when I lost my train of thought midsentence. Nessa, who was soon to take over for Craig as stewardship director and would therefore become my direct supervisor, covered for me more than a few times. "Been there, and not so long ago," she said sympathetically when she found me drooling on my keyboard one afternoon when I was supposed to be in a meeting.

Pascal called often—I do remember that, because he showed up at my office at the end of one workday in February to complain that I never picked up the phone. Then he dragged me to a steak house, where he ordered me a rib eye and fries. ("You look like a malnourished goat, and you don't smell much better, either," he muttered when I protested.) As I ate, he demanded that we devise a plan.

I blew him off, arguing that a plan was pointless when Lou was the one calling the shots.

"I'm not talking about Emerson or Lou," he retorted—typical Pascal. "I'm talking about *you*. As your friend, I have no choice but to insist that you cannot walk around looking like that."

"Like what?" I said, as though he had not just compared me to underfed livestock.

"You're not going to get anything you want if you can't think straight. And," he said, sniffing me, "you need a shower."

I laughed and ate my steak, but I still didn't see how any effort on my part would make a difference.

The following day, a box of books arrived at my office. Some were new; others were dog-eared and marked to high hell. I found a note scribbled on a piece of university stationery at the bottom of the box:

> *Kafka said a book must be the axe for the frozen sea within us. Start chopping.* —P

He had sent me at least a dozen volumes. Penelope Fitzgerald's *The Blue Flower*. Charles Baxter's *The Feast of Love*. Books I might have turned my nose up at during my MFA years, like Laurie Colwin's *Family Happiness*, proved to be page-turners. Others, like Rilke's *Possibility of Being*, were not as cathartic as I was anticipating.

No matter: I read them all, one after another like my life depended on it. Which I suppose it did. I pored over the pages in the morning and at night, on my lunch break and in the bath. When Lou would put the phone near your head (not too close—we were all half convinced cell phones caused brain tumors, and maybe by the time you read this that will have proved to be true) so you could hear my voice, I would read lines from Colette or Alice Munro, more of Pascal's picks.

Buoyed by the books and a slow but surging feeling that maybe I could find some way to make the most of our fractured family, I flew to New York for a long weekend.

~

I should have seen the signs, but I was so busy analyzing myself in relation to Lou that I failed to train a critical lens on her. Even leaking breast milk, exhausted and overwhelmed, she was beautiful to me—maybe more so than ever. But my heart no longer fluttered each time I looked at her. Was I just distracted by the baby, I wondered? Or maybe it was guilt at play. Even if Rob and I would go to our graves without reconciling, I owed it to him to not rekindle a relationship with Lou—regardless of whether she happened to be the mother of my child. Perhaps this, I reasoned, had finally managed to dampen my desire.

And so I disregarded her being up in the middle of the night, even when you slept through until the morning. I assured myself that her spending the better part of the day in bed, too, was normal. I ignored that the bagels, Brie, and chocolate penguins I brought her—all of her favorites—went uneaten. I told myself she just needed a break when she didn't want to go for a walk with us when the temperature rose to a glorious, sunny sixty-five.

It was so easy to focus on the immediate—that is to say, you. You lifted your head! You gained half a pound! You smiled. (Or did you? I wasn't always sure.) Everything you did was so fresh and fascinating that I couldn't believe I had ever thought having a child would be a bad idea.

When can I bring Emerson to meet my father, my sister, my extended family? I asked Lou. And when I received mumbled, inconclusive answers in return, I rationalized that away, too. For all intents and purposes, Lou was a single parent. Was it any surprise that her primary concern was how she would get through the next hour?

On Monday afternoon, just before I left for the airport, I asked Lou if I could return in a month or two.

"Sure," she said, her voice void of emotion.

"Are you okay?" I asked. She was in the same pair of pajamas she had been wearing since I had arrived, and her hair was matted at her shoulders. But maybe that was how new mothers looked. Who could be concerned about lustrous locks when there was an adorable if squalling child just across the room?

"Never better," she said, flashing a smile that was as hollow as it was brief.

And I, the half-wit, let it go.

"Come when you'd like," she told me. You were cradled in her arms like a football—you were still so incredibly small—and she held you forward, almost like a peace offering.

I took you, kissed you, and whispered that I would see you again soon. Then I kissed Lou on the cheek, promised to call, and returned to my life.

~

When Rob and I were kids, April Fools' Day was always a big production. One year I put part of a Hershey's bar on Rob's seat, and he walked around school half the day with a brown smear on the back of his pants. In retaliation, the next year he lay on my front porch, right under the door, his t-shirt coated in fake blood and his head bent at an extreme angle. But when I walked out the door, I didn't see him there and stepped directly on his stomach, which made him jump violently, and between his screaming and crimson-soaked shirt, and my screaming, half the neighborhood came out of their houses and started screaming, too. No surprise, my father threatened to whup my ass and Rob's, but that didn't stop us from running over to Wisnewski's and attempting to pull the same gag on him.

And so, when my doorbell rang the morning of April first, I didn't think, *Maybe I have a delivery* (back then, the UPS truck didn't swing by twice a day to drop off batteries and Bordeaux and the countless other things one now orders online). *No,* I thought, *someone's playing a joke on me.* And when I opened the door and Lou thrust you into my arms, I expected her to yell, "April Fools!"

Instead, she began to cry. "I can't do this, Jim," she said.

I glanced past her. She had parked her rental car in the driveway; from the doorway, I could see the car seat in the back. Was she saying she couldn't take care of you? As much as I was not ready to be a parent, I was even less ready to slip into the role of Mr. Mom. I looked at Lou again and ordered myself to stay cool.

"Come in," I said, ushering the two of you into the house. "Come in, come in."

I kept you in my arms as I got Lou arranged on the sofa; it seemed she was in no state to take you, and anyway, I was so thrilled to see you that I wasn't about to let you go. You had more hair than the month before, and your face already seemed so different that you could have been an older cousin or even an entirely different child.

"What do you mean, you can't do this?" I finally asked Lou.

In that moment, both my fear and my resolutions went up in smoke. I wanted Lou to say she couldn't be without me. That she had realized all along that I was the true love of her life. That if we were in for a penny, we were in for a pound, and we were going to create the full family experience, complete with loving parents who also happened to be madly in love with each other.

You see, Emerson, I suspect that what I really wanted was to give you the life I had not had. I must have believed, at least on a subconscious level, that having this stereotypical setup would make up for the unhappy childhood I had experienced and save you from the same fate in the process. Lou's expression alone could have told me my desires were not to come to pass, but here I was, the ultimate April fool, hope springing eternal in my irrational mind.

"I can't raise a child *alone*, Jim," she said. "I need your help." (And now I am crying over my keyboard; forgive me for my sappiness.)

"You don't have to," I told her. "I'll start looking for a job in New York right away, an apartment—whatever you need."

She shook her head. "No, I need to be here for a while. *We* need to. Em and me. With you. Is that okay?"

Yes—yes—a million times yes. "Of course," I said.

I nestled you in some blankets on the floor, which was probably three different varieties of death trap; I knew so little about parenting. Then I went to the kitchen to put tea on for Lou and tried not to dance around in joy.

When I returned, she was drowsy. She had a sip of tea, then placed her mug on the coffee table. "I drove through the night so that Emerson would sleep. I'm out-of-my mind exhausted. You have to go to work, though, don't you?"

Work . . . right. I had been on my way to the office, and in fact had a meeting with Nessa scheduled first thing, but that ship had long since left the port.

"I'll call in," I said, vowing to wow my team with übercompetence sometime in the very near future. "Let me get the guest bedroom ready. Did you bring a—what do you call those baby cages?"

She managed a small laugh. "A Pack 'n Play. It's in the car."

"Got it. Do you mind if I leave Emerson with you while I run out and get it, and then you can sleep?"

She looked deeply relieved at the suggestion of sleep. "No, of course not. Hey, Jim?"

"Yeah?"

She gave me a small smile. "Thank you."

NINETEEN

June–August 2009

Since when did it take two hours to pick up a pack of diapers?

"Are you okay?" I asked as Lou let herself in through the back door. I had just put you down for a nap—finally, and clad in the very last diaper we had in the house—and was about to unwind by washing dishes, emptying the trash, and paying the rest of the month's bills.

"I'm fine," she said slowly. "Why?"

I eyed the small shopping bag she had just set on the table. "Are the diapers in the car?"

Her hands flew up to her cheeks. "Oh my gosh."

"You forgot the diapers?"

She looked mortified. "I totally forgot the diapers."

"Um . . . where were you all that time?" I asked.

"I ran into one of the neighbors while I was picking out shampoo—you remember Yvonne? She runs that bookstore downtown that I love. And then we ended up chatting for a long time, and, well, you know how it goes."

I had forgotten how hard it was to live with someone. No—let me rephrase that. I had *no idea* how hard it was to live with someone, particularly when that person was co-parenting with you. For the love of all that was good and holy, *why* had I not appreciated how toilet paper and Q-tips magically appeared when I lived with Kathryn? How when she said she would do something, she did it? How she actually got in bed with me each night rather than retreating to the bedroom down the hall?

Stop it, I told myself. *This is the mother of your child.*

"I'm sorry," said Lou. She looked so pathetic standing there that the only thing I could do was hug her.

"Don't be," I said. "I'll run out and get them right now."

"Thanks, Jim. I'm sorry," she said again. "I'm trying."

I knew she was trying—and struggling, even if neither of us had fully admitted it. We three had been living together for several months, and each one had seemed to take more of a toll on Lou. She didn't open her computer, or write by hand, or even read. She didn't call her friends and rarely left the house; when she did, she would return with random items, like chocolate pudding, which neither of us liked, rather than the item she had gone out for in the first place. She did, however, sleep a great deal, and I would sometimes hear her crying softly before she passed out.

But it was all perfectly normal for a new mother: this was the lie that I clung to, the leaking life raft I had precariously put our family on.

And sometimes Lou made it easy to believe. I would come home from work and find her nursing you on the sofa, and she would smile up at me and tell me about some fantastic thing you had done while I had been out.

Living with others is a never-ending improv, and because I was out of practice, I often fumbled my response. But I would tell Lou a story about, say, Craig's latest attempts to woo the new hire—who clearly would have rather cuddled up to a rabid dog—and she would laugh heartily, like she used to, and I would think to myself with triumph, *See? Everything is almost as it should be.*

Yes, the awkwardness that we had experienced in New York was nearly gone. We had finally established an amiable companionship, and I didn't want to disrupt it by questioning her—not when comfort counted for so much.

~

Trouble is, Lou was not actually comfortable, and I am sorry it took her sobbing in front of your crib in order for me to recognize this.

She was in a ball on the floor making a terrible mewling noise. I had just rushed in thinking that maybe you were crying; it didn't *sound* like an infant's wail, but in my alarmed state I still thought something awful might have happened to you.

"Are you okay?" I said to Lou as I looked in the crib. You were reaching up for the musical mobile we had installed, safe and content; something else was amiss.

Lou's face was streaked with tears. "I didn't know you were home."

"I'm home," I said, at once sheepish and relieved. "My meeting let out early, so I took off. Are you okay?" I asked again.

"No," she said, and began to cry. "I'm not even a little okay, Jim. I don't think I should be a mother. You're going to have to take care of Emerson on your own."

"What? No, no," I told her. "You don't mean that."

"You don't understand," she said, and burst into tears again.

I didn't, in fact, and was forced to admit as much. It took her a minute to calm down enough to speak. "I'm not cut out for this," she said. "I come from a long line of women who aren't meant to be mothers, and now I've finally joined them. I couldn't even give birth like a normal woman. The female body is built to birth, and I couldn't even manage that."

"Lou," I said softly. "Don't something like one in three women have a C-section? And you know the cord was wrapped around Emerson's neck. You heard what your midwife said. That surgery saved her life."

"I somehow doubt it."

"You're not feeling like yourself."

She wiped her face with her hands. "I am afraid that I'm feeling a whole lot like myself. I'm going to fail Emerson, and I don't even know what to do about it. Get a place nearby but let you raise her? Find a full-time nanny who will mother her in a way that I can't? God, Jim," she said, putting her head in her hands. "Look at me! I'm just like my mother: unmarried, unstable, and without a real home to call my own."

I took her hands in mine. "Lou," I said. "Lou," I said again when she didn't meet my eyes, "please look at me."

Reluctantly, she lifted her head.

"Your home is here, always," I told her. "No matter what happens, this house is yours and Emerson's. If you decide one day that you don't want to live under the same roof as me, then I'll be the one to go. This place is yours as long as you want or need it."

"Jim, you don't have to—"

"I do have to, but it's not even that," I told her. "I *want* to. Let me give you one less thing to worry about."

She sniffed and looked at me. "Okay," she said quietly and began to cry again.

I wrapped my arms around her. "Lou, love, you are *not* your mother. Not even a little bit."

"I'm a terrible parent and an awful human being," she said, still crying.

I hugged her to me. "We screwed up, but you're a good person and an even better mother. Remember last week, how Em was screaming her head off, and within a minute you had found and pulled the sliver from her palm? It would have taken me two days to understand what was wrong with her and another three to remove the thing."

"You would have figured it out," she whispered. Even in her distressed state, she was so insistent, jutting her chin out, batting away every kind word.

"I want you to see someone," I told her.

"What kind of someone?"

"A therapist."

She made a face. "You know I tried that before; it only made me feel worse. If I wanted to revisit my childhood in painful detail, I'd go hang out near one of my mom's old trailers."

"Last I heard, therapy doesn't work that way."

"Hmph."

"Let's go see your midwife, then," I suggested. "Your primary care doctor. A psychiatrist, even."

"I *don't* want pills."

Behind us, you were kicking your feet against the crib mattress, and I could smell that your diaper needed to be changed. "Please, Lou," I pleaded. "Your hormones could be out of whack, and you don't even know it."

"My brain cells are out of whack," she said, pulling herself out of my embrace. She stood. "Maybe they've always been this way and I'm just realizing it. Maybe that's why—"

She stopped herself, but I was able to fill in the blanks: *Maybe that's why I left Rob. Maybe that's why I had an affair with you.* It was so sad I wanted to sob, too. "No," I insisted. "You just went through a difficult divorce, and you're raising a child with someone who isn't your partner. It's a lot. Enough to make a person feel awful even if she *hadn't* recently given birth."

"I'm not depressed," she argued. "I know what that looks like, and this isn't it."

You had begun to cry, and I picked you up and put you on the changing pad that we had attached to the dresser. I was fastening a fresh diaper on you when Lou came up next to me. "You have to do it tighter," she said quietly. She reattached the tab on one side, then did the other. "Otherwise pee goes everywhere."

Well, that explained why I was constantly changing diapers. "How'd you know that?" I asked.

She shrugged. "It's not rocket science. And does it matter when I still don't know how to make her smile?"

"Sure you do," I said. I'd seen you smile at Lou earlier that very morning.

But she just shook her head. "A four-year-old can diaper a baby."

It was not just the diapering, though. It was that she knew one burp was not enough; you needed two or three in order to not spit up ten minutes later. She knew the kind of cry you made when you were hungry, and the type you made when you were tired. She was a natural, intuitive mother. I only wished she could see it.

～

As it so often happens, things got worse first. I had to push Lou to see her doctor, who prescribed her an antidepressant and told her to walk for half an hour every day. Lou began taking you out in the stroller more often, but her pill bottle remained full.

"Rumor has it you have to actually swallow them for them to work," I joked one morning as I pointed to the container on the counter.

She shot me a look that would have made a raisin out of a grape. "I don't want to take them while I'm still nursing."

"The doctor said they were safe."

"The doctors said that about Thalidomide at one point."

"Lou."

"Jim."

"Are you feeling any better?"

"Sure."

The only sure thing was that she was still crying in the bathroom while the shower ran, thinking I couldn't hear her. That the gifts her friends sent stacked up in the dining room until I opened them. That sometimes, when you would giggle, she would smile but didn't laugh back, even though your laughter was the most contagious sound.

After you stopped nursing and switched to formula and solid food at the end of the summer, Lou switched from water to wine. She would have a glass as I was making dinner—*fine*, I would think—but then a few more glasses would follow, and by the time we said good night there was a wobble to her walk.

And what could I say? What could I do? It was such a strange space, to be living and co-parenting with someone who was not actually my life partner.

"Lou," I said once when she emptied a bottle of wine into her glass. She raised an eyebrow at me and I quickly muttered something that had nothing to do with alcohol or the sadness in her eyes. Maybe I had no *right* to speak up, I told myself. Maybe Lou just needed time.

~

Late one night, so late it was almost morning, I got out of bed to get a snack and found Lou at the kitchen table. She held a glass nearly filled to the brim with white wine and was bent over a black-and-white composition book, which she liked to write poems in. But the page beneath her was blank.

She looked dazed as she glanced up at me. "I've lost myself, Jim," she whispered. "I don't remember who I am, all I can think about is that I feel like I'm going to die, and I'm not even sure that's the worst outcome."

I took the wineglass out of one of her hands and the pen from the other. Then I picked her up—she was so light, hardly heavier than a child—and hugged her to me, almost like she *was* a child. My eyes filled with tears, and I was glad she couldn't see; I didn't want to make it any worse. "This is so hard, isn't it?" I whispered.

"The hardest thing I've ever done."

"And yet the best. Our girl is amazing."

"No thanks to me."

"Lou." I said her name over and over, like a chant, as I stroked her head. "Emerson is amazing because she *is* you. We are going to get you through this. We are going to get us all through this. You have to trust me."

"I do trust you," she said into my neck.

I had an urge to kiss her, which took me by surprise. But it passed as quickly as it had come on. Yes, she was too frail and vulnerable, curled up in my arms. It was more than that, though. When I had visited her in New York after your birth and noticed that my desire had waned, I assumed it was temporary. This no longer seemed to be the case. As much as I loved Lou, she was now but one part of my world, instead of the entirety of it.

As I pulled a blanket over her on the bed and closed the door quietly behind me, it struck me that this was not a disappointment, but rather an incredible relief.

TWENTY

Winter 2009–2010

"How's that book coming along?" asked my father. He was sitting at our kitchen table, jiggling you on his knee.

I was at the counter chopping peppers for fajitas. I paused, my knife suspended in midair. "What book?"

"You know," he said as you patted his cheek with your hand. He pretended you had slapped him, and you giggled. Then he turned back at me. "The one you were writing."

I turned back to the peppers. "There is no book." Yes, I had been keeping a journal of sorts, but it had been more than two years since I had attempted a word of fiction.

"What do you mean, 'there isn't'? You were working on one. What happened to it?"

I shook my head, thinking it had been a mistake to invite him over. Since Lou had been feeling better, we were trying to be more social; the doctor she was seeing said it was important for her to reconnect with people and the aspects of life that did not include bibs and baby talk. So we hired a sitter and went to dinner with Pascal. We invited Nessa, her partner, and their two children over for brunch. The Jennifer who had been with Lou at your birth, and who had made no effort to hide how baffled she was by our living arrangement, even flew in for a weekend.

But then Lou decided that it would be good to have my father over more regularly. "He's the only grandparent Emerson has," she said when I explained that I didn't really want to see him outside of, say, major holidays.

As far as I was concerned, he already came over too often. He was thrilled to have another grandchild, just as he said he would be, and expressed this by showering you with gifts and grandparenting with an enthusiasm that bore no resemblance to his performance as a father. Objectively, I understood that these were good things. But I was irritated over the way he had reacted to Lou's pregnancy and my having had a child with her. And now there he was, asking me about my writing.

You had started to squirm, so my father put you on the ground to crawl around. He walked over to the fridge. "It's just that I thought you would have written a book by now, even if you didn't have it published," he said, and stuck his head behind the fridge door. "I know that was important to you."

"Well, it's not anymore," I said, dropping the peppers onto the skillet. They cracked and sizzled as I pushed them around on the cast iron with a wood spatula. "I have bills to pay. A family to take care of."

He retrieved a beer and returned to the table without responding.

"I feel good about it," I insisted, though of course my insisting this only underscored the fact that I felt anything but.

"Okay," he said.

One of my earliest memories is of my father standing over me at the dining room table as I did my math homework. Back then, most parents' idea of getting involved with their kids' schooling involved signing report cards and attending the occasional conference; homework was a matter overseen by teachers. But there was my father, watching me arrive at one wrong conclusion after another.

"Come on, son," he said, pointing at the numbers I had just bungled. "You *can* do this. You *can* figure it out." His voice was stern, but I remember thinking that he must love me—not just to help me, but also to be so convinced that I actually had it in me to get the answer right in spite of all evidence to the contrary.

But that memory didn't come to mind as I angrily tossed the steak I had just seasoned onto a pan and placed it beneath the broiler. "Anyway, what do you care?" I asked. "I'm not writing about cars."

A stranger could have looked at my father and seen that I had wounded him. He stood and grabbed his beer. "I just thought it would be good for you to be doing what you claim to love so much," he said, and walked into the living room.

∼

"I'm a jerk," I told Lou that night. My father had spent dinner talking to everyone but me and had not even looked me in the eye when we said good night. Yes, he was stubborn, and yes, he could be selective in his affection. I still knew I had been wrong.

Lou was sitting in the armchair across from the sofa, her knees hugged to her chest. She had recently cut her hair so that it just barely reached her shoulders. I liked it better before, but it looked nice on her.

"You're not a jerk." Noting my skeptical expression, she said, "Okay, maybe that was a *little* jerky, but you've been programmed to respond that way. Why don't you apologize the next time you see him? Or even call him tomorrow. That would go a long way."

"Yeah. I guess an apology wouldn't be the worst idea." Beside me, there was a navy throw pillow embroidered with yellow stars, which made up some sort of constellation that I could not identify. "Is this new?" I asked, pointing to the pillow.

She nodded. "Do you hate it?"

"No, no, not at all. It's nice."

When Kathryn and I lived together, I remember wishing that our everyday involved more passion and less humdrum. Now the humdrum seemed its own sort of bliss, particularly where Lou and I were concerned. I didn't want to give up our comfortable living arrangement, and her small domestic acts—like buying throw pillows or rearranging the living room furniture—fueled my hope that she intended to stay in town, in our house, where we would raise our child. Together.

"So . . ." She scrunched up her nose. "I got my first alimony check today."

"Really?" I had not been expecting that. Their divorce had long been final, but the collapse of Rob's company had tangled up their postdivorce negotiations. He had to make a statement to a government panel, and Andrea had been called to testify before Congress. They had each emerged with their Teflon coating intact, and Rob had quickly found work at a small financial firm run by one of his old business-school classmates. I was glad; this seemed like a sign he was on his way to putting his life back together. I didn't know if he was still with Andrea. I didn't want to know.

"Yeah. Saturday would have been our eleven-year anniversary," she said quietly.

They could have made it, I thought. They could have come back together after their separation if I had not inserted myself between them. "Eleven. Wow."

"I know. Technically, we made it to ten; the divorce went through just after our anniversary. But I only think of us having been married for nine. For me, it was over from the minute I saw him with his hand on her lower back."

I looked at her with surprise. "When was this?"

"Two weeks before Jason's funeral, maybe? Three? I had been downtown, and I thought I would surprise him at the office, since he said he wouldn't be working super late. I was just outside the building and saw them coming through the revolving door." She bit her bottom lip. "They were going through together, instead of one at a time, like everyone else. When they came out, he was touching her back. That was the moment I knew it was over between us."

I shook my head, unsure of what to say.

"To this day, he swears they weren't fooling around then. But there was an intimacy between them, you know? It seemed like the first real nail in the coffin for us."

A year earlier, even six months before, I would have felt vindicated by this news. (See! He deserved it!) Now I felt sad for Lou, and for Rob, too. After all, if anyone knew about the aftershocks of an ill-advised decision, it was me. "I'm sorry, Lou."

"Thanks. And I'm sorry I never told you that before. I probably should have when I came over after Wisnewski's funeral."

"It's okay. Thanks for telling me now." What had driven him to Andrea? Had *he* been depressed? Wisnewski's death must have hit him pretty hard. And his work was taxing in a way that I had not fully appreciated until after his company collapsed. Maybe what I had registered as stress was really a crisis. Why hadn't I paid attention to the signs? Why hadn't I tried to intervene?

Because I had been busy obsessing over his wife, I realized with disgrace.

Lou sighed and stretched her legs out in front of her. "Anyway, the alimony isn't much, which is fine with me. It's almost enough to live on."

"Here? Or in New York?" I asked.

She looked at me with surprise. "I guess we should talk about that, huh?"

"I was hoping we would at some point."

"The longer I stay, the harder it will be if I leave."

"So don't," I said. "The schools are great here. It's better for you and Emerson to have me around. You . . . you've been doing so well."

"My mood, you mean."

I nodded. "We don't have to live together. We could find town houses in the same neighborhood or something like that, so I'd be there for you, but you and Emerson could have your own place."

"In this market? I couldn't get a decent mortgage to save my life."

"You could rent. I could help you. There are all kinds of options. Do you really want to go back?"

"I don't know that I do. New York feels like a city for premother-hood me. And . . ." She looked at her nails. "It was the place I shared with Rob. Going back would be incredibly painful. That's part of the reason I came to live with you—I just couldn't be there anymore."

She still loved him. That kept you near me for now. But one day it might be the very same thing that pulled her away. She added, "I'm not so sure this is it, either. Haven't you ever wanted to live anywhere else?"

"Of course. I've always wanted to live in a city. Chicago, maybe, or somewhere warmer, like Austin or New Orleans."

She smiled wistfully. "That sounds fun. Let's see how the next few months go."

~

A few weeks later, Lou got a job at our neighbor Yvonne's bookstore, and there was no more talk of her moving elsewhere. The bookstore was the kind of place that sold dream catchers and crystals and served fifty-two varieties of tea—but not espresso, which was apparently bad for one's root chakra, wherever that was located. She could take the bus there if I needed the car, and Yvonne had given her a flexible schedule.

"You're sure about this?" I asked Lou. She was sitting on the counter, looking pleased.

"Positive. I want to make sure I'm able to take care of Emerson. Given the pickle Rob got himself in, there's no saying if alimony will last, and poetry doesn't exactly pay the bills."

"But you have me," I said. It wasn't that I was making an incredible amount of money, but it was enough for the three of us. "And now that you're feeling better, wouldn't you rather use that time to write again? After all, your last book—"

"The publisher paid me two thousand dollars for it," she said, almost apologetic in tone. "And that was generous. I'm not exactly Maya Angelou."

"Oh," I said. "Well, know that I'm going to keep helping, and that won't change."

"I know, and I appreciate it. I'll write at night and on the weekends. Anyway, I don't have the drive I did before. I'm sure it will come back, but for now, the muse is missing." She eyed me. "What about you, Jim? Are you back at it?"

"Nothing more than the occasional paragraph, but maybe I'll try a novel again soon," I said, so confidently that I almost believed myself.

~

The first year of your life was the fastest long time I have ever lived through. When your birthday came, we did what parents do and threw you a big party you would never remember. We invited the neighbors and their kids, and Victoria and her boys flew in from Oregon. My father came over with Miriam, whom he had finally begun referring to as his girlfriend.

"Where is my princess?" he asked as he came shooting through the door. He scooped you up in his arms and then showed you the wooden rocking horse he had made for you, which you spent the next hour climbing on and falling off of.

Lou decorated the house with streamers and clusters of inflated balloons and made cupcakes with buttercream frosting and brightly colored sprinkles. Your face lit up as we sang "Happy Birthday"; you knew that song was for you, sung by the people who loved you most. I expected you to try to stick the whole cupcake in your mouth or maybe smash it with your palm, but you stuck a careful finger in, lifted it to your lips, and broke into a grin as the sugar dissolved on your tongue.

"Let's get a picture," my father said, clapping my shoulder. I had apologized for snapping at him months before, and we had since resumed our cordially distant relationship.

"Good idea," I said, motioning for everyone to come over.

My father shook his head. "No, I mean just the three of you."

I frowned, but he pushed me forward, firmly enough that I knew he meant business. "Could you trust me for a single second of your life?" he groused.

"Fine," I said, and sighed. I motioned for Lou to come toward me. "My father wants a picture of the three of us."

Lou and I positioned ourselves behind your high chair, but my father kept motioning for us to crouch lower and get closer. "Come on, pretend you like each other," he said with mock exasperation.

Lou put her arm around my back and pulled me toward her. "Who needs to pretend?" she shot back.

After everyone left and Lou and I had put you to bed, we were in the kitchen washing the dishes that hadn't fit into the dishwasher. I raised one of the wineglasses I had just rinsed. "To Emerson, and making it a year."

She lifted another goblet and clinked its edge against my glass. "To our girl, and making it. We did better than could be expected, considering the circumstances."

"Cheers to that." I hesitated, then decided that yes—your birthday was as good a time as any to demonstrate, even in a small way, that I was moving on, that I was working hard to really, truly, let her go. "Lou?"

She had just set down the glass and was reaching for a bowl of chips. "Yes?"

"I think I'm ready to start dating."

She dumped the leftover chips in the waste bin and looked at me questioningly.

"Other people," I clarified.

"Okay . . . ," she said, and handed me the bowl to wash. "What does that mean for us?"

"I'm not sure. Nothing has to change unless we want it to. Are you okay with that?" I asked.

I couldn't quite read the expression on her face. "Of course I am. I want you to be happy."

"You can, too, if you want. Date, I mean."

She grabbed a platter from the table and passed it to me. "I appreciate that, but I'm not there yet. I may not be for a while. I want to make sure I'm okay. It's been a rocky couple of years."

"That makes sense. And if that changes, that's okay, too."

Lou handed me the bottle of milk you had polished off before bed. It was mind-boggling to think that less than two years earlier, she and I had split a bottle of champagne and given in to the fantastical notion that nothing mattered but that moment.

Now I was constantly thinking ahead. In the next thirty minutes, I would check on you to make sure you weren't wet or twisted up in your blanket. I would need to get myself to bed within the next hour if I was going to make it to the office on time the following morning and begin to plow through the twenty-seven projects that were waiting for me. At the end of the month, the largest of those projects was due, and I was fairly certain it was a steaming hot pile of garbage that would eat up most of the next two workweeks. And so on and so forth.

But then I looked over at Lou, who gave me the same lopsided, dimpled smile that you have, Emerson. And for just a few seconds, I forgot all about what was next and was able to soak up the good fortune of here and now.

TWENTY-ONE

Winter 2010–Summer 2010

Having not truly dated in so long, I had serious reservations about the whole ordeal. I soon found it was easiest to be myself when I pretended to be someone else.

With Lilah, an attractive cellist who was about to go on tour in Europe, I carried myself like a man with innate confidence in his ability to delight women.

To Amy, a radio producer with a wicked wit, I was a writer who was on the verge of penning the next great Canadian novel (this, Amy and I agreed, seemed slightly less impossible than attempting the next great American novel; no matter that I had no claim on Canada and would have to go up against Margaret Atwood).

Mallory, who never did say what she did for a living, found in me an adept conversationalist. I quickly came to regret my conversation skills when it became apparent that Mallory only wanted to discuss her pet skunk. They're quite pleasant after you remove the glands that produce their signature scent, she informed me, showing me a picture of the striped beast lying prostrate on her bed. And as companions went, she said, they were as fun as any ferret. I didn't have it in me to tell Mallory that I found ferrets, skunks, and her terrifying.

You'd think that being a single father would put me at a disadvantage in the dating world, but no. Apparently using the phrase *shared custody* on one's online profile signifies a certain level of trustworthiness and reliability—or maybe it just highlighted my virility. And so I met many smart, captivating women. It was a shame that I wasn't interested in pursuing a long-term relationship with a single one of them.

"How was she?" Lou would ask after I came back from a date.

"Fine, but nothing to write home about," I'd say, and we would laugh. But when I went to bed alone each night, I wondered why I wasn't able to have a deeper connection with any of these women. Lilah, for example, had emailed from Prague to say she would like to see me again as soon as she returned to the States. Why could I not fall in love with her—or at least give it the old college try? Or what about Amy, or perhaps Bridget, who was cute and cultured and eager to bring me home with her?

And of course, there was my failure with Kathryn, which still played on a loop in the back of my mind. One evening I was sorting through my inbox and came upon an email she had sent me not long after we had started dating. The message was only inquiring about whether I would join her at a friend's art show, but it was so clever and warm that I found myself thinking that if we met for the first time now, and we were both single, I would want to be with her—even if marriage and children were what she was gunning for. What a terrible shame, I thought as I refiled the message, unable to bring myself to delete it.

"What are you even *doing*, my friend?" said Pascal when we met for drinks downtown one evening. "Surely there's at least one woman who you could see for, say, a third date."

"I've gone on third dates," I said, when in fact the only person I had seen three times was Lilah, and that was because I knew she was about to hop on a transatlantic flight. "Anyway, this coming from a serial dater."

"It all looks so shiny in the rearview mirror," he said in his songbird lilt. "I wouldn't wish my postdivorce years on my worst enemy. Now that Winnie has finally taken me back, I'm as happy as a clam in possession of the world's largest pearl."

I tipped my drink at him. "Isn't a pearl a trapped granule of debris that builds up with years of irritation?"

He rolled his eyes.

"The point is, Pascal, I've moved on from Lou. You should be proud of me."

"I'm glad you're feeling better, James. I am. But as long as you and Lou are living in the same house, can you really move on?"

Maybe he has a point, I thought that night as I heard Lou tinkering in the bathroom. But what would it do to you, Emerson, if we separated? This was the question that woke me at two in the morning, and again at four, and sometimes left me staring at the ceiling until my alarm went off hours later.

The night I had seen Pascal, Lou knocked on my bedroom door on her way to bed. "Jim?" she said without opening the door. "You check on Em yet?"

"Yes," I called.

"Thanks. Let me get her if she wakes up."

"I won't," I said, and she laughed.

"You're incorrigible."

"The worst," I agreed. "Hey, Lou?"

"Yes?"

"Do you think we should keep living together?"

Now she opened the door and stuck her head in. "Why do you ask?"

I had been reading, and put my book down on the pillow beside me. "I was just thinking about Em."

"I'm not sure. She seems so happy but . . ."

". . . if she gets too used to it as she gets older, it will be a harder transition for her when we have two houses," I said.

"Yeah." Lou opened her mouth to say something else, then shook her head.

"What is it?"

"I don't even know, really. But let's think about it some more, yes? Then maybe we can compare notes and figure out what's best."

"Good idea," I said.

But we didn't speak the next day or even the next month. We just kept on as we were, like everything would work out with no intervention on our part.

~

One June afternoon, I opened my email and found this at the top:

James,

It's been years; I hope you remember me. I looked you up online and saw that you're still living in Ann Arbor. I'll be in town for a job interview in two days. Any interest in grabbing a drink? Either way, I hope you're well.

All my best,

Nora

Nora Roderick. Of course I remembered her. I had even looked her up a few years ago; her digital résumé informed me that she had graduated at the top of her class at Loyola Law and was working at a big firm in Chicago.

I wrote back and suggested we grab drinks at a Mexican restaurant downtown, to which she responded, "Perfect," and listed her phone number.

"You don't mind if I go?" I asked Lou that evening over dinner.

You had started doing a rocking-lurching trick to attempt to catapult yourself out of your high chair and onto the floor, unaware that if you went down, the chair was going with you. As such, you were sitting in Lou's lap for safety's sake. She stopped passing you peas to eat and looked at me. "On your date? Of course not. You know I'm not working that night."

"It's not a date, and I just wanted to make sure you were okay with it," I said.

Lou smiled. "Isn't it?"

"She's my ex-student."

"That was a million years ago. She's in her thirties now, right?"

"I suppose so."

"Go enjoy yourself," she insisted, bouncing you on her knee. "We want Daddy to have fun, don't we?" she cooed at you, to which you slapped the table with a pea-coated hand and said, "Fun!"

"This is so weird sometimes," I said.

Lou looked at you again, then back up at me. "Rich life experiences, remember, Jim? Rich life experiences."

~

Nora was fifteen minutes late. My father felt tardiness was a character flaw, and though I didn't agree, I still hated when someone failed to show up on time. But when I saw Nora striding through the door in a purple dress and boots that brought to mind the pair she used to wear to class, I forgot I was irritated.

"Well, well, well," she said, making no effort to hide the fact that she was giving me the once-over. "James Hernandez. How is it that I've had to start injecting myself with Botox and you haven't aged a day?"

I was flustered, but in an oddly enjoyable way. "You have not."

She grinned at me. "No, I haven't. But really, you look good, James. It's great to see you."

"You, too, Nora."

The hostess led us to a cavernous booth.

"I feel like we're on opposite sides of the restaurant," said Nora after we slid into our respective sides.

"Hellooooo," I said, mock-echoing.

She cupped her hands around her mouth. "Want to go sit at the bar?" she echoed back.

"Thought you'd never ask."

We snagged a couple of bar stools and ordered margaritas. Then Nora swiveled toward me. "This is so much better."

I nodded. "It's good to see you. What made you think of reaching out after all this time?"

"The firm that's trying to recruit me is based in Detroit, and if I get the job, I'd be working in the Ann Arbor office. I figured it wouldn't hurt to reconnect with some of the people I know here, and I Googled you and saw that you were still at the university. Though I can't believe you're not teaching anymore. What's up with that?"

I shrugged. "I wasn't particularly good at it."

"No, you weren't," she said with another grin. "But at least you cared. Remember how you gave me another chance?"

"Who could forget?"

"So you didn't do that for all the students?" she said.

"I flunked everyone else."

"Sure you did."

I laughed heartily. "No, I didn't." I was feeling loose in the way that tequila can make a person, and I leaned in toward her. "I still remember reading your story. It was good, just like I thought it would be. Did you ever write anything else?"

"I appreciate the compliment, but I don't love fiction. Turns out that what I actually enjoy writing is legal briefs. I'm that rare lawyer who loves the law."

"Lucky. Though if you don't like fiction, I'm not sure we can be friends," I teased.

Her eyes twinkled. "Are you sure about that, James?" (I was not.) "Enough about me, though; tell me about you. What have you been up to for the past ten years?"

Interestingly—and maybe this was not just because of the tequila, but because Nora lit me up even as she put me at ease—I felt no urge to act like someone else around her.

So I gave her the warts-and-all update of my disappointments and unexpected success at the business school, my failed relationships and complicated family situation. She didn't seem put off that I had a child with a woman who was not my partner. In fact, she barely blinked when I explained that Lou and I were living together. I had just begun explaining that things in our house were humming along nicely when Nora leaned forward, put her hand on my knee, and kissed me.

Her lips were electric on mine, and as she leaned onto my leg, I felt a tug of something—passion, yes, but possibility, too—that I hadn't felt in a long time.

"Do you have anywhere to be?" she asked when we parted.

"Yes," I said, and leaned forward to kiss her again. "With you."

TWENTY-TWO

Summer–Fall 2010

Nora got the job and moved into a condo on the west side of town that July. Almost immediately, we began seeing each other most days. During the workweek, I went to her place after putting you to bed. Since Nora logged long hours at the office, this proved to be an ideal arrangement. Weekends were more complicated, both logistically and emotionally. Lou was often scheduled to be at the bookstore, where she had recently been promoted to manager, and I didn't want to leave you with a sitter during that time. Moreover, you, Lou, and I were in the habit of spending most of our free time together. We continued to do so, but increasingly I found myself wishing that Nora was with us. Yet when I was with her, I missed you—and yes, Lou. My heart was in perpetual limbo.

One evening in early August, Nora and I were unpacking the last of the boxes in her bedroom when she turned to me and said, "I don't want to ask you to be exclusive, because that might freak you out, but can we please not see other people?"

I laughed, put down the hangers I was holding, and embraced her. "I don't know when I'd see other people, given that I'm spending all my free time with you. But yes, for me, there's only you. Though my inner pessimist is telling me that it can't possibly be this simple."

Nora pulled back and made a face at me. "And why not? Is this about Lou?"

I had already told Nora everything: how I had loved Lou all those years, even when I should not have; how I had let that love take over so much of my life; how I had struggled with what I had done to Rob, whose angry face often surfaced in my dreams, and whom I thought about every single day. With a different woman, it might have been too early in the relationship for such confessions. But with Nora, it felt natural—necessary, even, in order for us to be intimate.

"No, I don't think so," I told her. "I think it's about me not trusting fate or maybe my subconscious."

"Okay, then trust *me*," she said. "This is simple because it's good, and good because it's simple."

Maybe she was right, but I suspected that it was actually good because it was complicated. Nora was both the spark and the warmth of the fire; she was the passion and the humdrum. As I put my lips to the back of her neck and felt her prickle with pleasure, it occurred to me that there was no comparing her to the two women I had loved before her. Because without Lou or Kathryn and what they had taught me about love—at great cost, yes, but all the same—there would have been no Nora.

~

"I'm thrilled for you, Jim," said Lou when I told her Nora and I were serious. "This is the best possible thing that could have happened to you."

"But is it the best thing to happen to *you*? And what about Emerson? There are three of us to consider now," I pointed out.

"Don't worry about us, right, baby love?" Lou cooed at you.

You clapped your hands together and said, "Worry about us!" and Lou and I looked at each other and laughed. (You were so funny; when, we asked ourselves in the way that new parents often do, had there ever before been a child so bright and wonderful?)

I did worry, though. Lou had come so far, but she still had dark days. And when she did, I was there to help pull her through.

When I told her I was worried about her leaving, she acted as though I were nuts. "My therapist thinks moving is a terrible idea," she said, waving a hand at me. "Things are stable now, which is what's most important."

I was glad that her psychologist thought a move was ill-advised, even if I suspected that my spending a few nights a week at Nora's house wasn't adding to Lou's sense of stability.

~

Clever empath that she was, Nora sensed my anxiety. "You know, you don't *have* to stay over so often if it makes you feel bad," she said one Saturday evening when I arrived with my overnight bag in tow. "We can take it slow."

"I don't *want* to take it slow." I dropped my bag and pulled her close to me. "Ah, Nora, how do I love thee?"

I was referencing the Elizabeth Barrett Browning poem, but before I could add "Let me count the ways," Nora met my eyes and said, "It's easy to do, James. Love me when I'm at my worst. Love me when you don't agree with me, and when this no longer feels new and surprising. Love me through it all."

It took me a few minutes to find my voice. When I could finally speak, I said quietly, "I love you, Nora. I really do. And I'm going to do my absolute best to keep loving you through it all."

She kissed me but did not say it back—that would come the following weekend, while we were eating pancakes in bed. It didn't matter; I already knew.

~

Remember the photo your grandfather took on your first birthday? It's the one that's on the mantel. He had emailed it to me the day after your party, but it wasn't until the following September that I finally had it printed and framed. I had planned to give it to Lou for her birthday, but she caught me bringing it in the house.

"Ooh, let me see!" she said, and held her hands out.

I reluctantly handed it to her. "You've seen it already. I was going to give you this framed version for your birthday."

"You still can," she said. She sat on the sofa, staring at the picture.

"What is it?" I asked. "You don't like it?" I looked kind of goofy, but it was one of the best photos of Lou I'd ever seen. And you, a smear of frosting on your cheek, that wild hair of yours in every direction: you were practically an advertisement for having children.

"We . . . look like a happy family."

I was about to make a joke about all happy families being the same until I caught her expression.

"I've never had a happy family before," she said quietly.

"I know," I said softly. "I'm not so sure I have, either." My upbringing had not been as traumatic as Lou's, but nonetheless, the unpleasant memories outnumbered the pleasant, at least where my parents were involved.

Really, all of my best moments from growing up included Rob, and more often than not, his parents. There was the time when our softball team won the citywide championship, and the four of us went out to an old-fashioned ice cream shop to celebrate. "Order anything on the menu, you two," Bobby had told us. Rob's pitching was the reason our team had claimed the title, but they made me feel the victory was mine, too.

When I won a young author's contest in sixth grade, Nancy saw the certificate on top of my homework on their counter and ran out and bought a frame for it. "That's a big deal, James. Be sure to hang it somewhere where you can see it," she said solemnly, and in doing so gave me permission to be proud rather than chagrined because it was not the right kind of award, as I had been telling myself.

Then there were the summer weeks at Rob's aunt's cabin, which gave me a chance to be a boy without constantly second-guessing myself for fear I was doing everything all wrong. For once, I wasn't flooded with shame when I thought about Rob and what we had shared. I only felt loss.

Lou's eyes were brimming with tears as she looked up at me. "God, Jim. I've really ruined everything, haven't I?"

I smiled sadly. "Isn't that my line?"

"No, you screwball. It's definitely mine." She wiped her eyes with a corner of her sweater. "We could have been good together, Jim."

"We *are* good together, Lou."

"You loved me for so long," she insisted. "Maybe that meant something."

"Maybe it meant I hurt both you and Rob terribly," I remarked. "Whoever said all's fair in love and war was not a student of history."

She was quiet for a moment. Then she said, "Well, I *am* glad you've found love. You deserve it."

"Thank you." I didn't know if I deserved it—it seemed to me that I still owed Karma a point or three—but it was wonderful to want to run off to some far-flung location with Nora rather than Lou. Heck, it was wonderful just to be able to confide in her at the end of the day.

Would we last? It was impossible to say. We had our troubles. She worked long hours and often continued to obsess about her cases during what should have been her downtime. She refused to change her mind over trivial issues, such as whether quilted toilet paper was superior to single-ply, to say nothing of the political squabbles we got into.

But I loved her in spite of these issues, and maybe even more because of them. For the first time, Nora had demonstrated to me that a strong relationship didn't require an absence of strife, that two people could hold opposing viewpoints (whether on toilet paper or public policy) and still be deeply in love and committed to their partnership.

"Can I ask you something?" I said to Lou.

"Sure," she said.

"Do you still love Rob?"

She froze, and for a split second I thought I had offended her. Then she walked to the mantel, set the picture on it, and turned back to me. "Don't you, Jim? Once you love someone all the way, you love them forever. That's just how it goes."

TWENTY-THREE

Winter 2010

That Christmas Eve, Lou and I decided to host dinner. Nora had never spent any extended amount of time with you and Lou, and I was—let's just say a bit apprehensive. In response, I may or may not have had a few too many eggnogs, each containing more bourbon than egg, and might have been a bit tipsy when Nora arrived.

She was wearing a sweaterdress, a delicate gold necklace, and another pair of tall boots. "Don't *you* look amazing," I said, kissing her hello.

She kissed me back, then looked at me with amusement. "That's some breath you've got going on. Trying to drink away the jitters?"

I grinned like a fool. "Me? Never."

"Introduce me to everyone," she said, putting her hand on the back of my arm to direct me into my own house, "then go find some rolls and eat as many as you can so I don't find you passed out under the Christmas tree an hour from now."

When I had told my father about Nora, he declared that the only person I should be having a relationship with was Lou, whom he was quite fond of. "You have a child together, for cripes' sake," he muttered, throwing his hands up in the air. "Is this how you kids do it these days? What's next? You all go live together on a commune and start adding more wives? If that's your plan, you're going to need another job. Even an engineer couldn't afford more than one woman."

But Nora cornered my father, who was sitting by the fireplace—"Javier? So nice to finally meet you. I've heard so many great things about you from James"—and suddenly he was singing a sweeter tune. I could all but see him thinking, *Well she's fantastic. What on God's green earth is she doing with my son?*

And when you saw Nora, you lifted your arms for her to hold you. She hoisted you onto her hip and the two of you followed me into the kitchen, where we found Lou desecrating an innocent pan of yams with mini marshmallows. "Hello, hello!" she said to Nora, waving with fluff-covered fingers. "Welcome!"

"Thank you so much for having me," said Nora. "How can I help?"

"We've got it!" chirped Lou, like the oven timer wasn't going off in the background and the green beans weren't smoking on the stove. She was more nervous than I was, even after I turned off the timer and pulled the beans from the burner, and she kept looking at Nora as though she were about to drop you.

"Please, sit, make yourself comfortable," she said, her voice an octave too high. "There's a bar set up in the three-season room, and appetizers in the dining room."

"Thank you. Wanna get some food, Emerson?" Nora asked, and you nodded.

"No cookies!" Lou called after the two of you. "Too much sugar and she turns into a monster."

Nora swiveled. "Got it. No cookies." She pressed the tip of your nose with her finger, and the two of you laughed like you were sharing a private joke.

Lou didn't love Nora. She wasn't rude, but neither was she her usual effusive self around her. Nora knew it and made it clear that while she would be cordial to Lou, she wasn't about to expend an iota of mental energy devoted to Lou's opinion of her. I worried that this forecasted future problems for our household, even as I envied Nora; I myself had never quite managed to not care what other people thought of me. As I watched the two of them exchange stale niceties over drinks, I wondered if they would ever come to actually enjoy each other's company. Then I wondered why this mattered to me. If they were fine with it, shouldn't I be, too?

Dinner went as well as anyone could have hoped. Your uncle Dan drank enough that I looked sober in comparison, and my uncle José and aunt Marie left as soon as the meal was over, which was longer than we had expected them to stay. When I showed my father our Christmas tree—it was the first I had ever put up in my house, and the first tree of my life that wasn't fabricated from petroleum—he responded by saying we had too many presents stashed beneath. Not only was it a fire hazard, he explained, it was a sure sign you would grow up spoiled, and that would be our fault—never mind that when it came to you, he was the most egregious gift-giver of all. Nora managed to defuse the situation by saying that her parents had spoiled her rotten, and yet she had turned out to be a minimalist (true: she didn't own a single thing she didn't use on a regular basis).

After dinner, everyone but Lou decamped to the living room. I found her in the kitchen, washing a platter.

"I thought we were going to do the dishes later on?" I asked.

"I just needed a minute."

Outside, snow was falling in thick, wet flakes, which had begun to form peaks on the windowsill. I touched her shoulder. "You okay? Is this about Nora?"

"Not at all."

"My father, then?" I pressed. "I know he can be difficult sometimes."

"If that's your idea of difficult, let's trade lives," she said, placing the platter on a towel.

Right—her family, I thought. The holidays had always been hard for her. I was about to ask if she had spoken with her uncle, who had recently gotten sober and had been making an effort to connect with her, when she turned off the faucet and said, "I heard from Rob this morning."

"You did? When were you going to tell me?"

"Now," she said plainly.

"What did he say?" I asked, my tone betraying my fear. "What did *you* say?"

She shrugged. "Merry Christmas."

"That's it?"

"That's it."

"When's the last time you heard from him?"

"Do we have to go into it right now?"

"You're the one who brought it up."

"You asked if everything was okay. I figured you'd want to know that it has nothing to do with your girlfriend. Who, for the record, is lovely."

Nothing to do with my girlfriend, and everything to do with Rob. I should have been happy for her; if he had emailed, then he didn't despise her. But there was no rationalizing away my racing pulse and the adrenaline pumping through my veins. Email now—but what next? She still loved him. He probably still loved her. I understood this; really, I envied it. But if they reunited, would she move back to New York with you—leaving me here alone or requiring me to move and leave Nora behind?

"Thanks," I said weakly.

Lou dried her hands on the dish towel. "Don't even give it another thought, Jim. Let's go join the others and try to enjoy ourselves, okay?"

But I did think about it. A lot—and even after Lou told me that aside from the Christmas email, her correspondence with Rob had been limited to brief exchanges regarding alimony and attorney fees.

Tension had been building between Lou and me, subtly but surely since right after Nora and I began dating. Lou used to tease me when I forgot things; now, if I didn't bring milk home after work, you'd think I had just sentenced you to a week without food. This drove me mad, since she herself was incapable of following a basic grocery list. And I couldn't understand why she insisted on getting up at six in the morning even after she'd gone to bed late—after all, she was the worst sort of grouch when she skimped on sleep.

Bigger fish went unfried. For example, we couldn't agree on whether or not you would start preschool the following summer. You were doing great with Lauren, the sitter who watched you a few hours a day, Lou argued, whereas I felt that a part-time preschool program was the best way to tap into your full genius.

Rob added yet another layer of tension. What did his reaching out to Lou mean for her—and for all of us?

TWENTY-FOUR

Spring–Summer 2011

Months went by, and nothing and everything changed. You turned two, and we threw you another party, this time with a few children from the neighborhood as well as our extended family. You began to use the tiny plastic toilet we bought you and speak in increasingly complex sentences ("Daddy, that's your pen!" "Mommy, I don't like that cereal!").

Lou didn't mention Rob, and I didn't ask. I met Nora's parents in February; in April, she and I went to Paris for five glorious days. We had coq au vin with a bottle of Bordeaux on Rue Balzac in the Eighth Arrondissement. We toured the modern art gallery at Centre Pompidou, and saw Picasso's collection of West African masks at his eponymous museum. We hung a lock on the Pont des Arts, even though the bridge was crumbling beneath the weight of so much love.

When we returned, Nora sat me down and told me that as much as she adored you, she never wanted children of her own. She wasn't so sure she wanted to get married anytime soon, either. "Neither has anything to do with you, James," she told me, squeezing my hand.

"Of course they do," I argued. I'll confess, I had spent a good part of our Parisian vacation thinking about how nice it would be to give you a sibling and have a child with Nora.

"No," she insisted. "I've always felt this way."

"And I'm not enough to change it," I said, dejected.

"That's not fair, James, and you know it."

"Isn't it?"

We argued for the better part of an hour. Nora, skilled litigator that she was, was ready to go at it with me until we reached an accord. I wanted to go to bed—and I did.

As I tossed and turned on Nora's sofa, I recalled how I had said no to Kathryn when she had asked me to have a child with her. At the time, I thought something was missing between us. Lo and behold, all these years later I knew that what was missing was my ability to fully buy into our relationship.

This wasn't the same—Nora was far more mature than I had been when I said no to Kathryn. Even so, it was enough to help me see that I should accept Nora's decision and stay with her rather than jeopardize what we had together. Around midnight, I climbed back into bed with her. "I'm sorry, sweetheart," I whispered.

Nora, who had been asleep on her stomach, turned over and draped her arm over my chest. "Thank you," she murmured. "I don't want this to be a deal breaker, but I don't want to lie to you, either."

"You shouldn't have to," I said, and wrapped my arms around her. "I want to be with you, and that's all that matters."

~

One blazing day in July, I had just returned from the grocery store when Lou announced she had good news.

Gone were the days of one-bag shopping; four hauls from the car to the kitchen had left me doused in sweat. "Tell me more," I said as I wiped my forehead with a paper towel.

"Yvonne just offered to let us use her house in Grand Marais for a week next month!" she exclaimed as she pulled a sack of potatoes from one of the bags I had set on the counter.

I eyed her skeptically. "You do know that's where I used to go on vacation with Rob and his family, yes?"

"I've been to his aunt's cottage. This would be a totally different week than when Nancy and Bob usually go up."

The Logans always vacationed the week of July Fourth, which had already passed. I knew this because I had joined them every summer from the time I was twelve to the year I graduated from college. His aunt's cottage was a postcard sort of place perched on a sandy hill overlooking Lake Superior, with miles of woods directly behind it. I had spent hundreds of hours of my life beachcombing and hiking there—with the man who had once been my closest friend.

"I don't know, Lou," I said. "Couldn't we go anywhere else?"

"Another place would cost thousands of dollars. This is free, and it would be so good for Em. Sun, fresh air, a chance to experience a piece of her father's childhood." She had opened the fridge to put something away and called back to me. "You can bring Nora."

I was feeling winded, and I pulled a chair away from the table and sat down. "I don't know if I have vacation time left after Paris. Maybe Jennifer could go with you? Or what about Cassie and Ben?" I said, referring to our neighbor and her son, with whom Lou had become close. "Then you would have company, and Em would have someone to play with."

"I don't really know Cassie well enough to travel with her. Anyway, I was hoping we could take a family vacation."

I wiped my brow again, this time with the back of my arm, and stood. "Can I give it a little thought before I say yes?"

"Of course."

But I already knew that I would be able to get the time off. The real issue was that I was fairly convinced that revisiting the vacation spot I had shared with Rob would inevitably be traumatic.

Or perhaps it would be healthy, I thought. Our friendship was over, but that didn't mean the memories we had were of no value. And as Lou had said, it would be an opportunity to share part of my childhood with you—the good part.

"Don't overthink it," said Nora, who couldn't join us because of a trial she was working on, when she kissed me good-bye. "Just go and try to enjoy yourself." I kissed her back and promised I would at least try.

~

You know how sometimes you picture something in your mind a particular way, but when you see it again, you're disappointed to discover that what you thought was blue is in fact green, and what should be left side was on the right all along? As we drove down the steep road leading into Grand Marais, I felt a curious mix of anticipation and trepidation.

Nearly everything about my life had changed since I had last visited with Rob. Yet the town was almost exactly the same. Sure, the tavern where Rob and I used to down baskets of battered whitefish and chips had been updated with a fresh coat of paint and a new name. But the post office was untouched, as were the bait and tackle and the old gas station. I blinked, remembering how Rob had run out of gas just half a mile from the station. Instead of walking to buy a canister of gas, we had the harebrained idea to put the car in neutral and let it roll down the hill. We almost ended up in the lake, and that was after we narrowly missed a collision with a pickup truck.

My throat tightened as the enormous bay the town was built around came into view. And just beyond the bay was Lake Superior, so vast you could mistake it for the sea—and indeed, when Bobby had told me that it was the Atlantic the first summer I came with them, I had actually believed him until Rob laughed and told me he was pulling my leg.

The town felt like the grave of an old friend who was still alive. It had been nearly three years since Rob and I had last spoken; it may as well have been three decades. There was so much that had happened and so much I had wanted to tell him.

"Turn right," Lou instructed, reading from the directions she had printed out (hard to believe that in a few short years, we would both own cell phones that served as both map and navigator). "Then left, and . . . keep going . . . and here we are!"

I pulled onto the dirt drive leading to a single-story cottage with white cedar shakes. It had a large wraparound porch and a yard adorned with all sorts of shrubs and flowering plants. A handful of tiny fairy houses were nestled in the garden, which you immediately spotted and ran to examine.

The cottage was standard-issue charming: white walls with unpainted wooden beams spanning the ceiling, a slip-covered sofa and rattan chairs, watercolor paintings of the lake and seashells. Here and there were items that made the house so clearly Yvonne's: a giant dream catcher hanging from one of the beams, a large chunk of purple quartz in the center of the dining room table, and books everywhere—beside the sofa, stacked at the end of the kitchen island, piled beneath the beds.

The kitchen and living room were connected, and the back of the house was made almost entirely of windows, save for a pair of

French doors. Lou unlatched them, and we walked out onto the deck. There was a hammock strung between two pines in the small backyard. Ten feet beyond the yard was the beach, which was on the bay. It was impossible to see another house unless you walked to the water's edge.

As Lou and I stood with our bare feet in the lake, she turned to me triumphantly. "See? I told you this would be perfect."

To my left, you were twirling in circles to a chorus of gulls and the rhythm of the early evening surf. To my right, an invisible Rob stood beside me, but I would have to do my best not to let him overshadow this vacation. I smiled at Lou. "And you were right."

~

Old haunts conjure up familiar ghosts, and I spent the first few days glancing over my shoulder, like Rob or one of the Logans would appear at any moment. After all, here was the bay where Rob had caught a twenty-inch bass. There was the diner where Bobby went every single day for a chocolate malted. And just over the way was the trail where Rob and Wisnewski rode four-wheelers, even though Nancy said they would kill themselves, if a bear didn't beat them to it. Every turn held another memory, but no sooner did I remember the good than the bad came rushing back.

I knew our sunny, schedule-free days would be over as soon as they began, so I worked hard to focus my attention on you and Lou. The minute I was alone, my thoughts returned to Rob. I hadn't tried to reach out to him since the email that he shot down with a single no. I suspected that extra effort would not lead him to forgive me. But there was more than a simple apology that remained to be said.

~

"I like to see you looking like this," said Lou. We were lying on the seemingly endless stretch of beach on Lake Superior's southern side. Rocks of all sizes, some glittering, others flat and gray, all ancient, were scattered across the sand. We had cleared a batch for our towels and a large beach umbrella, which you were asleep beneath.

"Looking like what?" I said.

"You know," she said, her face barely visible under her floppy straw hat. "You look like . . . yourself."

"And what's that, exactly? Nerdish? Flabby? Incompetent?"

"Stop it."

I grinned. "I'm just getting started."

"You look relaxed, Jim. Have you thought about your next book? This would be a good place to get started, don't you think?"

I had been propped up on my elbows, and I could feel my chest beginning to burn. This far north, the weather could become chilly without warning, even in August. But we had been sweating off our sunscreen for days and had yet to see a cloud. I sighed and flipped onto my stomach, then turned my head toward her. "The thing is, I'm not writing anymore."

Even behind her hat and sunglasses, Lou's disapproval was evident. "Since when?"

Should I try to put a bow on the ugly truth? And for what? I had stopped trying to impress Lou some time ago. I had stopped trying to impress anyone, really, unless me trying to wow you with my Elmo impression counted. "I don't know. It's been a few years now," I admitted.

"You haven't written for that long?" she said, making it sound far worse than it really was.

"Yes, but I don't really care," I said. "Writing feels like a younger man's game. At this juncture in life, with Emerson to think about, and my relationship with Nora, and work—well, I don't see how I can manage it. And just as well; I've lost my drive. I mean, I've been keeping a journal, and that's been enjoyable."

She pursed her lips, examined me for a minute, then said, "But that's your lifelong dream, Jim. You don't just *lose* that."

"Sure you do," I scoffed. "I'm living proof it's possible."

She eyed me skeptically. "Are you sure you're not just hung up on your own performance? You could have finished any one of the novels you were working on. Or written another in the meantime. I just wonder if you let fear hold you back."

"Don't psychoanalyze me, Lou," I warned.

"I'm not. I just want you to be happy and healthy. Have you been feeling okay?"

"Never better."

"Really? You barely touched your burger last night, and you've been losing weight."

Was this true? I supposed the burger bit was, but I had been tired. I was down a few pounds, but that was almost always the case in the summer. My appetite was perfectly normal.

"You've been slouching around a bit, too," she added.

"Slouching around? I'm not exactly known for my good posture, nor my radiant positivity." I shaded my eyes with a hand. "Listen, Lou, I appreciate your concern. I really do. But believe me—I'm as happy as I've ever been."

"Okay . . . ," she said, tilting her head quizzically. "But what occurs to me just now is that maybe I'm making you a little unhappy. After all, I dragged you here when you wanted to be home with Nora."

"She told me to go, and it turned out to be a great idea," I pointed out.

"I'm glad. Still, what I'm getting at is that maybe it would be better if you and Nora lived together."

"Pardon me?" I sputtered.

"It wouldn't have to be full time if you didn't want; we could work something out so that you spent almost as much time with Em as you always have. But living with me around the clock isn't good for you, Jim." She smoothed an invisible wrinkle on the front of her navy swimsuit. "I suppose you don't *have* to live with Nora. I could get an apartment for me and Emerson, and then Nora would feel more comfortable coming to our house. Or something. I just sense that things would be better if you and I had our own spaces."

"But the house is yours," I said. On the one hand, her suggestion made me sad. Yes, we had been bickering more than we used to, but I actually *liked* living with Lou; almost all the things that had made me love her kept me liking her, too.

On the other hand, it was as though someone had just dropped a key into my cage. The idea of living with Nora—officially, rather than this back-and-forth routine we had been doing for a full year—was appealing. And I suspected Nora would agree.

I stared out at the lake, which was pale and calm. A freighter grew smaller and smaller in the distance, until it finally disappeared from sight. "How will we manage that?" I said after a minute.

"The way we always have. We're flexible people, Jim. Aside from love, that's probably the primary reason Em's doing as well as she is."

I frowned. "Two homes for her, though? I'm not so sure that will keep her doing well."

"She's young, and two good homes are better than one bad."

"Our house isn't bad," I protested.

Lou gave me a small smile. "No, it's not. But if we want to keep it that way, something's got to change." She stood and shook the sand from her body. "Do you mind if I go for a walk?"

"Not at all."

"Thanks. I'll be back in a few."

I watched Lou stroll down the beach, past a pile of driftwood and around the bend, until she, like the ship, was no longer visible. *I owe her so much,* I thought as she came back into view. She had given me her love—only for a short while, true, but at great expense. She had given me a child. In many ways, she had given me the best years of her life.

As she walked toward me, growing larger on the horizon with every step, I thought, *There may be something I can give her in return.* I wasn't sure how exactly I would do it. But I had an idea of how I could try.

On the last day of our visit, as you and Lou napped in the hammock, I took out a legal pad and wrote a short letter. My handwriting was nearly illegible ("What is handwriting?" you will probably wonder as you read this), but Rob had been deciphering my chicken scratch for most of his life, I reasoned—at least up until he kicked me out of it. Before I could second-guess myself, I went to the post office, bought a book of stamps, and sent it on its way.

When we got home the next day, I wrote another letter, slightly longer this time, and mailed it, too.

The following week, I wrote a very long letter, and then a short one again, and so on and so forth, until I had mailed eight letters in two months.

~

Every letter was worded differently but contained essentially the same message:

> *I know you can't forgive me, and I don't expect you to. But you can forgive Lou. Please, even if you don't want to. Even if it's the hardest thing you'll ever have to do. It was* me *who led us down the wrong path, not her. I was too blind and stupid to understand that what she needed was to heal—not another wound. Now I understand that what I thought was a single act set a much larger chain of events in motion, and that has directly impacted the lives of every person I most care about in this world.*

Especially you and Lou.

Lou and I have a daughter, and I know that probably tears you apart even as it brings me joy. But I believe that if you meet our child, it would not hurt so much. She is so much of Lou, and you will adore her.

You and Lou were happy once. I used to envy that. Now I see that it took work, even if your love sometimes kept it from feeling that way.

Lou still loves you, Rob. She always will; she told me as much. I have a feeling you still love her, too. If that's true, please—even if it takes you next to forever—give it another shot. Don't make the biggest mistake of your life because of me.

TWENTY-FIVE

2012

"I! Want! Mamaaaaaa!"

I wanted Mama, too. You had been sick with strep throat and a double ear infection for days. Unfortunately, those days had coincided with Lou's four-day trip to New York, where she was meeting with her agent and seeing friends. And Rob, I hoped, though I didn't ask for fear of tipping my hand. I had not heard back from him, but my letters had not been returned. Knowing Rob as I once had, I suspected this meant he was mulling over what I had said.

"I can come home," Lou told me when I called to tell her how you were doing, but I insisted I had it under control. Now, as I attempted to get you to swallow thick pink goop that would kill the bacteria at the root of your distress, I was forced to admit that I was a liar and quite possibly an unfit parent.

"Emmy, love, will you open for me?" Nora said, crouching in front of you.

Nora and I had moved into a two-bedroom condo in her complex the previous fall. You spent weekends with us as well as the occasional weeknight when Lou had plans. But your main house was the one I had purchased, which now, for all intents and purposes, belonged to you and Lou.

It was strange to have to knock on my own front door. Still, splitting homes had worked out as Lou had anticipated (which is to say far better than I had been expecting). You had taken to the whole situation like it was completely normal, and any lingering tension between Lou and me dissipated not long after I moved.

Even if it had not gone well, I'm not so sure I would have reverted to our previous arrangement. Because I was, as Lou teased, "in looooooove." Living with Nora was not always a cakewalk. My standards of cleanliness did not meet hers, to say the least, and she was vocal about it. She read legal briefs at breakfast, in the bathroom, and even while we were supposed to be watching a movie together (and I, in turn, was vocal about this). But now I understood that these were normal conflicts, not a sign I had chosen the wrong partner.

"No!" you shouted, and slapped the plastic cup from Nora's hand, sending a spray of bubblegum-colored liquid across the bathroom.

"That's a bummer," said Nora, completely unfazed. She leaned in toward you conspiratorially. "What if I give you a popsicle after you take your medicine? That would help your throat feel better."

The demon in possession of your body immediately vacated at the mention of high-fructose corn syrup. "Okay," you agreed.

"Lou doesn't like her to have sweets," I pointed out. "Especially when she's sick."

"Lou isn't here," Nora said pleasantly. "And when you have strep, that's about the only thing that you can manage. I bought a pack of popsicles on the way home from work."

"Man, you are really the best."

She grinned. "I know."

After you were in bed, Nora and I sat side by side in our own bed. She was reviewing a brief, while I was reading a book. From the other room, you began to whimper. Within thirty seconds, you were crying.

"Want me to go?" said Nora.

"No, I've got it."

You were wailing by the time I reached you, and I rushed to your side. "What's wrong, love? What is it?" I asked, stroking your forehead, which was damp from sweat and tears.

You shook your head.

"Do your ears hurt?" I asked.

More vigorous shaking, more tears.

"You want water?"

You wailed in response.

I was starting to get desperate. "Your throat? Your nose? What is it, Em?"

You looked up at me with huge eyes. "Hug me, Daddy," you whimpered.

As it so often happens in life, the right answer happened to be the most obvious one. As I held you in my arms until you fell asleep again, I thought about how much you had changed in three short years. I promised you the world the day you were born, but as many a man before me, I had since learned that it is far easier to become a father than to be one.

Yet how lucky I was, that you became my daughter when you did. Like my mother, my father had not been affectionate. Perhaps if he himself had been born at a later time, when expectations for a parent were different, when it was acceptable and even expected that a man was to be tender with his own child, he could have loved me the way I loved you.

~

That September, Lou turned thirty-seven, and I turned forty. But how could I possibly be forty, I wondered the morning of my birthday, when I was just twenty-five a few days ago?

I peered in the mirror, trying to pinpoint the ravages of time. I was still barely gray, with only a few strands near my temples, but there was a flock of fine lines around my eyes that guaranteed I would never again be carded when ordering a drink. And while I was pleased to not yet have developed my father's drum of a gut, my once-muscled legs were not anymore. But I could mark the next decade of my life by joining a gym and lifting weights, like Rob always told me I should. I shook my head and turned away from the mirror, vowing to be more proactive in the coming years.

Nora threw a birthday party for me at our condo. At my request, it was a small affair—though let's face it, it couldn't have been any other way. As my family expanded, my circle of friends grew smaller, and so the usual suspects were in attendance: you and Lou, my father and Miriam, Pascal and Winnie, Nessa, Craig, and a couple other coworkers, Yvonne, Cassie, and a handful of Nora's friends.

As I greeted this person and got a drink for that one, I could not help ruminating about who was *not* there. My mother, for example. In the years since her passing, the rough edges of our relationship had grown smoother in my mind, and now I only missed her. Wisnewski, too, whose birthday would have been in June. How great it would have been to hear him holler birthday wishes at me.

And of course, Rob.

He had turned forty in May; I wondered how he had celebrated. There was so much I wanted to know. There was so much I wanted to say. I was still waiting to hear back from him—or if he would not directly respond to me, receive some sign that he was considering what I had written to him about Lou.

How he would adore you, I thought as I stopped to watch you in the living room. As the party went on around you, you were building a domed, multitiered building out of magnetic tiles. You positioned the last tile, took a look at your creation, then knocked it down and began to create a new, even more complex structure. You had that perfect mix of intelligence and creativity that Rob loved. And you were a miniature Lou, so much so that every once in a while I would look at you and think, *She could have been Rob's child.*

After we ate, Nora brought out a cake that she had baked with you the night before. It was dripping with chocolate ganache and coated in rainbow sprinkles—your finishing touch. You sat on my lap, with Nora just behind me, her hand on my shoulder. Lou was across the way, beside my father, both of them smiling widely at me. Candles blazing, the people closest to me in this world sang "Happy Birthday," and I grinned like a fool and tried not to cry because it was so wonderful and so disarming—almost like being transported back to a moment in childhood that I had not actually lived through.

I blew out the candles, and everyone cheered. "Thank you all for being here with me," I said, too choked up to manage more. It is so easy to go through your days stewing about someone stealing your parking spot without giving the same attention to your child's arms around your neck, to grumble about the ever-increasing cost of groceries without realizing just how good it is to have warm toast and a fresh cup of coffee while sitting across from the one you love.

But on that day—if only in that moment—I felt the full expanse of my blessings. Life had not turned out as I had hoped or expected it might. I don't know that I even had a clear vision in mind when I stepped into my twenties, but at forty, I at least knew that I had abandoned my dream of writing a book, which felt like a new failure each time I had to admit it aloud.

Smaller goals, too, had been discarded: I had never attempted a hundred-mile bike ride, for example, or lived in a big city, even though the opportunity had presented itself.

But it's not too late, I thought as I bit into a piece of the cake you had made just for me.

I would appreciate my life more. I would do more and love more in the years that followed. I would finish the things I had started.

~

The party petered out, until only Nora, Lou, Pascal, Winnie, and my father remained. We were standing in the kitchen when you wandered in from the living room, rubbing your eyes. I remember thinking I, too, was exhausted.

I held my arms out to you. "Come here, *pequeñita*," I said, using one of the nicknames my father had given you. It means "little one" in Spanish, and you were a tiny thing—surely no more than thirty-five pounds. But no sooner had I hoisted you into my arms than you slipped through my grasp and fell onto the ground.

You let out a yelp, then looked up at me from the tile with anger. "*Daddy!* You *dropped* me!"

What could I say? I *had* dropped you, which was the very thing I had told myself not to do the day you were born. It had not been a miscalculation or a result of you going boneless, as you sometimes did when you were upset. It was that I had not been able to maintain a grip on you—not with my arms, and not with my hands.

"One too many," said Pascal. His laughter was canned. "Happens to the best of us."

"Yeah," I said, trying to manage a laugh myself as I bent down to attend to you. In fact, I had been so busy making sure that everyone else's cup was full that I had only sipped one drink hours earlier. "I'm sorry, Em," I said, tilting your chin up with a finger. "Daddy needs to exercise more."

"Hmph," you said, arms crossed over your chest.

"Extra book before bed?" I said, though books would put you even further past your bedtime, which would likely lead you to have a complete meltdown before you passed out.

"Mommy puts me to bed!" you cried.

"Emerson, that's not very nice. It was an accident, and it's Daddy's birthday," scolded Lou. She looked at me and mouthed "sorry" like the only thing we were dealing with was a minor tantrum. (I would later learn that she hadn't seen me drop you and thought nothing of it at the time.)

But my father had seen everything. "Son?" he said, putting a hand on my shoulder. "You okay?"

Anxiety was spreading through me like spilled ink. Somehow I knew that I was not, in fact, okay. "I don't know, Pops," I said.

TWENTY-SIX

2013

I don't care if lovers swear it to each other and the devout sling it around as a future reward for their faithfulness. As far as I'm concerned, forever is the worst long time. At least with adversity and illness, there's a general idea of what to expect. We don't know a damn thing about the uncharted horrors of eternity.

Yet one day I was walking through our neighborhood with you; your warm little hand was in mine and the sun was shining on our backs. You stopped to examine a pill bug, which you gently set back on the ground. You bent to pick a dandelion, then to sniff a tulip that was the most extraordinary shade of purple.

And I thought to myself, *God—if there is a forever, please let this be what it feels like.*

I digress. I was not okay, as you know. And yet it took the better part of a year to confirm that. I spent the first few months in denial. "You're as healthy as can be expected for a man your age," said the prepubescent medical resident I had seen for my annual physical exam.

Well, that makes sense, I thought. If I had not been operating like I was still twenty-five, rather than the forty-year-old I had become, I would not have dropped you. After all, one of my colleagues, who was also in her forties, had recently had a seizure in the middle of a department store. A dozen tests later, it was determined she didn't have epilepsy or a brain tumor. In fact, her doctors couldn't find a single thing that was wrong with her. It was, they speculated, just one of those random things that mostly seemed to happen to people who were no longer young.

So I sought ways to stave off middle-aged decay. I began seeing Nora's personal trainer, a brute who sent me home with shaking legs and a sense of general incompetence. I traded alcohol for protein shakes and ate an obscene amount of egg whites and leafy greens. I even began taking multivitamins, which I had long regarded as encapsulated snake oil.

And wasn't the slight bulge in my biceps evidence that it was not for naught? Was waking at five without an alarm not evidence that I was bursting with vitality? I had color in my cheeks, a spring in my step, and new hope for my future.

I was the picture of perfect health—except that I found I could no longer type for more than ten to fifteen minutes before the words stopped appearing on the page as they should. My legs cramped, particularly at night, which is why I ended up getting out of bed at an hour that was too early for even Lou. That spring in my step? It was more like me overlifting my knees to compensate for my leaden legs. And as Lou had ascertained long before I ever did, eating was no longer all that fun. In fact, it felt a lot like a chore.

The signs were there, and still I put my head down and plowed forward.

~

Four was an explosive year for your mind; it was astounding to see you make the leap to a fully cognizant being. You had questions—so many questions. How do spiders make the silk for their webs? Do plants sleep? Do all animals have blood? What happened to woolly mammoths?

Bedtime was your favorite time to remind me of how little I knew. "What are people made out of?" you asked me one night.

"You know," I said, trying to figure out how best to explain human anatomy to a four-year-old. "Bones and blood and tissue. And lots and lots of water."

You were clutching your stuffed rabbit, who was already more gray than white, and bare in patches. I had bought the rabbit for you at a toy store in New York the day after you were born. At the time, it was almost as long as you were. Now it wasn't even the length of your torso. "Yeah, but what is all of *that* made out of?" you said insistently. "Where does it *come from?*"

I thought about this for a moment, trying to recall what I had read in a book a few years earlier. "Well, Em, experts think that much of what we are comes from the inside of a giant star that exploded billions of years ago. The star's parts contained material that makes up the parts in your body. The calcium in your teeth and bones, the iron in your blood, the carbon in your genes—"

"What are genes?"

"Um, like tiny Legos that make up your entire body. Parents pass them on to their children, so you come from my genes and Mommy's."

"Whoa."

I smiled. "I know. Pretty neat, right? Anyway, all that comes from the inside of a star. So we're basically made of star stuff."

"But not like those stars," you said, pointing to the plastic glow-in-the-dark constellations I had stuck to your ceiling a few months earlier.

"Nope," I said, pulling the cord to lift the wood blind over the window next to your bed.

Why is this blind so hard to open? And—oof—when did Emerson get so heavy? I thought as you threw yourself on my back to look over my shoulder at the night sky.

"More like those," I said, pointing up and out. It was early in the evening, and the moon would be full in another day or two, so we could only see a few stars.

"So *that's* what we're made of," you said knowingly and tightened your grip.

"Sort of, yeah."

"Cool."

"Isn't it? You and I are going to have to take a better look on a dark night."

I kissed your forehead, then tucked you in. As I pulled the blanket up to your chin, just how you liked me to, there it was again: a deep, base understanding that something was wrong. My hands and forearms felt too weak for someone who had just spent many months doing push-ups and planks. The twitching I felt in my muscles had nothing to do with my caffeine consumption. Something more ominous than middle age was at hand. As I said good night to you from your doorway, I understood that there would be no wishing away this ominous thing. Whatever it was, it was time to face it.

∼

I returned to the same health clinic. "It's likely a common problem, such as an iron deficiency," said the primary care physician who had been called in after I told the receptionist that I refused to see another resident.

"Didn't you just check for that on my physical exam?" I asked, not able to conceal my irritation.

"Oh right," he said, frowning at the computer screen that he had spent more time looking at than me. "Well, it could be anything. A thyroid problem, Lyme disease, a small tumor."

"Fantastic," I said.

He swiveled on his stool. "It beats the alternative."

"Which is . . . ?"

"A more serious condition," he said opaquely. "We'll cross that bridge if and when we get there."

There would be no "we"; I was sent to cross the bridge with a neurologist. I could not recall having ever spent more than twenty minutes with a physician. My neurology appointment lasted almost two hours. I went through reflex and strength tests and an exhaustive recalling of my health history (which had been, up until the previous year, completely normal, though there was the issue of my mother's early death).

When that was over, the neurologist—a fit woman in her fifties whose name escapes me—told me she wanted me to have more tests, including another blood panel, an MRI, and an electromyogram, which involved inserting tiny needles into my muscles to see if they had become too lazy to respond to stimuli.

"What is all this for?" I asked her.

"I want to rule out certain conditions."

"Such as what?" As with the previous physician, I was running low on patience.

"Spinal muscular atrophy. Or ALS," she said.

"ALS? Isn't that—"

"Amyotrophic lateral sclerosis. It's also known as Lou Gehrig's disease. After the baseball player who—"

"Yes, I know," I said. I sounded pathetic, even to myself. I had been thinking—what *was* I thinking? I don't know. A tumor on my spine, maybe. Multiple sclerosis.

"As I said, James, this could be a lot of things. But twitching and persistent, progressive muscle weakness on both sides of your body is indicative of this particular disease."

That was the last I saw of her, too. Two days after I had an MRI, she called to say that it looked normal. "That's good, right?" I said.

"Normally, yes. But in this case, I thought perhaps we would see some lesions or some such that would explain your weakness and fasciculations. That is, the twitching you're experiencing."

"And my electromyogram?"

"I'm afraid it appears you have definitive signs of muscle atrophy and nerve damage. That's a sign that you may have motor neuron degeneration. I'd like to send you to one of my colleagues."

Yet even when the receptionist called to tell me to bring a loved one to my next appointment—"It helps to have someone else take notes while you listen," she said, entirely too cheerfully—I still hoped for the best, because that is what you do when you have a family and no fewer than four thousand other reasons to want to remain among the living.

The specialist's name was Sarah Stevens. She looked to be about the same age as the resident.

"Let's hear it," I said as soon as I sat down.

"James, I like your attitude." Unlike the other doctors I had seen, she didn't bother turning on the computer. She didn't have a clipboard or chart with her, either. Based on the tenor of her voice, I decided that she was probably my peer and just had one of those preternaturally young faces. "From what I've seen, it seems there's a strong possibility that you may have ALS."

"May?"

"Unfortunately, there's no blood test or any other definitive test for ALS. It's a disease that makes itself known through symptoms. If your symptoms do, in fact, become worse, then we will have confirmation. I can say with some certainty that what you're experiencing, and what your test results have shown, fit the bill."

After my last neurology appointment, this diagnosis could not be called a surprise. And yet it was like I had just been sucker punched, and I let out a wretched noise.

Nora put her arm around my shoulders and pulled me close. "It's all right," she whispered. "It's all right." She kept saying it, like she was trying to convince us all, and as much as I appreciated the effort, I now knew that it was never going to be all right again, and I would have to spend the rest of whatever was left of my life dealing with that.

"James," said Dr. Stevens again, "I know this is terrible to hear, and I am so incredibly sorry. But I want you to know that there is much we can do to improve your quality of life over these next years. There's an FDA-approved medication called Rilutek that we can consider for treatment, and together we can explore the possibility of pursuing a clinical trial."

"It's fatal, though," I said flatly.

Her gaze was steady. "Yes. I'm afraid ALS is fatal."

~

It's funny, when someone close to you dies, it's almost impossible not to reflect on your own impending mortality. Death is nothing if not a reminder that no matter how long it may be, life is always too short.

But after the shock wears off, a sense of invincibility sets in. Aren't the odds slim, you might think, that I would die soon after someone else I knew and loved did? Certainly that was my reaction to Wisnewski's passing. If I'm honest, I'm pretty sure I spent several years thinking, *Poor Wisnewski; maybe one day I'll get to thank him for getting that early death thing out of the way for all of us.*

It's a shame that death doesn't actually observe a calendar or strictly adhere to statistical probability. Unless you live next to a nuclear plant or in a war zone, there is little correlation between your life span and that of those around you. It happens when it will, and like Wisnewski before me, my number had been called. I would have to wait in line for a while, but there was no mistaking which line I was in.

So many of my memories of that day and those that followed were washed away by confusion and grief. I do recall that as I left the doctor's office, one of my first instincts was to pick up the phone and call Rob, just as he had called me when his company collapsed. Mine was a different sort of disaster, but he must have felt a similar sense of shock and loss. But I had not heard back from him after sending him my letters, and I knew my call would not be welcome.

I remember sobbing in the car, too, and Nora pulling into a restaurant parking lot, climbing onto my lap, and sobbing with me. I remember driving myself to the house and trying not to break down when you came flying down the stairs at me, delighted that I had come to visit on an unscheduled day.

And I remember Lou's face—stoic, knowing—as I walked into the kitchen, took her hands, and told her that the very long story she and I now shared with you would soon belong to the two of you alone.

TWENTY-SEVEN

October–November 2013

"Of *course* he'll come live here," said Lou sharply. "This is his *home*. He needs to be with his daughter."

It was Sunday night, and Nora and I had dropped you off per the usual custody split, if the informal agreement I had with Lou could be called that. I should have known something was up when Lou suggested you turn on cartoons, given that she believed television sapped one's gray matter. (I was fairly certain you had gray matter to spare, which is why I may have let you spend a bit too much time vegetating in front of the tube when you were staying with Nora and me.)

As soon as you were out of the room, Lou asked us what our long-term plan was and if I might consider returning home. Nora had scoffed, Lou had balked at her scoffing, and instantly a barbed wire fence had been erected within the respectful distance they had given each other over the past several years.

"He *will* be with Emerson," said Nora. "She can spend more time with us. James can spend more time at your house. But him moving is out of the question. It will be . . . easier to get around at our place." She meant in a wheelchair. "Our condo's on the ground floor, and we can take the bedroom on the first floor."

Lou was perched on the kitchen counter, legs dangling off the edge. "And how long do you think that will last?"

"Indefinitely," said Nora, jutting her chin out. I could sense the rage churning in her, and I was already dreading the discussion we would have on the car ride home.

"Hello?" I interjected. "I'm right here. Do either of you have any interest in what I think might work?"

It had been four months since my diagnosis. I had disclosed my condition to Nessa (always fun to send a coworker into spontaneous sobbing in the middle of the workday), and together we had begun exploring the possibility of my transitioning to a reduced schedule. I suppose I could have quit outright and gone on long-term disability, but I would need to use that option soon enough.

Anyway, part of me wanted to preserve some semblance of normality while I still could. Nora seemed intent on it as well. Maybe too much so.

"What do you think, James?" she said now, turning to me. She expected me to side with her the way a partner should. After all, that was my role, and one that I had relished. But to my left there was Lou, and to look at her was to see you. And yes, Lou was right. I wanted—I *needed*—to spend as much time with you as possible.

"I think I can't make a decision like this on the spot," I said, and both Nora's and Lou's faces softened.

"Of course," said Lou quickly.

"Maybe we could set up an actual time to discuss this," said Nora, looking pointedly at Lou, who knew Nora well enough to understand that springing an important talk on her wasn't going to go over swimmingly. Then again, the last person Lou was likely thinking of was Nora.

Which is what I told Nora on the way home.

"Maybe, but it's still rotten of her," she said.

"Can we approach this rationally? This is hard for her, too. She just barely learned that she's going to be a single parent in very short order." I took a deep breath, not to calm myself, but because I had the sensation that a medium-size mammal—say, an obese wombat—was sitting on my chest. I thought we would have longer before my breathing became strained, but Dr. Stevens said that we should start talking about a BiPAP, a noninvasive device that would help pump air through my weakening throat. *"Your disease appears to be progressing,"* she had said.

Appears. May. Might. Probably. So many conditional words, all of which belied the inevitable truth.

"Of course. Look at you; Dr. Stevens herself said you're doing great," said Nora, touching my shoulder lightly before moving her hand back to the steering wheel.

"Except the whole foot-drop thing," I said. "The you'll-need-to-use-a-walker-soon thing. And the breathing—"

"It could be anxiety."

Could: another white lie.

"Sure," I said, and took a deep breath.

~

I met Lou for lunch at a Japanese restaurant downtown the following week.

"It's good to see you. You know, sans the chaos of the drop-off routine," she said once we had been seated.

"You, too."

Her face lit up. "You know what I was thinking about on the drive over?"

"Hit me."

"Remember that time you, me, and Rob went to the Iggy Pop concert at Irving Plaza a year or so after we got married? Do you remember how Rob wanted to rage all night and told us to go home alone, and then we ended up going to a bar instead and he beat us home? I'll never forget the look on his face."

I laughed. "I haven't thought about that in years. He wanted to murder us."

"He wasn't even an Iggy fan!"

"Those were happy days," I said wistfully. The longer I went without hearing back from him, the more I felt that our parting had truly been final. Knowing that I was not long for this world made this feel particularly heartbreaking, but I was determined not to use my disease as a bargaining chip. If he reached out, I would tell him, but not a second sooner. "Do you miss him?"

She pressed her lips together and looked across the restaurant, then back at me. "Yeah, I do. It's—well, I don't say this to make you feel bad."

"Come on, Lou. I think we know each other better than that by this point, don't we?"

She smiled. "We do. It's just . . . hard to be alone sometimes. Especially when Em's staying with you and Nora."

The waiter appeared. Lou ordered sushi; I chose a noodle dish that would not require me to use chopsticks, which I was certain I could not maneuver; even gripping a toothbrush had become an undertaking that required concentration and more than a small dose of willpower.

"You don't have to stay alone," I said. "You could date again."

"I'm a bit of a bald eagle in that regard."

I looked at her quizzically.

"I mate for life," she explained. "You know that I really never had a serious boyfriend before Rob?"

"You're kidding me."

"I kid you not."

The waiter set small black bowls before us, each filled with a foggy broth. "So would you go back to Rob?" I asked in what I hoped was not a too obvious way.

"I heard from him again recently."

I lifted my head, which felt like it had recently doubled in weight. "Did you? And what did he say?"

Her smile was resigned, and I quickly began to tell her that she shouldn't go on—I shouldn't have asked and didn't need details. But she put up a hand to stop me. "No, Jim, it's okay. We share almost everything now, don't we? Especially this, really."

"I suppose," I said.

"He didn't say much, to be honest. He asked how I was doing and what I was up to. And he asked if I might send a photo of Em. I didn't send it yet, of course," she added hastily. "I wanted to ask you first."

I tried not to grin; if he was asking for photos, my letters must have had *some* effect. "Of course you can," I told her.

"Thanks."

"Do you think you might reconcile with him?" I asked in what I hoped was a casual way.

She gave me a small smile. "I'd rather see *you* go back to him. The two of you should make up."

"Before it's too late," I said bitterly. As soon as I said this, my spoon slid through my pointer and middle fingers and fell to the floor, sending a splatter of miso every which way. "Crap," I muttered.

"No worries. I've got it." She wiped the mess in front of me with her napkin, signaled for the waiter, then continued as though nothing had happened. "Yes, I'd like to reconnect with him, but I don't know what I want out of it. Over the past couple years, I've started to see that I played a big role in why we split."

I had, and Rob had, too. But Lou? She hadn't, and I told her as much.

"No, Jim, really I did," she insisted. "I could have asked him to work harder on our relationship. When I felt he was cheating, I should have made him talk about it—and talk some more until we got to the bottom of why he was acting that way. I wanted so badly to have a partner who wouldn't abandon me that the minute it seemed like he wasn't going to be there for me, I ran in the other direction to try to save myself that loss. In the end, it only hurt worse."

"A quest for perfection at the cost of everything," I said. "I know it well."

She reached across the table and squeezed my forearm. "Which reminds me, I didn't ask you to lunch so we could talk about me. What's next for you, Jim?"

"Let's see," I said slowly. "What's next is a walker, then a wheelchair. Dropping my utensils, then being spoon-fed by someone else. Labored breathing, then a ventilator. Decay, then death."

Lou looked wounded.

"I'm sorry," I said quickly. "I wasn't trying to be a jackass. I'm just not feeling particularly optimistic right now."

"Don't apologize. I can't begin to imagine how you're feeling. But— you're not there yet. When I was so depressed after Em's birth that I was fantasizing about accidentally overdosing on sleeping pills—"

"You were contemplating suicide? I had no idea it was that bad."

"Of course you didn't, Jim." She took my hand. "I needed you to keep seeing me as something better than I was. I don't think I would have made it through otherwise. My doctor told me that if I would just focus on doing what was most important, what brought me the most joy, then the days would string together to become something coher-ent—something better. There's still time, Jim. I can't tell you what to do with it, but I'm going to be blunt: it still feels to me like you and Nora are both operating as though everything's going to remain the same. Maybe it's none of my business, but as the mother of your child, I'd like to think it is. Yes, the terrible things you mention may well come to pass. But in the meantime, I'd like to see you try to make the days more joyful. Do you really want to keep writing copy for the business school? What about taking another stab at a book? What about having a few more adventures? And what about marrying Nora? I suspect that would make both of you very happy, and Em, too."

I said nothing. Instead, I thought, *How has Lou yet again given voice to the longings within me that I could not admit to myself?*

She squeezed my hand. "You spend good time with Emerson, and that is what matters most. But as someone who has known you for so long now, I think you should think even more broadly. Make it count."

~

The drive back from the restaurant would be one of the last I would make; my reflexes were slowing, and I could not continue to take the wheel if I couldn't be certain I could maintain control. So I took the long way—through downtown, out along the Huron River, until I hit the rolling hills at the city's border. The roads were canopied by magnificently colored leaves, and I thought again how I had loved living in this particular pocket of the Midwest. Staying, at least, had not been a regret.

As I drove back to my condo, I considered what Lou had said. It was true that I had loved and been loved, and that mattered more than any unmet goals. I no longer cared that I had not lived in a big city or ever attempted that hundred-mile bike ride.

Still, it rankled that I had not ever written a whole book. And yes, Lou was right about Nora. She had said she wasn't sure she wanted to get married, and I had let it go at that rather than risk the failure of being turned down. But it was not too late.

~

"Hey, Nor?"

It was a few days after I had lunch with Lou, and Nora and I were sitting on the small deck, enjoying the warmth of an Indian summer evening. Her long legs were stretched out in front of her, and she was holding a beer on her stomach.

"What is it?

"Do you want to get married?"

"Yes," she said, without hesitating. "When?"

"Right away."

"Let's do it."

"Are you sure? You said at one point you didn't know if you ever wanted to get married."

She gave me one of her don't-mess-with-me looks. "Now I know."

"There are a few things we should probably talk through before you say yes for sure." I explained that I would leave everything to you and entrust the house to Lou until you were old enough to inherit it, so that she could raise you there as long as she saw fit.

She got up and sat on my lap, her eyes filled with tears. "James, I don't need anything from you but you," she said.

I opened my mouth, then hesitated; what I was about to say next was the one thing that could change everything—that could make Nora say "No, maybe let's not get married, after all." "I would like to move back into the house with Lou and Em," I told her. "Not right away, but . . . toward the end."

She nodded. "I had a feeling that was the case."

Neither of us said anything for a while.

"It would be easier on you," I finally said.

"Screw easy."

"You used to think that was one of the better parts of our relationship."

"Our relationship has changed."

"Yes, because my body had to go and quit on me."

Nora put her hand on my face. "No, James, because I love you so much. You're the best thing that ever happened to me."

I kissed her tenderly. "I hope that won't always be the case. When I'm gone, I want you to find someone else to love. I know you can, if only you'll try."

"Please don't say that."

I thought of what Lou had said. "We have to start facing the facts about what this is going to mean for us. Sticking our heads in the sand doesn't do anyone any favors."

She bit the sides of her cheeks, trying not to cry harder.

"Nora?" I said softly. "You don't have to decide right now, but when the time comes, I'd like you to move in with me. With *us*. Keep the condo, but come to the house."

"Won't that be awful for Lou, having me underfoot?"

"No," I said, and I knew without having to ask Lou that she would say the same. "I think it will be easier for her in a way. Anyway, we've never been all that conventional, have we? This will be no different."

~

Maybe you'll remember this; maybe you won't—I'm not sure what the mind of an almost-five-year-old retains. On November 30, at Nora's parents' house in Bloomfield Hills, she and I exchanged vows and rings before our family and friends.

Fifteen years earlier, almost to the day, I had spoken about happiness and meaning to an ecstatic Rob and Lou. Lou was again at the center of this wedding. Only this time she was pronouncing Nora and me husband and wife, as she had been ordained by God-knows-what mail-order church in order to marry us.

I gripped Nora's arm and held your hand with my free hand as the three of us made our way down the center of the great room, where guests had gathered for our nuptials. I allowed myself to cry without reservation. Aside from the day you were born, it was the most joyful day of my life. But like your birthday, it too was punctuated by the absence of the best man I had ever known.

Even as a new chapter began, another came to a close. On December 1, just a day before we were set to fly to the Florida Keys for our honeymoon, Nora and I went to a medical supply store and purchased my first walker.

TWENTY-EIGHT

Spring 2014

"Daddy?" you called. You were in the middle of the kitchen floor, a notepad and crayons spread out before you.

I looked up from the bowl of pancake batter I had been stirring. Every mundane act now seemed monumental: Would this be one of the last times I was able to effectively scrape the side of the bowl with a wooden spoon, ensuring that the heart-shaped pancakes I was about to make weren't teeming with tiny pockets of flour? "Yes, love?"

"Will you still be alive when I'm an adult?"

I took a deep breath. How to answer such a question? "I don't know, Emerson." *Probably not.* "Why do you ask?"

You held up a crayon to examine, then traded it for another. "Ivy said parents can die," you said, referring to one of your classmates.

"Yes, they can." It took me a minute, but I lowered myself from the chair so that I was beside you on the ground. "Emerson, sweetie, I'm sorry to tell you this, but I'm pretty sure I won't be around when you're my age."

"Really?"

"Yeah. It's a bummer, sweetheart. Because wherever I end up, I'm going to miss you like crazy."

You stuck your bottom lip out, then looked down at the picture of the unicorn you were drawing. After a moment, you raised your head again and looked at me with sad eyes. "Daddy? If you're not here, I hope I remember you."

I pulled you into my arms. You smelled like strawberries and soap. "I hope so, too, love. I really do."

~

Shortly after I was diagnosed, I questioned whether it would have been better if I had waited to see a doctor—or simply never found out what was wrong with me. After all, I had the misfortune of developing a disease so unfortunate that when you tell others you have it, they don't dare suggest you pray it away or seek the assistance of a desert-dwelling shaman. With ALS, there are no stories of someone's cousin's wife being cured by a caveman-style diet or green juice infused with activated charcoal, whatever the hell that is.

As I write this, there is but one medication available to me. It will add maybe a month to my life, three if I'm lucky, which I'm clearly not. There is simply nothing to be done but accept and endure. Not necessarily in that order.

Yet I have come to find some comfort in knowing what it is that's killing me. ALS has no known cause. While you may have inherited my knobby knees and long fingers, the odds of me passing this horrible condition on to you are extremely slim. I remind myself of this several times a day and again before I go to bed at night; it keeps the nightmares at bay.

Then there is the matter of this book. The very day Lou challenged me to begin to come to terms with my fate, I opened the journal I had been keeping and set about to turn it into something coherent.

It is different from my previous attempts, because this time, I wrote about the fractured marriage and impending apocalypse of which I knew. That is to say, my life.

It is an incomplete history. I have allotted few words to my life after diagnosis. That's not what I want to think about; that's not what I want you to remember.

And just as well. As the days go by, it becomes harder to write at length. I was lucky enough to have unloaded the bulk of these pages during the months in which I could still type. More recently, I've had to dictate to my computer, then attempt to move the mouse, delete ill-conceived words and sentences and paragraphs, and say what I meant to write the first time while hoping it comes out right.

I am not sure it is coming out right.

Surely this recollection is somewhat inaccurate, but I suspect that there's no such thing as absolute truth. Every event is different to those who have lived it, those who have witnessed it, and those who only later read of it.

It has been worth it to try. Madeleine L'Engle—you may remember, she wrote *A Wrinkle in Time*, which I read to you the year you were five, even though it was probably a little too soon and a lot too scary, because who knew if I would still have the chance the following year?—said, "A book, too, can be a star . . . a living fire to lighten the darkness, leading out into the expanding universe."

I began this story for you, Emerson. But in these dark days, it is for me, too.

~

"Jim?" Lou's voice roused me from a shallow slumber one morning. Ten already, I realized as I eyed the clock on the other side of the room.

I had recently left my job and gone on full-time disability. I didn't miss writing the press releases or puff profiles, but I missed my coworkers and the feeling of being needed.

Now it was I who needed. Help me get this shirt on; help me get it off. I'm hungry; can you make sure I don't spill oatmeal all over myself? Can you help me get up, sit down, pick that up, scratch this itch? The blessing of ALS is also the torture of the disease: you can feel everything. Your limbs and digits don't work the way they should, and your throat and vocal cords fail you. But temperature, pain, numbness, itching—each sensation remains intact, even as you can do less and less about it.

Anyway, I was still using a walker at that point and had not yet begun my stint in solitary confinement, as I would come to think of my wheelchair. Yet with every passing week it was harder to get around. And so Nora, Lou, and I decided it was time for Nora and me to move into the house.

I expected the move to be a major upheaval, but I had forgotten just how adaptable we humans can be when change is not a choice. Just as the four of us had adjusted to my illness, our shared home life almost instantly became our new normal.

Lou had converted the family room at the back of the house into a bedroom for Nora and me, and it soon felt as welcoming as our room at the condo. The four of us usually ate breakfast and dinner together. We planned activities together, too, and traded duties: Nora watching you so Lou could take me for a walk, Nora staying with me so Lou could go out with you. The days were long; the days were short.

"Jim," said Lou again.

I had closed my eyes, maybe even fallen back asleep. I had been sleeping a lot—too much—and often wondered if it was true fatigue or just my mind's attempt to block out reality. I turned to Lou drowsily. "What is it?"

"There's someone here to see you."

I rolled onto my side and pushed myself upright the best I could. I sometimes caught myself in a mirror or the reflection of a window. It was like watching a newborn foal try to get about. Messy business, this deteriorating.

"Who is it?" I asked.

"Me," said a voice I had not heard in quite some time.

Now I was awake. I tried to fully right myself, too quickly, and almost tumbled off the bed. I pulled my sweatpants into place, then tugged my t-shirt down over my stomach, which was concave, as though I was again a skinny teen who shot up before he filled out.

Lou disappeared into the kitchen, and Rob appeared in the doorway. "Hi."

"Were you going to warn me you were coming?" I said, only half joking. "My bits and pieces could be hanging out."

"Good to see you, too, dick widget," he said.

"So having a degenerative disease has put me back in your good graces?" I cringed at the sound of my own voice, which had already begun to sound flat and nasal. But at least Rob had called me by one of my nicknames. You didn't do that to someone you hated.

Rob laughed uncomfortably. "Yeah, I guess so."

"Well then hey, douche nozzle," I said, standing. As I reached for the walker beside my bed, I spotted Lou standing a few feet behind Rob, no doubt hanging around to see how this would play out. It was uncanny, seeing them together—almost as though we had just rewound a decade.

I leaned into the plastic arm cuffs attached to the top of my walker, which helped me maintain control with a weak grip. I had no choice but to move at a snail's pace. Catching my foot or the walker on the edge of a rug could send me tumbling to the ground, and I was neither fast nor strong enough to break my own fall. I had learned this the hard way the month before, in the middle of the grocery store. Humiliating doesn't begin to cut it; something in my mind continued to resist the reality that I would never again be the person I once was.

"God, James," said Rob. When I reached the doorway, he put his arms around me, squeezing me hard, and what could I do but be grateful for the pain?

"It's been too long," I said gruffly.

"I know," he said. "I know."

"Let's go sit down."

He followed me into the kitchen. Lou was nowhere to be seen, but she had left two fresh cups of coffee on the table, as well as the sugar bowl for Rob and a small ceramic pitcher with cream for me.

"So you got my letters."

Rob leaned back in his chair, his long legs spilling out past the edge of the table. "Yes. Though you didn't tell me you were sick."

"I didn't know then. Anyway, I prefer to think of it as less an illness and more an expedited expiration." I cleared my throat. "I'm—I'm glad you came."

"Me, too." His hair was as gray as it was black, and his beard was peppered, too. But something in his face had softened, like he was at ease with himself for the first time in a while.

"It's a shame that it took finding out I'm about to self-destruct in order for you to forgive me."

"Who said I forgive you?"

My laugh came out as a grunt. "And if I said I was sorry?"

"I may have heard it before. But now that we're face-to-face—are you? Really?"

"Of course I am. But . . ."

Just behind Rob's head, the fridge was covered with your preschool art projects. A crayon drawing of Lou with butterfly wings. A painting of you, me, Lou, Nora, and the kitten you had been begging for but had not yet been given, in front of the house. A large, bejeweled mural that said DAD.

"I am sorry," I continued, "but I guess you should know that I don't regret it. You were right that Lou and I weren't supposed to be together. But our girl, Emerson—she's everything. I would do it all again if I had the choice."

Sadness, unmistakable in its depth, surfaced on Rob's face. He steeled himself. "I understand. I'm looking forward to meeting her."

"Me, too. You're going to love her."

"I would tell you I'll never understand why you did it, but—" He looked over his shoulder, maybe to make sure Lou was out of earshot. "The more I thought about it, the more I realized it's in character for you. I mean really, it's your classic move."

"And how's that?" I remarked. If anything, pursuing Lou had been the least me-like thing I had ever done in my life.

"Come on, James. You get obsessed with the perfect—not because it's perfect, but because if you can't have it, you don't actually have to try."

I had come to a similar conclusion myself. Still, my face grew warm as Rob reminded me that I wasn't the only one who knew about this flaw of mine. "Maybe when it comes to Lou, sure," I said. "But that's in the past now."

"Maybe when it comes to everything," he said, not unkindly. "Remember how you quit the JV soccer team because you were pissed you didn't make the cut for varsity? Or when you didn't get into that one writing program you had your heart set on, you almost didn't apply to Michigan? I can go on, if you'd like."

"Don't," I said, only half joking. "But what about you? What's your excuse?"

He stared at me. "Don't have one. I was in a dark place, and I let that take me over. When I finally came out of it, Lou was gone. I'll spend the rest of my life paying for that mistake."

"From the looks of you, the only thing you're paying for is luxury goods," I said, sending a pointed look in the direction of his tasseled loafers, which appeared to have been handcrafted by a cobbler in Milan.

But as Longfellow said, every heart has its secret sorrows that the world knows not. "Yes, my life's a frickin' fairy tale," said Rob. "I loathe my job, and that makes me increasingly mediocre at it. I don't have a single friend who I don't know through work. My colleagues' second wives set me up with women who know my net worth down to the penny and have only agreed to date me because their most fertile years are behind them and they have to lower their standards if they want to procreate with someone who can cover their kids' college tuition."

"At least you're not dying," I noted.

"I was wondering how long you'd wait to pull that one out."

We both broke into smiles.

"You're an awful human being," I said.

"You're even awful-er. And don't you dare correct my grammar, nerd wad," he said.

I laughed, and this time I actually sounded like myself. "Nerd wad! Now there's one I haven't heard in ages."

"Get used to it."

The tension between us finally defused, and we sat at the table talking for a good long time. He and Lou had been emailing back and forth for months now. She had told him about my diagnosis, and he had debated how to react, if he did at all. He had flown to Michigan to see his parents; Bobby had had a hip replaced, and Nancy was beginning to show the early signs of dementia, though she swore she was as sharp as a tack. Visiting me had been a whim. He had only just called Lou that morning to make sure I would be here.

What else did we discuss? I don't remember all of it. He told me he was thinking about quitting finance and trying to find a career that would actually bring him some sort of satisfaction, though he had no idea what that was. He spoke of leaving New York, maybe for Rhode Island or Tennessee. (*Or Michigan,* I thought.)

In turn, I told him about Nora and our wedding, and of course, my diagnosis and what had changed.

At some point, Lou wandered back into the kitchen. She was as lithe as the day we had met, and she looked calm and content; by that point, it had been years since she had suffered a bout of severe depression. But she, too, was beginning to gray around the temples, and her eyes were set deeper in her face. It was impossible for me not to wonder how much of her aging owed to the stress of my illness and how much was from everyday life.

"You guys doing okay?" she asked. "Nora should be getting Em from ballet any minute now. Rob, what do you think? You up for a meet and greet?"

"Yeah," he said, running a hand through his hair. "That would be great."

We heard you before we saw you; you were singing "Old MacDonald Had a Farm," a song I myself learned when I was about your age. As soon as you spotted Rob, you stopped singing and hid behind Nora's legs.

"It's okay, love," she said. "I'm guessing this is Rob, yes? I'm Nora."

"Yes," said Rob, rising. He held out a hand to Nora, who shook it firmly. "Really nice to meet you. James has been telling me all about you. Congratulations on your wedding."

"Thank you," she said. "And it's nice to meet you. I've heard so much about you from James."

Reluctantly, you peered your head out from behind Nora. "Wow," you finally said to Rob. "You're *big*."

He laughed heartily. "I get that a lot. You must be the famous Emerson."

You turned to me with a curious look. "Daddy? What's 'famous' mean?"

"The opposite of Daddy. It means everyone knows about you."

You scrunched up your nose, just like Lou. "That's not me. What's your name again?" you said to Rob.

"Rob."

"Want to see my blanket fort?" you said, and he nodded, suddenly shy himself.

You took him by the hand and tugged him in the direction of the living room, narrating as you went: "This is our hallway, that's the sofa—you can't jump on it—that's the lamp I broke, but Mommy glued it back together . . ."

Rob was so tall that he almost had to duck to get through the doorways, but he ambled along behind you.

"She appears to trust him," Lou noted from behind me.

"She should," I said.

And I meant it. While we were talking in the kitchen, I kept thinking about what he had done after my mother died. The day of her death, my father called me and simply said, "Your mother is gone."

"What do you mean?" I asked him. "Gone where?"

"She's dead," he said flatly.

"What—what happened?"

"Her heart gave out. Service is being held in two days at Chester's in Southfield. Funeral's the following day. I'll call you later."

I stared at the phone, semiconvinced that the news I had just received was meant for someone else. My mother? Dead? She couldn't be; I owed her a phone call. I had not seen her in two months, but I was going to, just as soon as I finished another chapter on my thesis. When was the last time I told her I loved her? I couldn't remember.

I don't know how long I sat there afterward. Eventually I found myself dialing Rob's number. "My mother," I said numbly. "She—she died."

"Oh God, James. That's horrible. Are you okay?"

"Yes," I said, because I did not yet understand that this pain was not the fleeting kind; I would never have a mother again.

But Rob knew better. "Hold tight. I'll be there tomorrow," he said, and even though I knew he was in the middle of his hazing year—he had just been hired at his firm and had six months to demonstrate that he was competent and another six to prove he could rake in millions for the company—he showed up at my apartment the following morning and did not leave until the day after my mother was lowered into the ground.

This particular occasion stands out in my mind, but it's one of many. Rob made many mistakes, as did I. They do not mean he isn't a good man.

Yet when you and he returned to the kitchen—the two of you hand in hand, clearly enchanted with each other—a piece of me died right there. Because there was my oldest friend, yet again with a person I loved so deeply I could not explain it for the life of me, playing a role I could not.

But as soon as I acknowledged that odious jealousy—how deep it went, how very corrosive it was for all of us—it began to fade.

"Let me see you to the door," I said when it was time for him to go.

"You sure?" he said.

"I'm not an invalid yet," I said.

He gave me an amused look. "Good to know you haven't lost your sense of humor, if it can be called that."

"The brain remains as the body withers," I said.

"And just as melodramatic as ever, I see."

"Hmph. Will we see you again?" I asked.

"I'd like that. I'll be back next month; maybe I could plan a longer visit or even swing by a few times. We could do dinner or something."

A rush of emotion surged through my chest and rose in my neck, and I thought for a moment I would sob. I swallowed as well as I could and attempted to clear my throat. "That sounds good."

Rob reached for the doorknob. "I'm glad we did this."

Me, too, I thought as he began down the stairs.

He was already on the walk when I called his name. He spun around. "Yeah?"

A better man might have let it go. But I had to ask. "Why didn't you fight to get Lou back?"

He shook his head. "I honestly don't know. Maybe because she had already chosen you."

"Chose me? Not quite," I said. More like I had put her in a situation in which I was her only option, which was no choice at all. "Not unless you count one fated night back in 2008," I added.

He looked around at the yard, at the house, then back at me. "You share a life, James. A child. It may not be everything you ever wanted, but it's an awful lot."

I stood on the porch and watched him drive away. I stayed there for a while, even though my legs were weak, thinking about what he had said. When I finally let myself back in the house, you, Nora, and Lou embraced me, as though I had been gone a very long time.

TWENTY-NINE

Early 2015

Snow whipped horizontally through the air, coating our world in white. Meteorologists had just upgraded the storm to blizzard status, and Nora, who had the misfortune to attend a meeting at her company's Detroit office that morning, had decided it was safer to spend the night at a hotel in town than attempt to make the treacherous drive back.

"We'll be fine," I assured her when she second-guessed her decision to stay in the city. "Try to enjoy it. Take a long bath, order food in. You could use a break." *From me,* I added mentally.

She sighed, like she knew what I was thinking; she hated when I pointed out that my condition was difficult for her, even though there was no way for it to be anything but. "Okay," she relented. "Hopefully I'll be home tomorrow afternoon, if not sooner."

"No rush; be safe. Love you."

"Love you, too. Tell Lou I say hi, and give Emmy a big smooch for me."

I promised her I would and hung up.

It had been a long, cold winter, and my health was taking a toll on all of us. Lou worked at the bookstore while you were at school during the day, then cared for you and helped me until Nora came home around five. She had not said as much, but it was clear Nora had been granted some sort of arrangement at work that allowed her to maintain a partner-track pace but leave the office at a reasonable hour. She often worked after I went to bed and sometimes in the early hours of the morning, too.

During the workweek, I was usually alone from nine to four. In better weather, I didn't mind so much; then, at least, I could go outside, if only to attempt to walk down the block. Every once in a while, Pascal would take me to lunch or the library.

But the snow and ice had been relentless since November. It was too easy for me to slip on the walkways, so I holed up and wrote as much as I was able. I video-chatted with Pascal, too, and read all the books I had never had time to get through. By midwinter, though, even reading became dull, as any activity repeated too often is wont to do. So on that frigid February morning, I was happy for a snow day, if only because it meant I had company.

"Daddy, let's *make* a story," you said, clapping your hands together with delight.

"Okay," I said. "Like a book?"

"Well, we can just say it out loud, and then you can write it down later."

"You going to take notes?" I asked Lou.

She was typing furiously—not poetry, I knew, because there wasn't a notebook at her side, and anyway, her fingers never moved that fast when she was transcribing her poems. I wondered if she was talking to Rob. He emailed me every few weeks, and Lou chatted with him more frequently. He had come for dinner several times since his first visit, too, and even showed up at Christmas. It wasn't romantic, Lou claimed—they were just getting to know each other again. But his hand lingered on her arm a beat longer than it would have if she were another person; she looked up at him across the table, then looked down, only to glance up again. It was clear that the old feelings were resurfacing for both of them, which in turn made me feel—well, if not absolved, then at least hopeful.

"Sure," she said in a way that suggested she had no idea what she had just committed to.

"So what's our story?" I asked you, shifting slightly in the recliner; as usual, I had been sitting in the same position too long.

You gave me a mischievous smile, and I wondered what sassy suggestion you were about to make. But then you said, "The story of a girl and her family. Mommy!"

"Yes, dear!" chirped Lou.

"We *need* you to make this story with us. Okay!" You clapped your hands together with authority. "So once upon a time, there was a family that was only sort of a family."

"Okay . . . ," I said, afraid of where this was going.

"And that's because they weren't really people! They were really stars that had fallen to the ground," you declared. "Daddy? Your turn."

I paused, took a deep breath, and prayed this wouldn't be one of those times that my voice conked out on me. "All the members of this family knew the secret of the universe. And that was that *everyone* was secretly made of stars. And . . . Lou, you're up!"

"This is your doing, isn't it?" she said to me in a mock whisper. "Em told me all about you telling her what people are made out of."

"I know nothing," I said. At an earlier time in life, I would have held my hands up to demonstrate my innocence. Now I just gave her a lopsided smile.

Lou turned to you. "So . . . the secret was really hard for them to keep, but the family did it anyway . . . because they were good people."

"Mom*my*," you protested. "The secret has to give them some sort of *superpower*."

"Um. So, their being stars meant that they would live forever," Lou said. She smiled at this thought, then added, "As soon as their lives were over, they shot back up to the sky, leaving a trail of glittering light behind them. And now anyone who looks up at night can see them twinkling above."

"Perfect!" you declared. "Mommy, Daddy, you got this?"

"We've got it," Lou assured you, and I nodded compliantly.

As you ran off into the other room, Lou looked at me tenderly. "Jim?" she said.

"Yeah?"

"We did good."

"Yes, Lou. We did."

I pushed myself up, reached for the walker, then used it to move to the sofa where Lou was sitting. Through the windows, I saw that it had finally stopped snowing.

"Lou," I said, and held my hand out to her. Our eyes met as she grasped my fingers in her palm. "Will you be okay without me?"

She squeezed my hand. I wondered if she was going to tell me it would all be fine, that I shouldn't worry about her. "It's going to be hard, Jim," she said quietly. "So hard that I can't even imagine it right now."

Above us, you were running through the hallway like we were constantly telling you not to. Neither Lou nor I called out for you to stop.

"I know. I'm worried." Here I was, ripping the stability rug out from under her feet yet again.

"In what regard?" she asked.

"In every regard. I worry you'll be depressed again, and I won't be there to help you. I worry about leaving you to raise a child on your own."

"I won't be alone. I have your dad, and Nora, and Victoria and Dan, and . . ." She looked up at me. "I'm not the same person I was after Em was born. Or even before. I'm stronger now, Jim."

"But stability—"

She shook her head vigorously. "That doesn't mean the same thing to me that it once did. Stability for me is a family that loves me. I have that, and that's thanks to you."

I clenched my jaw. "Do you regret it, at least a little?" I asked. "Your life could have been better without me. Or at the very least, easier."

She moved closer to me on the sofa. I thought she was going to hug me, but then she leaned in and kissed me, lightly and tenderly. "I don't regret a thing, Jim," she said. "I just wish it could all last a little longer."

Me, too, I thought. *Me, too.*

~

As winter turned to spring, things went downhill fast. *Rapidly progressing,* said Dr. Stevens, though she was quick to add that my disease progression could occur in fits and starts. My breathing was labored, and though I could still speak and swallow, I needed to use a breathing machine much of the day.

That March, I made the switch from a walker to a wheelchair. I didn't have to use it all the time, said the occupational therapist who got me set up with my motorized rig.

Not yet was what he meant. I cried the first time I sat in it, grateful that the therapist was the only one to see me break down.

Nora picked me up from the therapist's in the wheelchair-accessible minivan we had recently purchased. When she pulled into the driveway of our home, fresh tears pricked at the back of my lids. But as soon as I wheeled myself up the ramp that had just been affixed to the front of the house and through the front door, you perched yourself on my lap.

"Go, Daddy, go!" you said with delight. And when I began to move, you said, "Keep going! Keep going!"

Yes, I thought. *I must keep going as long as I'm able.*

~

Which brings us to now. Nora bought me a computer stand that attaches to my wheelchair, and I work on this book a few hours most days. Between pages, I look out the large picture windows of the family room, which is where I spend most of my time. I can see the flower beds and vegetable gardens Lou planted, and the weeping willow I put in the year you were born, which is already taller than you are—at least the six-year-old you that I know. And beyond the willow, there's that damn black walnut tree that drops the golf ball–size walnuts that kill the grass and everything else they hit.

I have started sleeping more. Too much. Mostly I hate my dreams, which come at me more as fragments of scenes than actual narratives. Black holes, entrapment, suffocation. But running, biking, walking: these are actually worse than confinement or loss of control. Because when I open my eyes and remember again that my body is no longer in coordination with my mind, it is a fresh terror every time.

But the other night, I dreamed I was in a baseball field, one that looked a lot like the field at the far end of the elementary school I attended. Wisnewski was there, and Rob, too. We weren't playing ball. Instead, Rob and I were looking for Wisnewski, who was hiding from us. He was not behind the benches; he was not in the trees at the perimeter of the outfield. Just when we were about to give up, he came bounding out from behind the dugout, where I had sworn I had just looked. "I was here the whole time, you idiots!" he said, giving us each a hug, and in typical Wisnewski style, a noogie. Laughing, we ran off; where we were headed, I never learned. All I know is that we were young, we were alive, and we were together. This dream—

I did not want it to end.

～

Dr. Stevens says that about ten percent of people with ALS live ten years or longer. By the time you read this, that number might be much higher—at least that is my hope. Maybe researchers will have even found a cure.

I don't say this to Dr. Stevens, but I won't be a part of that ten percent. I'm pretty sure we all know that. This is not born of my innate pessimism or some secret superstition that expecting the worst will leave me pleasantly surprised. It says nothing about my belief in miracles. (For the record, I think they look nothing like a touchdown in the last seven seconds of the game or even missing a flight that then mistook the side of a mountain for a runway. A miracle is the first time you touch your child's downy skin; it is every time you hear her laughter. It is a mouth you love upon your own; it is the life you purposefully forge with another person.)

As to this disease, it is what it is. I've always hated that expression, and yet it's the one I have used again and again while attempting to explain to others how I have come to terms with what is happening to me. This horror that's devouring me one neuron at a time is just a variation on a theme. Each story is different. Every story ends with loss.

THIRTY

September 2015

As I begin this chapter, we are again in Grand Marais. The four of us are staying at Yvonne's cottage. My father and Miriam have rented a house a block away, and Rob is at his aunt's, half a mile down the road. Terry, the gregarious young nurse who now shows up most days to care for me, has come, too, though he's housed at an inn at the top of the hill.

Yes, the gang's all here to celebrate me having had one more go around the sun. I'm not sure if I am honored or embarrassed by this communal gathering. I am at least glad to be sharing the celebration with Lou, who will turn forty next week.

So I have lived to see forty-three. In a few months, you will be seven. I'm fairly certain I will live to see that, too, but I won't be writing then. Every page takes more energy, and I need it for other things.

There you are now, skipping into the living room in a sundress and rubber flip-flops. Light spills through the windows, turning your curls into a golden halo.

"Hi, Daddy," you say, gently putting your arms around my neck, then giving me a kiss on the cheek. "You getting enough air?"

I hate that you have to worry about this, even if I love that you do. I nod, pull my head back from my BiPAP machine that pushes air through my flaccid throat into my lungs. "Yes. Thank you," I said. "How are you, Em?"

"Good! Mommy says we can get ice cream again later."

"Yum." I practically live on the stuff these days; it's high in calories, which I have a hard time getting enough of, and almost effortless to eat.

"Mint chip?" you ask.

I make a noise that is meant to be a laugh. "You remembered." It has always been my go-to flavor. "Blue moon? Or rocky road?" I ask you, referring to yesterday's choice.

"Maybe," you say, putting a finger on your chin—another habit you've picked up from your mother. "Or lemon custard, or strawberry."

You hug me again, and how I wish we could stay in this moment forever.

But that wish is insignificant to the others that have been flooding my mind this week. It's been said that every good parent wants only for his child to be happy. I want happiness for you, but so much more. I want you to not know the pain that awaits you. I want you to roar back at the things that scare you. I want for you a life that is not just happy, but meaningful.

But above all, I want you to embrace the love you find yourself drawn to, whatever that may be. I hope this book will show you that if you can find it in you to push past the fear of loving another person— if you can learn to live with the inevitable loss that comes with doing so—you will know a good and meaningful life.

∿

The week goes by in a blur of sun and laughter and yes, tears. We have ice cream every day and watch the tide rise, recede, and repeat. As you collect rocks and shells at the beach, I stay on the patch of grass that meets the sand. I develop a deep sunburn, which proves to be a pleasant sting; it may well be the last time my skin will be scorched, and there's no worrying about wrinkles or melanoma now. *It is a shame,* I think, as Lou and Nora polish off a bottle of wine in the same time it takes for me to nurse half a beer, *that I cannot enjoy more destructive pleasures in my current state, when there is no real damage left to be done.*

Two days before we are scheduled to return to our various homes and lives, we gather at the shore in front of the cottage.

You can't push a wheelchair through sand, so Rob, lug that he is, hoists me into his arms and carries me to a set of Adirondack chairs arranged in a semicircle near the shoreline.

My father trails behind him with the BiPAP. After getting me set up, he takes the chair to my right.

Nora is on my left, telling me about the case she will begin working on when she returns to the office next week. Her practicality, her ability to move forward with what she has—these are just a few of the things I love about her. What grace she has demonstrated as she has watched my body give up its fight. What love, to feed me at meals like a mother to a child, only to curl around my body at night as a wife. Keep Nora in your life, Em; she is one of the best parts of me.

Lou is with you at the water's edge, helping you build—well, I won't call it a sand castle, because it is more complex than that. You have created a multilevel structure with edges that you scalloped with a clamshell. A foot away, you've built a smaller, near-identical building. Both are surrounded by the same deep moat you spent fifteen minutes digging out. Beside you, Lou's head thrown back in laughter in response to something you just said. She is never happier or more beautiful than when she is with you.

How I will miss her. I still sometimes question my love for her. Where did it come from, and why did it take me so long to let it go, if I really have at all? All I can do is accept that it has woven itself into the fabric of who I am. I could be wrong, but I suspect that the people we are drawn to are the ones we need most, even if we are never able to fully comprehend why. Maybe in Lou, I saw the possibility of you. Maybe in me, she saw you, too, and that became our fate and future.

Rob is standing off to the side, watching the water. Every once in a while he turns to quietly observe you and Lou. Just yesterday, he told me he will be moving back to Michigan before the year is out. He and Lou are dating again—just dating, she says firmly. Yet already I see them old and gray, sitting hand in hand, speaking of the time they were apart as merely a blip on the radar of their lives. In the interim, they could even have a child and give you a sibling. As I told Rob, it's not too late.

Of course, I don't know if that will come to pass. You remember what Pascal said about the wonder of life being that anything can happen? That infinite possibility is exactly what makes living so damn heartbreaking. But I believe Rob is a better man and that he still loves Lou, just as she still loves him. And I know he would be good to you.

Even if they don't come together as a couple, I'm happy to have Rob in your life. He of all people will be able to share with you the parts of my past that I wasn't able to include here. Surely this book is incomplete in ways, but so it goes. As much as we crave a concise, linear narrative, life happens as it will, often in a haphazard fashion that feels anything but finished. We must cobble together our most important moments and call them our story.

"Daddy, look!" you call, waving to me. You point excitedly at the sand structures you've just completed.

It takes everything in me to say, "Good work, Em!" as loud as I'm able, so that you will hear me over the waves breaching the shore.

"You doing all right, son?" my father says. He takes my hand and squeezes it. I don't squeeze back—I can't—but I pull my mouth away from my breathing device and say, "Yes." I take another breath and add, "Love you, Pops."

"I love you, son," he tells me. "I . . . I hope you know I've done the best I can."

I nod. It is not an apology, but it is enough.

After the sun sets—it always disappears below the horizon so quickly, doesn't it?—I ask to be taken in. Normally I would be ready for bed, but tonight I have Rob and Lou set me up in front of my computer. It is time for me to bring this to an end.

It is almost eerily dark in this barely populated area of Michigan's northernmost border. But it is the darkness that makes the stars so bright that I can still see them piercing the blackness when I close my eyes. As I stare out the window, trying to absorb the moment before turning back to my computer monitor, I find myself again thinking of my father.

"I'm going to tell you for the last time," he used to yell at your aunt Victoria and me when we failed to obey him. When we were little, those words frightened us—just as they were intended to. But as we grew older, we came to understand that he didn't mean what he said. Threats were his way of dealing with us without walloping us upside the head or worse, as his own father had with him. We would screw up again, and we would be yelled at again—if not for the same thing, then for something else. It was never really the last time.

Emerson, this is me telling you for the last time—yet hoping that because I have written it down, it won't be—that I love you.

To have been placed on this planet with you and your mother at the same time in a universe billions of years old and more vast than we will ever begin to comprehend—this is the gift of my life.

I know, having myself lost a parent too soon, that being without a father will not be easy for you. But try to remember that loss is an incredible stroke of luck.

Yes, luck. For loss carries with it two truths: that you have loved, and that you yourself have had the good fortune to live a little longer.

So try not to grieve me too much. But when you do, take down this book and know that my love endures, and I am with you—

Always.

James Javier Hernandez
September 2, 1972–September 23, 2016

~

James Bell Logan
Born August 30, 2016

AUTHOR'S NOTE

Though I consulted medical literature and physicians about amyotrophic lateral sclerosis (ALS), the experience detailed in this book is still a fictionalized account and should not be used for reference purposes. For more information, visit the ALS Association at alsa.org.

ACKNOWLEDGMENTS

Danielle Marshall, thank you for believing in this novel when it was still just an idea floating around in my head. I'm incredibly fortunate to call you my editor.

Elisabeth Weed, you're truly the best. Thanks for sticking with me all these years.

Tiffany Yates Martin, thank you doesn't begin to cut it; this story owes so much to your guidance.

My deep gratitude to the entire team at Lake Union and Amazon, especially Gabriella Dumpit and Dennelle Catlett.

Michelle Weiner and Creative Artists Agency, a million thanks for championing my work.

Shannon Callahan, I couldn't have done it without you. Julie Lawson Timmer and Dan Timmer, thank you for your kindness and giving me a place to finish this book. Kristy Barrett, Cynthia D'Amour, Stefanie and Craig Galban, Dee Lamphear and David Gubbini, Jennifer and Jeff Lamb, Laurel and Joe Lambert, Anna and Vince Massey, Stevany and Tim Peters, Alex Ralph, Sara Reistad-Long, Nicole and

Matt Sampson, Michelle and Mike Stone, Pam Sullivan, and Darci and Mike Swisher, your support means the world to me.

To my family—the Noes, Lamberts, Lizarribars, Monterossos, Pagáns, Nelson-Pietrzaks, Pietrzaks, and Sunadhars: thank you.

And to JP, Indira, and Xavi, all of my love—always.

READING QUESTIONS FOR BOOK CLUBS

1. Why do you think James is drawn to Lou? Is it really love at first sight and therefore something he can't control—or is his love a choice?

2. How does James' view of love evolve over time—and why?

3. James' mother says to him, "You do what you can with whatever you get." This viewpoint seems to reflect his friend Wisnewski's approach to life—which James suspects is the secret to happiness. Do you think he's right? And do you agree with his mother?

4. What role do names and nicknames play in this novel?

5. James says that the difference between love and loss is so slight that it's almost impossible to perceive. What does he mean by this? And does his fear of loss hold him back from fully loving others, such as Kathryn?

6. In recalling his affair with Lou, James says, "It was a small series of choices that snowballed into a much bigger decision, which then became an outcome that none of us saw

coming." Do you think this is an accurate recollection of what happened between him and Lou?

7. At the end of the novel, James tells Emerson she should trust Rob, even though he cheated on Lou: "Rob made many mistakes, as did I. They do not mean he isn't a good man." Do our choices make us "good" or "bad"? Why do you think both Rob and James failed the people they most loved?

8. Why do you think Rob ultimately forgives James? How big of a role does James' illness play in their reconciliation?

9. Echoing the opening line of the novel, James later notes, "Every story ends with loss." Is that true?

10. What do you think was James' purpose in writing this book for Emerson?

ABOUT THE AUTHOR

Photo © 2015 Joni Strickfaden

Camille Pagán is the author of the bestselling novel *Life and Other Near-Death Experiences*, which was recently optioned for film, and the international bestselling novel *The Art of Forgetting*. Her work has appeared in *Forbes*; *Men's Health*; *O, The Oprah Magazine*; *Real Simple*; WebMD.com; and many other publications and websites. She lives in the Midwest with her husband, two children, and too many animals. Visit her at www.camillenoepagan.com.